Acclaim for Chuck Palahniuk's

DIARY

"The closest thing to a plain old mystery Palahniuk has ever written. . . . Stunning, funky stuff."

—*Entertainment Weekly*

"Daring. . . . Palahniuk's inspiration comes from a love of the vernacular of subcultures, a black but not cynical sense of humor, and a fondness for unusual plot twists. . . . Ominous, shocking."

—*Chicago Sun-Times*

"Intriguing. . . . Must reading for art lovers and those who love a good puzzle." —*The Baltimore Sun*

"Palahniuk continues to redefine 'scary' for his readers. Recalling such classic horror tales as Shirley Jackson's *The Lottery*, *Diary*'s dark side reveals itself slowly, quietly. . . . Unraveling the mystery that [Misty's] life has become is as eye-opening for us as it is for her."

—*Chicago Tribune*

"In his inimitable style, Palahniuk has forged another chilling tale out of our deepest fears and given readers a *Rosemary's Baby* for the new millennium. . . . *Diary* is Palahniuk at his harrowing best."

—*BookPage*

ALSO BY CHUCK PALAHNIUK

Fight Club
Survivor
Invisible Monsters
Choke
Lullaby
Fugitives and Refugees
Stranger Than Fiction

DIARY

WHERE DO YOU GET
YOUR INSPIRATION?

DIARY

A Novel

CHUCK PALAHNIUK

Anchor Books
A Division of Random House, Inc.
New York

For my grandfather,
Joseph Tallent,
who told me to be
whatever I wanted.
1910–2003

FIRST ANCHOR BOOKS EDITION, SEPTEMBER 2004

Published in the United States by Anchor Books, a division of Random House, Inc., New York, and simultaneously in Canada by Random House of Canada Limited, Toronto. Originally published in hardcover in the United States by Doubleday, a division of Random House, Inc., New York, in 2003.

The Library of Congress has cataloged the Doubleday edition as follows:
Palahniuk, Chuck.
Diary: a novel / Chuck Palahniuk.—1st ed.
p. cm.
1. Women painters—Fiction. 2. Suicidal behavior—Fiction. 3. Coma—Patients—Fiction. 4. Married women—Fiction. 5. Contractors—Fiction. 6. Islands—Fiction.
I. Title.
PS3566.A4554 D53 2003
813'.54—dc21
2003043900

Anchor ISBN: 1-4000-3281-4

Book design by Dana Leigh Treglia
Paintbrush on Black Background by Steve Huschle/Getty Images
Painter's Palette by Anne-Marie Weber/Getty Images
Fish illustration by Dana Leigh Treglia

www.anchorbooks.com

Printed in the United States of America
10 9 8 7 6 5 4 3

DIARY

June 21—
The Three-Quarter Moon

TODAY, A MAN CALLED from Long Beach. He left a long message on the answering machine, mumbling and shouting, talking fast and slow, swearing and threatening to call the police, to have you arrested.

Today is the longest day of the year—but anymore, every day is.

The weather today is increasing concern followed by full-blown dread.

The man calling from Long Beach, he says his bathroom is missing.

June 22

BY THE TIME you read this, you'll be older than you remember.

The official name for your liver spots is *hyperpigmented lentigines*. The official anatomy word for a wrinkle is *rhytide*. Those creases in the top half of your face, the rhytides plowed across your forehead and around your eyes, this is *dynamic wrinkling*, also called *hyperfunctional facial lines*, caused by the movement of underlying muscles. Most wrinkles in the lower half of the face are *static rhytides*, caused by sun and gravity.

Let's look in the mirror. Really look at your face. Look at your eyes, your mouth.

This is what you think you know best.

Your skin comes in three basic layers. What you can touch is the *stratum corneum*, a layer of flat, dead skin cells pushed up by the new cells under them. What you feel, that greasy feeling, is your *acid* mantle, the coating of oil and sweat that protects you from germs and fungus. Under that is your dermis. Below the dermis is a layer of fat. Below the fat are the muscles of your face.

Maybe you remember all this from art school, from Figure Anatomy 201. But then, maybe not.

When you pull up your upper lip—when you show that one top tooth, the one the museum guard broke—this is your *levator labii superioris* muscle at work. Your sneer muscle. Let's pretend you smell some old stale urine. Imagine your husband's just killed himself in your family car. Imagine you have to go out and sponge his piss out of the driver's seat. Pretend you still have to drive this stinking rusted junk pile to work, with everyone watching, everyone knowing, because it's the only car you have.

Does any of this ring a bell?

When a normal person, some normal innocent person who sure as hell deserved a lot better, when she comes home from waiting tables all day and finds her husband suffocated in the family car, his bladder leaking, and she screams, this is simply her orbicularis oris stretched to the very limit.

That deep crease from each corner of your mouth to your nose is your *nasolabial fold*. Sometimes called your "sneer pocket." As you age, the little round cushion of fat inside your cheek, the official anatomy word is *malar fat pad*, it slides lower and lower until it comes to rest against your nasolabial fold—making your face a permanent sneer.

This is just a little refresher course. A little step-by-step.

Just a little brushing up. In case you don't recognize yourself.

Now frown. This is your triangularis muscle pulling down the corners of your orbicularis oris muscle.

Pretend you're a twelve-year-old girl who loved her father like crazy. You're a little preteen girl who needs her dad more than ever before. Who counted on her father always to be there. Imagine you go to bed crying every night, your eyes clamped shut so hard they swell.

The "orange peel" texture of your chin, these "popply" bumps are caused by your mentalis muscle. Your "pouting" muscle. Those frown lines you see every morning, getting deeper, running from each corner of your mouth down to the edge of your chin, those are called *marionette lines*. The wrinkles between your eyebrows, they're *glabellar furrows*. The way your swollen eyelids sag down is called *ptosis*. Your *lateral canthal rhytides*, your "crow's-feet," are worse every day and *you're only twelve fucking years old for God's sake*.

Don't pretend you don't know what this is about.

This is your face.

Now, smile—if you still can.

This is your zygomatic major muscle. Each contraction pulls your flesh apart the way tiebacks hold open the drapes in your living room window. The way cables pull aside a theater curtain, your every smile is an opening night. A premiere. You unveiling yourself.

Now, smile the way an elderly mother would when her only son kills himself. Smile and pat the hand of his wife and his preteen daughter and tell them not to worry—everything really will work out for the best. Just keep smiling and pin up your long gray hair. Go play bridge with your old lady friends. Powder your nose.

That huge horrible wad of fat you see hanging under your chin, your jowls, getting bigger and jigglier every day, that's *submental* fat. That crinkly ring of wrinkles around your neck is a *platysmal band*. The whole slow slide of your face, your chin and neck is caused by gravity dragging down on your *superficial musculo-aponeurotic system*.

Sound familiar?

If you're a little confused right now, relax. Don't worry. All you need to know is this is your face. This is what you think you know best.

These are the three layers of your skin.

These are the three women in your life.

The epidermis, the dermis, and the fat.

Your wife, your daughter, and your mother.

If you're reading this, welcome back to reality. This is where all that glorious, unlimited potential of your youth has led. All that unfulfilled promise. Here's what you've done with your life.

Your name is Peter Wilmot.

All you need to understand is you turned out to be one sorry sack of shit.

June 23

A WOMAN CALLS FROM Seaview to say her linen closet is missing. Last September, her house had six bedrooms, two linen closets. She's sure of it. Now she's only got one. She comes to open her beach house for the summer. She drives out from the city with the kids and the nanny and the dog, and here they are with all their luggage, and all their towels are gone. Disappeared. Poof.

Bermuda triangulated.

Her voice on the answering machine, the way her voice screeches up, high, until it's an air-raid siren by the end of every sentence, you can tell she's shaking mad, but mostly she's scared. She says, "Is this some kind of joke? Please tell me somebody paid you to do this."

Her voice on the machine, she says, "Please, I won't call the police. Just put it back the way it was, okay?"

Behind her voice, faint in the background, you can hear a boy's voice saying, "Mom?"

The woman, away from the phone, she says, "Everything's going to be fine." She says, "Now let's not panic."

The weather today is an increasing trend toward denial.

Her voice on the answering machine, she says, "Just call me back, okay?" She leaves her phone number. She says, "Please . . ."

June 25

PICTURE THE WAY a little kid would draw a fish bone—the skeleton of a fish, with the skull at one end and the tail at the other. The long spine in between, it's crossed with rib bones. It's the kind of fish skeleton you'd see in the mouth of a cartoon cat.

Picture this fish as an island covered with houses. Picture the kind of castle houses that a little girl living in a trailer park would draw—big stone houses, each with a forest of chimneys, each a mountain range of different rooflines, wings and towers and gables, all of them going up and up to a lightning rod at the top. Slate roofs. Fancy wrought-iron fences. Fantasy houses, lumpy with bay windows and dormers. All around them, perfect pine trees, rose gardens, and red brick sidewalks.

The bourgeois daydreams of some poor white trash kid.

The whole island was exactly what a kid growing up in some trailer park—say some dump like Tecumseh Lake, Georgia—would dream about. This kid would turn out all the lights in the trailer while her mom was at work. She'd lie down flat on her back, on the matted-down orange shag carpet in the living room. The carpet smelling like somebody stepped in a dog pile. The orange melted black in spots from cigarette burns. The ceiling was water-stained. She'd fold her arms across her chest, and she could picture life in this kind of place.

It would be that time—late at night—when your ears reach out for any sound. When you can see more with your eyes closed than open.

The fish skeleton. From the first time she held a crayon, that's what she'd draw.

The whole time this kid's growing up, maybe her mom was never home. She never knew her dad, and maybe her mom worked two jobs. One at a shitty fiberglass insulation factory, one slopping food in a hospital cafeteria. Of course, this kid dreams of a place like this island, where nobody works except to keep house and pick wild blueberries and beachcomb. Embroider handkerchiefs. Arrange flowers. Where every day doesn't start with an alarm clock and end with the television. She's imagined these houses, every house, every room, the carved edge of each fireplace mantel. The pattern in every parquet floor. Imagined it out of thin air. The curve of each light fixture or faucet. Every tile, she could picture. Imagine it, late at night. Every wallpaper pattern. Every shingle and stairway and downspout, she's drawn it with pastels. Colored it with crayons. Every brick sidewalk and boxwood hedge, she's sketched it. Filled in the red and green with watercolors. She's seen it, pictured it, dreamed of it. She's wanted it so bad.

Since as early as she could pick up a pencil, this was all she ever drew.

Picture this fish with the skull pointed north and the tail south. The spine is crossed with sixteen rib bones, running east and west. The skull is the village square, with the ferry-boat coming and going from the harbor that's the fish's mouth. The fish's eye would be the hotel, and around it, the grocery store, the hardware supply, the library and church.

She painted the streets with ice in the bare trees. She painted it with birds coming back, each gathering beach grass and pine needles to build a nest. Then, with foxgloves in bloom, taller than people. Then with even taller sunflowers. Then with the leaves spiraling down and the ground under them lumpy with walnuts and chestnuts.

She could see it so clear. She could picture every room, in-side every house.

And the more she could imagine this island, the less she liked the real world. The more she could imagine the people, the less she liked any real people. Especially not her own hip-pie mom, always tired and smelling like French fries and ciga-rette smoke.

It got until Misty Kleinman gave up on ever being a happy person. Everything was ugly. Everyone was crass and just . . . wrong.

Her name was Misty Kleinman.

In case she's not around when you read this, she was your wife. In case you're not just playing dumb—your poor wife, she was born Misty Marie Kleinman.

The poor idiot girl, when she was drawing a bonfire on the beach, she could taste ears of corn and boiled crabs. Drawing the herb garden of one house, she could smell the rosemary and thyme.

Still, the better she could draw, the worse her life got—un-til nothing in her real world was good enough. It got until she didn't belong anywhere. It got so nobody was good enough, refined enough, real enough. Not the boys in high school. Not the other girls. Nothing was as *real* as her imagined world. This got until she was going to student counseling and stealing money from her mom's purse to spend on dope.

So people wouldn't say she was crazy, she made her life about the art instead of the visions. Really, she just wanted the skill to record them. To make her imagined world more and more accurate. More real.

And in art school, she met a boy named Peter Wilmot. She met you, a boy from a place called Waytansea Island.

And the first time you see the island, coming from anyplace else in the entire world, you think you're dead. You're dead and gone to heaven, safe forever.

The fish's spine is Division Avenue. The fish's ribs are streets, starting with Alder, one block south of the village square. Next is Birch Street, Cedar Street, Dogwood, Elm, Fir, Gum, Hornbeam, all of them alphabetical until Oak and Poplar Streets, just before the fish's tail. There, the south end of Division Avenue turns to gravel, and then mud, then disappears into the trees of Waytansea Point.

This isn't a bad description. That's how the harbor looks when you arrive for the first time on the ferryboat from the mainland. Narrow and long, the harbor looks like the mouth of a fish, waiting to gobble you up in a story from the Bible.

You can walk the length of Division Avenue, if you've got all day. Have breakfast at the Waytansea Hotel and then walk a block south, past the church on Alder Street. Past the Wilmot house, the only house on East Birch, with sixteen acres of lawn going right down to the water. Past the Burton house on East Juniper Street. The woodlots dense with oaks, each tree twisted and tall as a moss-covered lightning bolt. The sky above Division Avenue, in summer it's green with dense, shifting layers of maple and oak and elm leaves.

You come here for the first time, and you think all your hopes and dreams have come true. Your life will end happily ever after.

The point is, for a kid who's only ever lived in a house with wheels under it, this looks like the special safe place where she'll live, loved and cared for, forever.

For a kid who used to sit on shag carpet with a box of colored pencils or crayons and draw pictures of these houses, houses she'd never seen. Just pictures of the way she imagined them with their porches and stained-glass windows. For this little girl to one day see these houses for real. These exact houses. Houses she thought she'd only ever imagined . . .

Since the first time she could draw, little Misty Marie knew the wet secrets of the septic tanks behind each house. She knew the wiring inside their walls was old, cloth-wrapped for insulation and strung through china tubes and along china posts. She could draw the inside of every front door, where every island family marked the names and height of each child.

Even from the mainland, from the ferry dock in Long Beach, across three miles of salt water, the island looks like paradise. The pines so dark green they look black, the waves breaking against the brown rocks, it's like everything she could ever want. Protected. Quiet and alone.

Nowadays, this is how the island looks to a lot of people. A lot of rich strangers.

For this kid who'd never swam in anything bigger than the trailer park pool, blinded by too much chlorine, for her to ride the ferry into Waytansea Harbor with the birds singing and the sun bouncing bright off the rows and rows of the hotel windows. For her to hear the ocean rolling into the side of the breakwater, and feel the sun so warm and the clean wind in her hair, smelling the roses in full bloom . . . the thyme and rosemary . . .

This pathetic teenager who'd never seen the ocean, she'd

already painted the headlands and the cliffs that hung high above the rocks. And she'd got them perfect.

Poor little Misty Marie Kleinman.

This girl came here as a bride, and the whole island came out to greet her. Forty, fifty families, all of them smiling and waiting their turn to shake her hand. A choir of grade school kids sang. They threw rice. There was a big dinner in her honor at the hotel, and everyone toasted her with champagne.

From its hillside up above Merchant Street, the windows of the Waytansea Hotel, all six stories of them, the rows of windows and glassed-in porches, the zigzag lines of dormers in the steep roof, they were all watching her arrive. Everyone was watching her come to live in one of the big houses in the shady, tree-lined belly of the fish.

Just one look at Waytansea Island, and Misty Kleinman figured it was worth kissing off her blue-collar mom. The dog piles and shag carpet. She swore never to set foot in the old trailer park. She put her plans for being a painter on hold.

The point is, when you're a kid, even when you're a little older, maybe twenty and enrolled in art school, you don't know anything about the real world. You want to believe somebody when he says he loves you. He only wants to marry you and take you home to live in some perfect island paradise. A big stone house on East Birch Street. He says he only wants to make you happy.

And no, honestly, he won't ever torture you to death.

And poor Misty Kleinman, she told herself, it wasn't a career as an artist that she wanted. What she really wanted, all along, was the house, the family, the peace.

Then she came to Waytansea Island, where everything was so right.

Then it turned out *she* was wrong.

June 26

A MAN CALLS FROM the mainland, from Ocean Park, to complain that his kitchen is gone.

It's natural not to notice at first. After you live anywhere long enough—a house, an apartment, a nation—it just seems too small.

Ocean Park, Oysterville, Long Beach, Ocean Shores, these are all mainland towns. The woman with the missing closet. The man with his bathroom gone. These people, they're all messages on the answering machine, people who had some remodeling done on their vacation places. Mainland places, summer people. You have a nine-bedroom house you only see two weeks each year, it might take you a few seasons to notice you're missing part. Most of these people have at least a half dozen houses. These aren't really homes. These are investments. They have condos and co-ops. They have apartments in London and Hong Kong. A different toothbrush waits in every time zone. A pile of dirty clothes on every continent.

This voice complaining on Peter's answering machine, he says there was a kitchen with a gas range. A double oven in one wall. A big two-door refrigerator.

Listening to him gripe, your wife, Misty Marie, she nods yes, a lot of things used to be different around here.

It used to be you could catch the ferry just by showing up. It runs every half hour, to the mainland and back. Every half hour. Now you get in line. You wait your turn. Sit in the parking lot with a mob of strangers in their shiny sports cars that don't smell like urine. The ferry comes and goes three or four times before there's room for you on board. You, sitting all that time in the hot sun, in that smell.

It takes you all morning just to get off the island.

You used to walk into the Waytansea Hotel and get a window table, no problem. It used to be you never saw litter on Waytansea Island. Or traffic. Or tattoos. Pierced noses. Syringes washed up on the beach. Sticky used condoms in the sand. Billboards. Corporate tagging.

The man in Ocean Park, he said how his dining room wall is nothing but perfect oak wainscoting and blue-striped wallpaper. The baseboard and picture molding and cove molding run seamless and unbroken from corner to corner. He knocked, and the wall is solid, plaster drywall on wood-frame construction. In the middle of this perfect wall is where he swears the kitchen door used to be.

Over the phone, the Ocean Park man says, "Maybe this is my mistake, but a house *has* to have a kitchen? Doesn't it? Isn't that in the building code or something?"

The lady in Seaview only missed her linen closet when she couldn't find a clean towel.

The man in Ocean Park, he said how he took a corkscrew from the dining room sideboard. He screwed a little hole where he remembered the kitchen door. He got a steak knife from the sideboard and stabbed the hole a little bigger. He has a little flashlight on his key chain, and he pressed his cheek to the wall and peeked through the hole he'd made. He squinted, and in the darkness was a room with words written across the walls. He squinted and let his eyes adjust, and there in the dark, all he could read were snatches:

"... set foot on the island and you will die ..." the words said. "... run as fast as you can from this place. They will kill all of God's children if it means saving their own ..."

In where his kitchen should be, it says: "... all of you butchered ..."

The man in Ocean Park says, "You'd better come see what I found." His voice on the answering machine says, "The handwriting alone is worth the trip."

June 28

THE DINING ROOM at the Waytansea Hotel, it's named the Wood and Gold Dining Room because of its walnut paneling and gold brocade upholstery. The fireplace mantel is carved walnut with polished brass andirons. You have to keep the fire burning even when the wind blows from the mainland; then smoke backs up and coughs out the front. Soot and smoke slip out until you have to pull the batteries from every smoke detector. By then the whole hotel smells a little on fire.

Every time someone asks for table nine or ten by the fireplace and then bitches about the smoke and how it's too hot, and asks for a new table, you need to take a drink. Just a sip of whatever you've got. Cooking sherry works for your poor fat wife.

This is a day in the life of Misty Marie, queen of the slaves.

Another longest day of the year.

It's a game anybody can play. This is just Misty's own personal coma.

A couple drinks. A couple aspirin. Repeat.

In the Wood and Gold Dining Room, across from the fireplace, are windows that look down the coastline. Half the glazing putty has dried hard and crumbled until the cold wind whistles inside. The windows sweat. Moisture inside the room collects on the glass and trickles down into a puddle until the floor is soaked through and the carpet smells bad as a whale washed up on the beach for the last two weeks of July. The view outside, the horizon is cluttered with billboards, the same brand names, for fast food, sunglasses, tennis shoes, that you see printed on the litter that marks the tide line.

Floating in every wave, you see cigarette butts.

Every time someone asks for table fourteen, fifteen, or sixteen by the windows and then complains about the cold draft and the stink of the squishy wet carpet, when they whine for a new table, you need to take a drink.

These summer people, their holy grail is the perfect table. The power seat. Placement. The place they're sitting is never as good as where they aren't. It's so crowded, just getting across the dining room, you're punched in the stomach by elbows and hipbones. Slapped with purses.

Before we go any further, you might want to put on some extra clothes. You might want to stock up on some extra B vitamins. Maybe some extra brain cells. If you're reading this in public, stop until you're wearing your best good underwear.

Even before this, you might want to get on the list somewhere for a donor liver.

You can see where this is going.

This is where Misty Marie Kleinman's whole life has gone.

You have endless ways you can commit suicide without *dying* dying.

Whenever anyone from the mainland comes in with a group of her friends, all of them thin and tanned and sighing at the woodwork and white tablecloths, the crystal bud vases filled with roses and fern and the silver-plate antique everything, anytime someone says, "Well, you should serve *tofu* instead of veal!" take a drink.

These thin women, maybe on the weekends you'll see a husband, short and dumpy, sweating so hard the black flock he sprays on his bald spot is running down the back of his neck. Thick rivers of dark sludge that stain the back of his shirt collar.

Whenever one of the local sea turtles comes in clutching her pearls at her withered throat, old Mrs. Burton or Mrs. Seymour or Mrs. Perry, when she sees some skinny tanned summer women at her own personal favorite table since 1865 and says, "Misty, how *could* you? You know I'm always a regular here at noon on Tuesdays and Thursdays. Really, Misty . . ." then you need to take two drinks.

When the summer people ask for coffee drinks with foamed milk or chelated silver or carob sprinkles or soy-based anything, take another drink.

If they don't tip, take another.

These summer women. They wear so much black eyeliner they could be wearing glasses. They wear dark brown lip liner, then eat until the lipstick inside is worn away. What's left is a table of skinny children, each with a dirty ring around her mouth. Their long hooked fingernails the pastel color of Jordan almonds.

When it's summer and you still have to stoke the smoking fireplace, remove an article of clothing.

When it's raining and the windows rattle in the cold draft, put on an article of clothing.

A couple drinks. A couple aspirin. Repeat.

When Peter's mother comes in with your daughter, Tabbi,

and expects you to wait on your own mother-in-law and your own kid like their own personal slave, take two drinks. When they both sit there at table eight, Granmy Wilmot telling Tabbi, "Your mother would be a famous artist if she'd only *try*," take a drink.

The summer women, their diamond rings and pendants and tennis bracelets, all their diamonds dull and greasy with sun-block, when they ask you to sing "Happy Birthday" to them, take a drink.

When your twelve-year-old looks up at you and calls you "ma'am" instead of Mom . . .

When her grandmother, Grace, says, "Misty dear, you'd have more money and dignity if you'd go back to painting . . ."

When the whole dining room hears this . . .

A couple drinks. A couple aspirin. Repeat.

Anytime Grace Wilmot orders the deluxe selection of tea sandwiches with cream cheese and goat cheese and walnuts chopped into a fine paste and spread on paper-thin toast, then she eats only a couple bites and leaves the rest to waste and then charges this and a pot of Earl Grey tea and a piece of carrot cake, she charges all this to you and you don't even know she's done this until your paycheck is only seventy-five cents because of all the deductions and some weeks you actually end up *owing* the Waytansea Hotel money, and you realize you're a sharecropper trapped in the Wood and Gold Dining Room probably for the rest of your life, then take five drinks.

Anytime the dining room is crowded with every little gold brocade chair filled with some woman, local or mainland, and they're all bitching about how the ferry ride takes too long and there's not enough parking on the island and how you never used to need a reservation for lunch and how come some people don't just stay home because it's just too, too much, all these elbows and needy, strident voices asking for directions and asking for nondairy creamer and sundresses in size 2, and the fireplace still has to be blazing away because that's hotel tradition, then remove another article of clothing.

If you're not drunk and half naked by this point, you're not paying attention.

When Raymon the busboy catches you in the walk-in freezer putting a bottle of sherry in your mouth and says, "Misty, *cariño*. *Salud*!"

When that happens, toast him with the bottle, saying, "To my brain-dead husband. To the daughter I never see. To our house, about to go to the Catholic church. To my batty mother-in-law, who nibbles Brie and green onion finger sandwiches . . ." then say, "*Te amo*, Raymon."

Then take a bonus drink.

Anytime some crusty old fossil from a good island family tries to explain how she's a Burton but her mother was a Seymour and her father was a Tupper and *his* mother was a Carlyle and somehow that makes her your second cousin once removed, and then she flops a cold, soft, withered hand on your wrist while you're trying to clear the dirty salad plates and she says, "Misty, why aren't you painting anymore?" and you can see yourself just getting older and older, your whole life spiraling down the garbage disposal, then take two drinks.

What they don't teach you in art school is never, ever to tell people you wanted to be an artist. Just so you know, for the rest of your life, people will torture you by saying how you used to love to draw when you were young. You used to love to paint.

A couple drinks. A couple aspirin. Repeat.

Just for the record, today your poor wife, she drops a butter knife in the hotel dining room. When she bends to pick it up, something's reflected in the silver blade. It's some words written on the underside of table six. On her hands and knees, she lifts the edge of the tablecloth. On the wood, there with the dried chewing gum and crumbs of snot, it says, "Don't let them trick you again."

Written in pencil, it says, "Choose any book at the library."

Somebody's homemade immortality. Their lasting effect. This is their life after death.

Just for the record, the weather today is partly soused with occasional bursts of despair and irritation.

The message under table six, the faint penciled handwriting, it's signed *Maura Kincaid*.

June 29—
The New Moon

IN OCEAN PARK, the man answers his front door, a wineglass in one hand, some kind of bright orange wine filling it up to his index finger on the side of the glass. He's wearing a white terry cloth bathrobe with "Angel" stitched on the lapel. He wears a gold chain tangled in his gray chest hair and smells like plaster dust. His other hand holds the flashlight. The man drinks the wine down to his middle finger, and his face looks puffy with dark chin stubble. His eyebrows are bleached or plucked until they're almost not there.

Just for the record, this is how they met, Mr. Angel Delaporte and Misty Marie.

In art school, you learn that Leonardo da Vinci's painting, the Mona Lisa, it has no eyebrows because they were the last detail the artist added. He was putting wet paint onto dry. In the seventeenth century, a restorer used the wrong solvent and wiped them off forever.

A pile of suitcases sits just inside the front door, the real leather kind, and the man points past them, back into the house with his flashlight in hand, and says, "You can tell Peter Wilmot that his grammar is atrocious."

These summer people, Misty Marie tells them carpenters are always writing inside walls. It's the same idea every man gets, to write his name and the date before he seals the wall with Sheetrock. Sometimes they leave the day's newspaper. It's tradition to leave a bottle of beer or wine. Roofers will write on the decking before they cover it with tar paper and shingles. Framers will write on the sheathing before they cover it with clapboard or stucco. Their name and the date. Some little part of themselves for someone in the future to discover. Maybe a thought. We were here. We built this. A reminder.

Call it custom or superstition or feng shui.

It's a kind of sweet homespun immortality.

In art history, they teach how Pope Pius V asked El Greco to paint over some nude figures Michelangelo had painted on the ceiling of the Sistine Chapel. El Greco agreed, but only if he could paint over the entire ceiling. They teach that El Greco is only famous because of his astigmatism. That's why he distorted his human bodies, because he couldn't see right, he stretched everybody's arms and legs and got famous for the dramatic effect.

From famous artists to building contractors, we all want to leave our signature. Our lasting effect. Your life after death.

We all want to explain ourselves. Nobody wants to be forgotten.

That day in Ocean Park, Angel Delaporte shows Misty the dining room, the wainscoting and blue-striped wallpaper. Halfway up one wall is a busted hole of curling, torn paper and plaster dust.

Masons, she tells him, they'll mortar a charm, a religious medal on a chain, to hang inside a chimney and keep evil spirits from coming down the flue. Masons in the Middle Ages would seal a live cat inside the walls of a new building to bring good luck. Or a live woman. To give the building a soul.

Misty, she's watching his glass of wine. She's talking to it instead of his face, following it around with her eyes, hoping he'll notice and offer her a drink.

Angel Delaporte puts his puffy face, his plucked eyebrow, on the hole and says, ". . . the people of Waytansea Island will kill you the way they've killed everyone before . . ." He holds the little flashlight tight to the side of his head so it shines into the darkness. The bristling brass and silver keys hang down to his shoulder, bright as costume jewelry. He says, "You should see what's written in here."

Slow, the way a child learns to read, Angel Delaporte stares into the dark and says, ". . . now I see my wife working at the Waytansea Hotel, cleaning rooms and turning into a fat fucking slob in a pink plastic uniform . . ."

Mr. Delaporte says, ". . . She comes home and her hands smell like the latex gloves she has to wear to pick up your used rubbers . . . her blond hair's gone gray and smells like the shit she uses to scrub out your toilets when she crawls into bed next to me . . ."

"Hmm," he says, and drinks his wine down to his ring finger. "That's a misplaced modifier."

He reads, ". . . her tits hang down the front of her like a couple of dead carp. We haven't had sex in three years . . ."

It gets so quiet Misty tries to make a little laugh.

Angel Delaporte holds out the flashlight. He drinks his bright orange wine down to where his pinkie finger is on the side of the glass, and he nods at the hole in the wall and says, "Read it for yourself."

His ring of keys is so heavy Misty has to make a muscle to

lift the little flashlight, and when she puts her eye to the small, dark hole, the words painted on the far wall say:

". . . you'll die wishing you'd never set foot . . ."

The missing linen closet in Seaview, the missing bathroom in Long Beach, the family room in Oysterville, whenever people go poking around, this is what they find. It's always Peter's same tantrum.

Your same old tantrum.

". . . you'll die and the world will be a better place for . . ."

In all these mainland houses Peter worked on, these investments, it's the same filth written and sealed inside.

". . . die screaming in terible . . ."

And behind her, Angel Delaporte says, "Tell Mr. Wilmot that he spelled *terrible* wrong."

These summer people, poor Misty, she tells them, Mr. Wilmot wasn't himself for the last year or so. He had a brain tumor he didn't know about for—we don't know how long. Her face still pressed to the hole in the wallpaper, she tells this Angel Delaporte how Mr. Wilmot did some work in the old Waytansea Hotel, and now the room numbers jump from 312 to 314. Where there used to be a room, there's just perfect, seamless hallway, chair molding, baseboard, new power outlets every six feet, top-quality work. All of it code, except the room sealed inside.

And this Ocean Park man swirls the wine in his glass and says, "I hope room 313 wasn't occupied at the time."

Out in her car, there's a crowbar. They can have this doorway opened back up in five minutes. It's just drywall is all, she tells the man. Just Mr. Wilmot going crazy.

When she puts her nose in the hole and sniffs, the wallpaper smells like a million cigarettes came here to die. Inside the hole, you can smell cinnamon and dust and paint. Somewhere inside the dark, you can hear a refrigerator hum. A clock ticks.

Written around and around the walls, it's always this same

rant. In all these vacation houses. Written in a big spiral that starts at the ceiling and spins to the floor, around and around so you have to stand in the center of the room and turn to read it until you're dizzy. Until it makes you sick. In the light from the key ring, it says:

"... murdered despite all your money and status ..."

"Look," she says. "There's your stove. Right where you thought." And she steps back and gives him the little flashlight.

Every contractor, Misty tells him, they'll sign their work. Mark their territory. Finish carpenters will write on the subfloor before they lay the hardwood parquet or the carpet pad. They'll write on the walls before the wallpaper or tile. This is what's inside everybody's walls, this record of pictures, prayers, names. Dates. A time capsule. Or worse, you could find lead pipes, asbestos, toxic mold, bad wiring. Brain tumors. Time bombs.

Proof that no investment is yours forever.

What you don't really want to know—but you don't dare forget.

Angel Delaporte, his face pressed to the hole, he reads, "... I love my wife and I love my kid ..." He reads, "... I won't see my family pushed down and down the ladder by you low-life parasites ..."

He leans into the wall, his face twisting hard against the hole, and says, "This handwriting is so compelling. The way he writes the letter *f* in 'set foot' and 'fat fucking slob,' the top line is so long it overhangs the rest of the word. That means he's actually a very loving, protective man." He says, "See the *k* in 'kill you'? The way the front leg is extralong shows he's worried about something."

Grinding his face against the hole, Angel Delaporte reads, "... Waytansea Island will kill every last one of God's children if it means saving our own ..."

He says, the way the capital *I*'s are thin and pointed proves Peter's got a keen sharp mind but he's scared to death of his mother.

His keys jingle as he pokes the little flashlight around and reads, ". . . I have danced with your toothbrush stuck up my dirty asshole . . ."

His face jerks back from the wallpaper, and he says, "Yeah, that's my stove all right." He drinks the last of the wine, swishing it around, loud, in his mouth. He swallows it, saying, "I knew I had a kitchen in this house."

Poor Misty, she says she's sorry. She'll rip open the doorway. Mr. Delaporte, he probably wants to go get his teeth cleaned this afternoon. That, and maybe a tetanus shot. Maybe a gamma globulin, too.

With one finger, Mr. Delaporte touches a big wet smear next to the hole in the wall. He puts his wineglass to his mouth and goes cross-eyed to find it empty. The dark, wet smear on the blue wallpaper, he touches it. Then he makes a nasty face and wipes his finger on the side of his bathrobe and says, "I hope Mr. Wilmot is heavily insured and bonded."

"Mr. Wilmot has been unconscious in the hospital for the last few days," Misty says.

Reaching a pack of cigarettes from his bathrobe pocket, he shakes one out and says, "So you run his remodeling firm now?"

And Misty tries to laugh. "I'm the fat fucking slob," she says.

And the man, Mr. Delaporte says, "Pardon?"

"I'm Mrs. Peter Wilmot."

Misty Marie Wilmot, the original shrewish bitch monster in the flesh. She tells him, "I was working at the Waytansea Hotel when you called this morning."

Angel Delaporte nods, looking at his empty wineglass. The glass, sweaty and smeared with fingerprints. He holds the wineglass up between them and says, "You want I should get you a drink?"

He looks at where she pressed her face to his dining room wall, where she let one tear leak out and smeared his blue-striped wallpaper. A wet print of her eye, the crow's-feet around her eye, her obicularis oculi behind bars. Still holding the unlit cigarette in one hand, he takes his white terry cloth belt in his other hand and scrubs at the tearstain. And he says, "I'll give you a book. It's called *Graphology*. You know, handwriting analysis."

And Misty, who really did think the Wilmot house, the sixteen acres on Birch Street, meant happily ever after, she says, "You want to maybe *rent* a place for the summer?" She looks at his wineglass and says, "A big old stone house. Not on the mainland, but out on the *island*?"

And Angel Delaporte, he looks back over his shoulder at her, at Misty's hips, then her breasts inside her pink uniform, then her face. He squints and shakes his head a little and says, "Don't worry, your hair's not that gray."

His cheek and temple, all around his eye, he's powdered with white plaster dust.

And Misty, your wife, she reaches toward him, her fingers held open. Her palm turned up, the skin rashy and red, she tells him, "Hey, if you don't believe I'm me," she says, "you can smell my hand."

June 30

YOUR POOR WIFE, she's racing from the dining room to the music room, grabbing up silver candlesticks, little gilded mantel clocks, and Dresden figurines and stuffing them in a pillowcase. Misty Marie Wilmot, after working the breakfast shift, now she's looting the big Wilmot house on Birch Street. Like she's a goddamn burglar in her own house, she's snatching up silver cigarette boxes and pillboxes and snuffboxes. Off fireplace mantels and nightstands, she's collecting saltcellars and carved-ivory knickknacks. She's lugging around the pillowcase, heavy and clanking with gilded-bronze gravy boats and hand-painted porcelain platters.

Still in her pink plastic uniform, sweat stains wet under each arm. Her name tag pinned to her chest, it lets all the strangers in the hotel call her Misty. Your poor wife. She works the same kind of shitty restaurant job her mom did.

Unhappily ever after.

After that, she's running home to pack. She's slinging around a string of keys as noisy as anchor chains. A string of keys like a cluster of iron grapes. These are long and short keys. Fancy notched skeleton keys. Brass and steel keys. Some are barrel keys, hollow like the barrel of a gun, some of them as big as a pistol, the kind a pissed-off wife might tuck in her garter and use to shoot an idiot husband.

Misty is jabbing keys into locks to see if they'll turn. She's trying the locks on cabinets and closet doors. She's trying key after key. Stab and twist. Jab and turn. And each time a lock pops open, she dumps the pillowcase inside, the gilded mantel clocks and silver napkin rings and lead crystal compotes, and she locks the door.

Today is moving-out day. It's another longest day of the year.

In the big house on East Birch Street, everybody's supposed to be packing, but no. Your daughter comes downstairs with a total of nothing to wear for the rest of her life. Your loony mother, she's still cleaning. She's somewhere in the house, dragging the old vacuum cleaner around, on her hands and knees, picking threads and bits of lint out of the rugs and feeding them into the vacuum hose. Like it matters a good goddamn how the rugs look. Like the Wilmot family will ever live here ever again.

Your poor wife, that silly girl who came here a million years ago from some trailer park in Georgia, she doesn't know where to begin.

It's not like the Wilmot family couldn't see this coming. You don't just wake up one day and find the trust fund empty. All the family money gone.

It's only noon, and she's trying to put off her second drink. The second is never as good as the first. The first one is so perfect. Just a little breather. A little something to keep her company. It's only four hours until the renter comes for the keys. Mr. Delaporte. Until they need to vacate.

It's not even a real *drink* drink. It's a glass of wine, and she's only had one, maybe two swallows. Still, just knowing it's nearby. Just knowing the glass is still at least half full. It's a comfort.

After the second drink, she'll take a couple aspirin. Another couple drinks, another couple aspirin, and this will get her through today.

In the big Wilmot house on East Birch Street, just inside the front door, you'll find what looks like graffiti. Your wife, she's dragging around her pillowcase of loot when she sees it—some words scribbled on the back of the front door. The pencil marks there, the names and dates on the white paint. Starting from knee high, you can see dark little straight lines, and along each line a name and number:

Tabbi, age five.

Tabbi, who's twelve now with lateral canthal rhytides around her eyes from crying.

Or: Peter, age seven.

That's *you, age seven.* Little Peter Wilmot.

Some scribbles say: Grace, age six, age eight, age twelve. They go up to Grace, age seventeen. Grace with her baggy jowls of submental fat and deep playsmal bands around her neck.

Sound familiar?

Does any of this ring a bell?

These pencil lines, the crest of a flood tide. The years 1795 . . . 1850 . . . 1979 . . . 2003. Old pencils were thin sticks of wax mixed with soot and wrapped with string to keep your hands clean. Before that are just notches and initials carved in the thick wood and white paint of the door.

Some other names on the back of the door, you won't recognize. Herbert and Caroline and Edna, a lot of strangers who lived here, grown and gone. Infants, then children, adolescents, adults, then dead. Your blood relations, your family, but strangers. Your legacy. Gone, but not gone. Forgotten but still here to be discovered.

Your poor wife, she's standing just inside the front door, looking at the names and dates just one last time. Her own name not among them. Poor white trash Misty Marie, with her rashy red hands and her pink scalp showing through her hair.

All this history and tradition she used to think would keep her safe. Insulate her, forever.

This isn't typical. She's not a boozer. In case anybody needs to be reminded, she's under a lot of stress. Forty-one fucking years old, and now she has no husband. No college degree. No real work experience—unless you count scrubbing the toilet . . . stringing cranberries for the Wilmot Christmas tree . . . All she's got is a kid and a mother-in-law to support. It's noon, and she's got four hours to pack everything of value in the house. Starting with the silverware, the paintings, the china. Everything they can't trust to a renter.

Your daughter, Tabitha, comes down from upstairs. Twelve years old, and all she's carrying is one little suitcase and a shoe box wrapped with rubber bands. With none of her winter clothes or boots. She's packed just a half dozen sundresses, some jeans, and her swimsuit. A pair of sandals, the tennis shoes she's wearing.

Your wife, she's snatching up a bristling ancient ship model, the sails stiff and yellowed, the rigging as fine as cobwebs, and she says, "Tabbi, you know we're not coming back."

Tabitha stands in the front hallway and shrugs. She says, "Granmy says we are."

Granmy is what she calls Grace Wilmot. Her grandmother, your mother.

Your wife, your daughter, and your mother. The three women in your life.

Stuffing a sterling silver toast rack into her pillowcase, your wife yells, "Grace!"

The only sound is the roar of the vacuum cleaner from somewhere deep in the big house. The parlor, maybe the sunporch.

Your wife drags her pillowcase into the dining room. Grabbing a crystal bone dish, your wife yells, "Grace, we need to talk! Now!"

On the back of the door, the name "Peter" climbs as high as your wife can remember, just higher than her lips can stretch when she stands on tiptoe in her black pair of high heels. Written there, it says "Peter, age eighteen."

The other names, Weston and Dorothy and Alice, are faded on the door. Smudged with fingerprints, but not painted over. Relics. Immortal. The heritage she's about to abandon.

Twisting a key in the lock of a closet, your wife throws back her head and yells, "Grace!"

Tabbi says, "What's wrong?"

"It's this goddamn key," Misty says, "it won't work."

And Tabbi says, "Let me see." She says, "Relax, Mom. That's the key to wind up the grandfather clock."

And somewhere the roar of the vacuum cleaner goes quiet.

Outside, a car rolls down the street, slow and quiet, with the driver leaning forward over the steering wheel. His sunglasses pushed up on top of his face, he stretches his head around, looking for a place to park. Stenciled down the side of his car, it says, "Silber International—Beyond the Limits of Being *You*."

Paper napkins and plastic cups blow up from the beach with the deep thump and the word "fuck" set to dance music.

Standing beside the front door is Grace Wilmot, smelling like lemon oil and floor wax. Her smoothed gray head of hair stops a little below the height she was at age fifteen. Proof she's shrinking. You could take a pencil and mark behind the top of her head. You could write: "Grace, age seventy-two."

Your poor, bitter wife looks at a wooden box in Grace's hands. Pale wood under yellowed varnish with brass corners and hinges tarnished almost black, the box has legs that fold out from each side to make it an easel.

Grace offers the box, gripped in both her blue, lumpy hands, and says, "You'll be needing these." She shakes the box. The stiff brushes and old tubes of dried-up paint and broken pastels rattle inside. "To start painting," Grace says. "When it's time."

And your wife, who doesn't have the spare time to throw a fit, she just says, "Leave it."

Peter Wilmot, your mother is fucking useless.

Grace smiles and opens her eyes wide. She holds the box higher, saying, "Isn't that your dream?" Her eyebrows lifted, her corrugator muscle at work, she says, "Ever since you were a little girl, didn't you always want to paint?"

The dream of every girl in art school. Where you learn about wax pencils and anatomy and wrinkles.

Why Grace Wilmot is even cleaning, God only knows. What they need to do is pack. This house: your house: the sterling silver tableware, the forks and spoons are as big as garden tools. Above the dining room fireplace is an oil painting of Some Dead Wilmot. In the basement is a glittering poisonous museum of petrified jams and jellies, antique homemade wines, Early American pears fossilized in amber syrup. The sticky residue of wealth and free time.

Of all the priceless objects left behind, this is what we rescue. These artifacts. Memory cues. Useless souvenirs. Nothing you could auction. The scars left from happiness.

Instead of packing anything of value, something they could sell, Grace brings this old box of paints. Tabbi has her shoe box of junk jewelry, her dress-up jewelry, brooches and rings and necklaces. A layer of loose rhinestones and pearls roll around in the bottom of the shoe box. A box of sharp rusted pins and broken glass. Tabbi stands against Grace's arm. Behind her, just even with the top of Tabbi's head, the door says "Tabbi, age twelve" and this year's date written in fluorescent pink felt-tipped pen.

The junk jewelry, Tabbi's jewelry, it belonged to these names.

All that Grace has packed is her diary. Her red leather diary and some light summer clothes, most of them pastel hand-knit sweaters and pleated silk skirts. The diary, it's cracked red leather with a little brass lock to keep it shut. Stamped in gold across the cover, it says "Diary."

Grace Wilmot, she's always after your wife to start a diary.

Grace says, Start painting again.

Grace says, Go. Get out and visit the hospital more.

Grace says, Smile at the tourists.

Peter, your poor, frowning ogre of a wife looks at your mother and daughter and she says, "Four o'clock. That's when Mr. Delaporte comes to get the keys."

This isn't their house, not anymore. Your wife, she says, "When the big hand is on the twelve and the little hand is on the four, if it's not packed or locked up by then, you'll never see it again."

Misty Marie, her wineglass has at least a couple swallows left in it. And seeing it there on the dining room table, it looks like the answer. It looks like happiness and peace and comfort. Like Waytansea Island used to look.

Standing here inside the front door, Grace smiles and says, "No Wilmot ever leaves this house forever." She says, "And no one who comes here from the outside stays for long."

Tabbi looks at Grace and says, "Granmy, *quand est-ce qu'on revient*?"

And her grandmother says, "*En trois mois,*" and pats Tabbi's head. Your old, useless mother goes back to feeding lint to the vacuum cleaner.

Tabbi starts to open the front door, to take her suitcase to the car. That rusted junk pile stinking of her father's piss.

Your piss.

And your wife asks her, "What did your grandmother just tell you?"

And Tabbi turns to look back. She rolls her eyes and says, "God! Relax, Mom. She only said you look pretty this morning."

Tabbi's lying. Your wife's not stupid. These days, she knows how she really looks.

What you don't understand you can make mean anything.

Then, when she's alone again, Mrs. Misty Marie Wilmot, when no one's there to see, your wife goes up on her tiptoes and stretches her lips toward the back of the door. Her fingers spread against the years and ancestors. The box of dead paints at her feet, she kisses the dirty place under your name where she remembers your lips would be.

July 1

JUST FOR THE RECORD, Peter, it really sucks how you tell everybody your wife's a hotel maid. Yeah, maybe two years ago she used to be a maid.

Now she happens to be the assistant supervisor of the dining room servers. She's "Employee of the Month" at the Waytansea Hotel. She's your wife, Misty Marie Wilmot, mother of your child, Tabbi. She almost, just about, nearly has an undergraduate degree in fine art. She votes and pays taxes. She's queen of the fucking slaves, and you're a brain-dead vegetable with a tube up your ass in a coma, hooked to a zillion very expensive gadgets that keep you alive.

Dear sweet Peter, you're in no position to call anybody a fat fucking slob.

With your kind of coma victims, all the muscles contract. The tendons cinch in tighter and tighter. Your knees pull up to the chest. Your arms fold in, close to your gut. Your feet, the calves contract until the toes point screaming straight down, painful to even look at. Your hands, the fingers curl under with the fingernails cutting the inside of each wrist. Every muscle and tendon getting shorter and shorter. The muscles in your back, your spinal erectors, they shrink and pull your head back until it's almost touching your ass.

Can you feel this?

You all twisted and knotted up, this is the mess Misty drives three hours to see in the hospital. And that doesn't count the ferry ride. You're the mess Misty's married to.

This is the worst part of her day, writing this. It was your mother, Grace, who had the bright idea about Misty keeping a coma diary. It's what sailors and their wives used to do, Grace said, keep a diary of every day they were apart. It's a treasured old seafaring tradition. A golden old Waytansea Island tradition. After all those months apart, when they come back together, the sailors and wives, they trade diaries and catch up on what they missed. How the kids grew up. What the weather did. A record of everything. Here's the everyday shit you and Misty would bore each other with over dinner. Your mother said it would be good for you, to help you process through your recovery. Someday, God willing, you'll open your eyes and take Misty in your arms and kiss her, your loving wife, and here will be all your lost years, written here in loving detail, all the details of your kid growing up and your wife longing for you, and you can sit under a tree with a nice lemonade and have a nice time catching up.

Your mother, Grace Wilmot, she needs to wake up from her own kind of coma.

Dear sweet Peter. Can you feel this?

Everyone's in their own personal coma.

What you'll remember from before, nobody knows. One possibility is all your memory is wiped out. Bermuda triangulated. You're brain-damaged. You'll be born a whole new person. Different, but the same. Reborn.

Just for the record, you and Misty met in art school. You got her pregnant, and you two moved back to live with your mother on Waytansea Island. If this is stuff you know already, just skip ahead. Skim over it.

What they don't teach you in art school is how your whole life can end when you get pregnant.

You have endless ways you can commit suicide without *dying* dying.

And just in case you forgot, you're one chicken-shit piece of work. You're a selfish, half-assed, lazy, spineless piece of crap. In case you don't remember, you ran the fucking car in the fucking garage and tried to suffocate your sorry ass with exhaust fumes, but no, you couldn't even do that right. It helps if you start with a full gas tank.

Just so you know how bad you look, any person in a coma longer than two weeks, doctors call this a persistent vegetative state. Your face swells and turns red. Your teeth start to drop out. If you're not turned every few hours, you get bedsores.

Today, your wife's writing this on your one hundredth day as a vegetable.

As for Misty's breasts looking like a couple dead carp, you should talk.

A surgeon implanted a feeding tube in your stomach. You've got a thin tube inserted into your arm to measure blood pressure. It measures oxygen and carbon dioxide in your arteries. You've got another tube inserted into your neck to measure blood pressure in the veins returning to your heart. You've got a catheter. A tube between your lungs and your rib cage drains any fluids that might collect. Little round electrodes stuck to your chest monitor your heart. Headphones over your ears send sound waves to stimulate your brain stem. A tube forced down your nose pumps air into you from a respirator. Another tube plugs into your veins, dripping fluids and medication. To keep them from drying out, your eyes are taped shut.

Just so you know how you're paying for this, Misty's promised the house to the Sisters of Care and Mercy. The big old house on Birch Street, all sixteen acres, the second you die the Catholic church gets the deed. A hundred years of your precious family history, and it goes right into their pocket.

The second you stop breathing, your family is homeless.

But don't sweat it, between the respirator and the feeding tube and the medication, you're not going to die. You couldn't die if you wanted to. They're going to keep you alive until you're a withered skeleton with machines just pumping air and vitamins through you.

Dear sweet stupid Peter. Can you feel this?

Besides, when people talk about *pulling the plug*, that's pretty much just a figure of speech. This stuff all looks to be hardwired. Plus there's the backup generators, the fail-safe alarms, the batteries, the ten-digit secret codes, the passwords. You'd need a special key to turn off the respirator. You'd need a court order, a malpractice liability waiver, five witnesses, the consent of three doctors.

So sit tight. Nobody's pulling any plugs until Misty figures a way out of this crappy mess you've left her in.

Just in case you don't remember, every time she comes to visit you, she wears one of those old junk jewelry brooches you gave her. Misty takes it off her coat and opens the pin of it. It's sterilized with rubbing alcohol, of course. God forbid you get any scars or staph infections. She pokes the pin of the hairy old brooch—real, real slow—through the meat of your hand or your foot or arm. Until she hits a bone or it pokes out the other side. When there's any blood, Misty cleans it up.

It's so nostalgic.

Some visits, she sticks the needle in you, stabbing again and again. And she whispers, "Can you feel this?"

It's not as if you've never been stuck with a pin.

She whispers, "You're still alive, Peter. How about *this*?"

You sipping your lemonade, reading this under a tree a dozen years from now, a hundred years from now, you need to know that the best part of each visit is sticking in that pin.

Misty, she gave you the best years of her life. Misty owes you nothing but a big fat divorce. Stupid, cheap fuck that you were, you were going to leave her with an empty gas tank like you always do. Plus, you left your hate messages inside everyone's walls. You promised to love, honor, and cherish. You said you'd make Misty Marie Kleinman into a famous artist, but you left her poor and hated and alone.

Can you feel this?

You dear sweet stupid liar. Your Tabbi sends her daddy hugs and kisses. She turns thirteen in two weeks. A teenager.

Today's weather is partly furious with occasional fits of rage.

In case you don't remember, Misty brought you lambskin boots to keep your feet warm. You wear tight orthopedic stockings to force the blood back up to your heart. She's saving your teeth as they fall out.

Just for the record, she still loves you. She wouldn't bother to torture you if she didn't.

You fucker. Can you feel this?

July 2

OKAY, OKAY. FUCK.

Just for the record, a big part of this mess is Misty's fault. Poor little Misty Marie Kleinman. The little latchkey product of divorce with no parent at home most days.

Everybody in college, all her friends in the fine arts program, they told her:

Don't.

No, her friends said. Not Peter Wilmot. Not "the walking peter."

The Eastern School of Art, the Meadows Academy of Fine Arts, the Wilson Art Institute, rumor was Peter Wilmot had flunked out of them all.

You'd flunked out.

Every art school in eleven states, Peter went there and didn't go to class. He never spent any time in his studio. The

Wilmots had to be rich because he'd been in school almost five years and his portfolio was still empty. Peter just flirted with young women full-time. Peter Wilmot, he had long black hair, and he wore these stretched-out cable-knit sweaters the color of blue dirt. The seam was always coming open in one shoulder, and the hem hung down below his crotch.

Fat, thin, young, or old women, Peter wore his ratty blue sweater and slouched around campus all day, flirting with every girl student. Creepy Peter Wilmot. Misty's girlfriends, they pointed him out one day, his sweater unraveling at the elbows and along the bottom.

Your sweater.

Stitches had broken and holes were hanging open in the back, showing Peter's black T-shirt underneath.

Your black T-shirt.

The only difference between Peter and a homeless mental outpatient with limited access to soap was his jewelry. Or maybe not. It was just weird cruddy old brooches and necklaces made from rhinestones. Crusted with fake pearls and rhinestones, these are big scratchy old wads of colored glass that hang off the front of Peter's sweater. Big grandma brooches. A different brooch every day. Some days, it was a big pinwheel of fake emeralds. Then it would be a snowflake made of chipped glass diamonds and rubies, the wire parts turned green from his sweat.

From your sweat.

Junk jewelry.

For the record, the first time Misty met Peter was at a freshman art exhibit where some friends and her were looking at a painting of a craggy stone house. On one side, the house opened into a big glass room, a conservatory full of palm trees. In through the windows, you could see a piano. You could see a man reading a book. A private little paradise. Her friends were saying how nice it looked, the colors and everything, and then somebody said, "Don't turn around, but the walking peter is headed over here."

Misty said, "The what?"

And somebody said, "Peter Wilmot."

Someone else said, "Do not make eye contact."

All her girlfriends said, Misty, do not even encourage him. Anytime Peter came into the room, every woman remembered a reason to leave. He didn't really stink, but you still tried to hide behind your hands. He didn't stare at your breasts, but most women still folded their arms. Watching any woman talk to Peter Wilmot, you could see how her frontalis muscle lifted her forehead into wrinkles, proof she was scared. Peter's top eyelids would be half shut, more like someone angry than looking to fall in love.

Then Misty's friends, in the gallery that night, they scattered.

Then she was standing alone with Peter in his greasy hair and the sweater and the old junk jewelry, who rocked back on his heels, his hands on his hips, and looking at the painting, he said, "So?"

Not looking at her, he said, "You going to be a chicken and run away with your little friends?"

He said this with his chest stuck out. His upper eyelids were half closed, and his jaw worked back and forth. His teeth ground together. He turned and fell back against the wall so hard the painting beside him went crooked. He leaned back, his shoulders squared against the wall, his hands shoved into the front pockets of his jeans. Peter shut his eyes and took a deep breath. He let it out, slow, opened his eyes to stare at her, and said, "So? What do you think?"

"About the painting?" Misty said. The craggy stone house. She reached out and turned it straight again.

And Peter looked sideways without turning his head. His eyes rolled to see the painting just past his shoulder, and he said, “I grew up next door to that house. The guy with the book, that’s Brett Petersen.” Then loud, he said, too loud, “I want to know if you’ll marry me.”

That’s how Peter proposed.

How you proposed. The first time.

He was from the island, everybody said. The whole wax museum of Waytansea Island, all those fine old island families going back to the Mayflower Compact. Those fine old family trees where everybody was everybody’s cousin once removed. Where nobody’s had to buy any silverware since two hundred years ago. They ate something meat with every meal, and all the sons seemed to wear the same shabby old jewelry. Their kind-of regional fashion statement. Their old shingle and stone family houses towered along Elm Street, Juniper Street, Hornbeam Street, weathered just so by the salt air.

Even all their golden retrievers were inbred cousins to each other.

People said everything on Waytansea Island was just-so museum quality. The funky old ferryboat that held six cars. The three blocks of red brick buildings along Merchant Street, the grocer, the old library clock tower, the shops. The white clapboards and wraparound porches of the closed old Waytansea Hotel. The Waytansea church, all granite and stained glass.

There in the art school gallery, Peter was wearing a brooch made from a circle of dirty blue rhinestones. Inside that was a circle of fake pearls. Some blue stones were gone, and the empty fittings looked sharp with ragged little teeth. The metal was silver, but bent and turning black. The point of the long pin, it stuck out from under one edge and looked pimpled with rust.

Peter held a big plastic mug of beer with some sports team stenciled on the side, and he took a drink. He said, “If you’d never consider marrying me, there’s no point in me taking you to dinner, is there?” He looked at the ceiling and then at her and said, "I find this approach saves everybody a shitload of time."

"Just for the record," Misty told him, "that house doesn't exist. I made it up."

Misty told you.

And you said, "You remember that house because it's still in your heart."

And Misty said, "How the fuck do you know what's in my goddamn heart?"

The big stone houses. Moss on the trees. Ocean waves that hiss and burst below cliffs of brown rock. All that was in her little white trash heart.

Maybe because Misty was still standing here, maybe because you thought she was fat and lonely and she hadn't run away, you looked down at the brooch on your chest and smiled. You looked at her and said, "You like it?"

And Misty said, "How old is it?"

And you said, "Old."

"What kind of stones are those?" she said.

And you said, "Blue."

Just for the record, it wasn't easy to fall in love with Peter Wilmot. With you.

Misty said, "Where did it come from?"

And Peter shook his head a little bit, grinning at the floor. He chewed his bottom lip. He looked around at the few people left in the gallery, his eyes narrow, and he looked at Misty and said, "You promise you won't be grossed out if I show you something?"

She looked back over her shoulder at her friends; they were off by a picture across the room, but they were watching.

And Peter whispered, his butt still against the wall, he leaned forward toward her and whispered, "You'll need to suffer to make any real art."

Just for the record, Peter once asked Misty if she knew why

she liked the art she liked. Why is it a terrible battle scene like Picasso's *Guernica* can be beautiful, while a painting of two unicorns kissing in a flower garden can look like crap.

Does anybody really know why they like anything?

Why people do anything?

There in the gallery, with her friends spying, one of the paintings had to be Peter's, so Misty said, "Yeah. Show me some real art."

And Peter chugged some of his beer and handed her the plastic mug. He said, "Remember. You promised." With both hands, he grabbed the ragged hem of his sweater and pulled it up. A theater curtain lifting. An unveiling. The sweater showed his skinny belly with a little hair going up the middle. Then his navel. The hair spread out sideways around two pink nipples starting to show.

The sweater stopped, Peter's face hidden behind it, and one nipple lifted up in a long point off his chest, red and scabbed, sticking to the inside of the old sweater.

"Look," Peter's voice said from behind, "the brooch pins through my nipple."

Somebody let out a little scream, and Misty spun around to look at her friends. The plastic mug dropped out of her hands, hitting the floor with an explosion of beer.

Peter dropped his sweater and said, "You promised."

It was her. The rusted pin was sunk in under one edge of the nipple, jabbed all the way under and coming out the other edge. The skin around it, smeared with blood. The hair pasted down flat with dried blood. It was Misty. She screamed.

"I make a different hole every day," Peter said, and he stooped to pick up the mug. He said, "It's so every day I feel new pain."

Looking now, the sweater around the brooch was crusted stiff and darker with bloodstain. Still, this was art school. She'd seen worse. Maybe she hadn't.

"You," Misty said, "you're crazy." For no reason, maybe shock, she laughed and said, "I mean it. You are vile." Her feet in sandals, sticky and splashed with beer.

Who knows why we like what we like?

And Peter said, "You ever hear of the painter Maura Kincaid?" He twisted the brooch, pinned through his chest, to make it glitter in the white gallery light. To make it bleed. "Or the Waytansea school of painters?" he said.

Why do we do what we do?

Misty looked back at her friends, and they looked at her, their eyebrows raised, ready to come to the rescue.

And she looked at Peter and said, "My name's Misty," and she held out her hand.

And slow, Peter's eyes still on hers, he reached up and opened the clasp behind the brooch. His face winced, every muscle pulled tight for a second. His eyes sewed shut with wrinkles, he pulled the long pin out of his sweater. Out of his chest.

Out of your chest. Smeared with your blood.

He snapped the pin closed and put the brooch in her palm.

He said, "So, you want to marry me?"

He said this like a challenge, like he was picking a fight, like a gauntlet thrown down at her feet. Like a dare. A duel. His eyes handled her all over, her hair, her breasts, her legs, her arms and hands, like Misty Kleinman was the rest of his life.

Dear sweet Peter, can you feel this?

And the little trailer park idiot, she took the brooch.

July 3

ANGEL SAYS TO MAKE a fist. He says, "Hold out your index finger as if you're about to pick your nose."

He takes Misty's hand, her finger pointed straight, and he holds it so her fingertip just touches the black paint on the wall. He moves her finger so it traces the trail of black spray paint, the sentence fragments and doodles, the drips and smears, and Angel says, "Can you feel anything?"

Just for the record, they're a man and a woman standing close together in a small dark room. They've crawled in through a hole in the wall, and the homeowner's waiting outside. Just so you know this in the future, Angel's wearing these tight brown leather pants that smell the way shoe polish smells. The way leather car seats smell. The way your wallet smells, soaked with sweat after it's in your back pocket while you're driving on a hot summer day. That smell Misty used to pretend to hate, that's how Angel's leather pants smell pressed up against her.

Every so often the homeowner standing outside, she kicks the wall and shouts, "You want to tell me what you two are up to in there?"

Today's weather is warm and sunny with a few scattered clouds and some homeowner called from Pleasant Beach to say she'd found her missing breakfast nook, and somebody had better come see right away. Misty called Angel Delaporte, and he met her when the ferry docked so they could drive together. He brings his camera and a bag full of lenses and film.

Angel, you might remember, he lives in Ocean Park. Here's a hint: You sealed off his kitchen. He says the way you write your *m*'s, with the first hump larger than the second, that proves you value your own opinion above public opinion. How you do your lowercase *h*'s, with the last stroke cutting back underneath the hump, shows you're never willing to compromise. It's graphology, and it's a bona fide science, Angel says. After seeing these words in his missing kitchen, he asked to see some other houses.

Just for the record, he says the way you make your lowercase *g*'s and *y*'s, with the bottom loop pulling to the left, that shows you're very attached to your mother.

And Misty told him, he got that part right.

Angel and her, they drove to Pleasant Beach, and a woman opened the front door. She looked at them, her head tilted back so her eyes looked down her nose, her chin pushed forward and her lips pressed together thin, with the muscle at each corner of her jaw, each masseter muscle clenched into a little fist, and she said, "Is Peter Wilmot too lazy to show his face here?"

That little muscle from her lower lip to her chin, the mentalis, it was so tense her chin looked pitted with a million tiny dimples, and she said, "My husband hasn't stopped gargling since this morning."

The mentalis, the corrugator, all those little muscles of the face, those are the first things you learn in art school anatomy. After that, you can tell a fake smile because the risorius and platysma muscles pull the lower lip down and out, squaring it and exposing the lower teeth.

Just for the record, knowing when people are only pretending to like you isn't such a great skill to have.

In her kitchen, the yellow wallpaper peels back from a hole near the floor. The floor's yellow tile is covered in newspapers and white plaster dust. Next to the hole's a shopping bag bulging with scraps of busted plasterboard. Ribbons of torn yellow wallpaper curl out of the bag. Yellow dotted with little orange sunflowers.

The woman stood next to the hole, her arms folded across her chest. She nodded at the hole and said, "It's right in there."

Steelworkers, Misty told her, they'll tie a branch to the highest peak of a new skyscraper or bridge to celebrate the fact that no one has died during construction. Or to bring prosperity to the new building. It's called "tree topping." A quaint tradition.

They're full of irrational superstitions, building contractors.

Misty told the homeowner not to worry.

Her corrugator muscle pulls her eyebrows together above her nose. Her levator labii superioris pulls her upper lip up into a sneer and flares her nostrils. Her depressor labii inferioris pulls her bottom lip down to show her lower teeth, and she says, "It's you who should be worried."

Inside the hole, the dark little room's lined on three sides with yellow built-in bench seats, sort of a restaurant booth with no table. It's what the homeowner calls a breakfast nook. The yellow is yellow vinyl and the walls above the benches are yellow wallpaper. Scrawled across all this is the black spray paint, and Angel moves her hand along the wall where it says:

"... save our world by killing this army of invaders..."

It's Peter's black spray paint, broken sentences and squiggles. Doodles. The paint loops across the framed art, the lace pillows, the yellow vinyl bench seats. On the floor are empty cans with Peter's black handprints, his spiraling fingerprints in paint, they're still clutching each can.

The spray-painted words loop across the little framed pictures of flowers and birds. The black words trail over the little lace throw pillows. The words run around the room in every direction, across the tiled floor, over the ceiling.

Angel says, "Give me your hand." And he balls Misty's fingers together into a fist with just her index finger sticking out straight. He puts her fingertip against the black writing on the wall and makes her trace each word.

His hand tight around hers, guiding her finger. The dark creep of sweat around the collar and under the arms of his white T-shirt. The wine on his breath, collecting against the side of Misty's neck. The way Angel's eyes stay on her while she keeps her eyes on the black painted words. This is how the whole room feels.

Angel holds her finger against the wall, moving her touch along the painted words there, and he says, "Can you feel how your husband felt?"

According to graphology, if you take your index finger and trace someone's handwriting, maybe you take a wooden spoon or chopstick and you just write on top of the written words, you can feel exactly how the writer felt at the time he wrote. You have to study the pressure and speed of the writing, pressing as hard as the writer pressed. Writing as fast as it seems the writer did. Angel says this is all similar to Method acting. What he calls Konstantin Stanislavski's method of physical actions.

Handwriting analysis and Method acting, Angel says they both got popular at the same time. Stanislavski studied the work of Pavlov and his drooling dog and the work of neurophysiologist I. M. Sechenov. Before that, Edgar Allan Poe studied graphology. Everybody was trying to link the physical and the emotional. The body and the mind. The world and the imagination. This world and the next.

Moving Misty's finger along the wall, he has her trace the words: ". . . the flood of you, with your bottomless hunger and noisy demands . . ."

Whispering, Angel says, "If emotion can create a physical action, then duplicating the physical action can re-create the emotion."

Stanislavski, Sechenov, Poe, everybody was looking for some scientific method to produce miracles on demand, he says. An endless way to repeat the accidental. An assembly line to plan and manufacture the spontaneous.

The mystical meets the Industrial Revolution.

The way the rag smells after you polish your boots, that's how the whole room smells. The way the inside of a heavy belt smells. A catcher's mitt. A dog's collar. The faint vinegar smell of your sweaty watchband.

The sound of Angel's breath, the side of her face damp from his whispering. His hand stiff and hard as a trap around her, squeezing her hand. His fingernails dig into Misty's skin. And Angel says, "Feel. Feel and tell me what your husband felt." The words: ". . . your blood is our gold . . ."

The way reading something can be a slap in your face.

Outside the hole, the homeowner says something. She knocks on the wall and says, louder, "Whatever it is you have to do, you'd better be doing it."

Angel whispers, "Say it."

The words say: ". . . you, a plague, trailing your failures and garbage . . ."

Forcing your wife's fingers along each letter, Angel whispers, "Say it."

And Misty says, "No." She says, "It's just crazy talk."

Steering her fingers wrapped tight inside his, Angel shoulders her along, saying, "It's just words. You can say it."

And Misty says, "They're evil. They don't make sense."

The words: ". . . to slaughter all of you as an offering, every fourth generation . . ."

Angel's skin warm and tight around her fingers, he whispers, "Then why did you come see them?"

The words: ". . . my wife's fat legs are crawling with varicose veins . . ."

Your wife's fat legs.

Angel whispers, "Why bother coming?"

Because her dear sweet stupid husband, he didn't leave a suicide note.

Because this is part of him she never knew.

Because she wants to understand who he was. She wants to find out what happened.

Misty tells Angel, "I don't know."

Old-school building contractors, she tells him, they'd never start a new house on a Monday. Only on a Saturday. After the foundation is laid, they'll toss in a handful of rye seed. After three days, if the seed doesn't sprout, they'll build the house. They'll bury an old Bible under the floor or seal it inside the walls. They'll always leave one wall unpainted until the owners arrive. That way the devil won't know the house is done until it's already being lived in.

Out of a pocket in the side of his camera bag, Angel takes something flat and silver, the size of a paperback book. It's square and shining, a flask, curved so your reflection in the concave side is tall and thin. Your reflection in the convex side is squat and fat. He hands it to Misty, and the metal's smooth and heavy with a round cap on one end. The weight shifts as something sloshes inside. His camera bag is scratchy gray fabric, covered with zippers.

On the tall thin side of the flask, it's engraved: *To Angel—Te Amo.*

Misty says, "So? Why are *you* here?"

As she takes the flask, their fingers touch. Physical contact. Flirting.

Just for the record, the weather today is partly suspicious with chances of betrayal.

And Angel says, "It's gin."

The cap unscrews and swings away on a little arm that keeps it attached to the flask. What's inside smells like a good time, and Angel says, "Drink," and his fingerprints are all over her tall, thin reflection in the polish. Through the hole in the wall, you can see the homeowner's feet wearing suede loafers. Angel sets his camera bag so it covers the hole.

Somewhere beyond all this, you can hear each ocean wave hiss and burst. Hiss and burst.

Graphology says the three aspects of any personality show in our handwriting. Anything that falls below the bottom of a word, the tail of a lowercase *g* or *y* for example, that hints at your subconscious. What Freud would call your id. This is your most animal side. If it swings to the right, it means you lean to the future and the world outside yourself. If the tail swings to the left, it means you're stuck in the past and looking at yourself.

You writing, you walking down the street, your whole life shows in every physical action. How you hold your shoulders, Angel says. It's all art. What you do with your hands, you're always blabbing your life story.

It's gin inside the flask, the good kind that you can feel cold and thin down the whole length of your throat.

Angel says the way your tall letters look, anything that rises above the regular lowercase *e* or *x*, those tall letters hint at your greater spiritual self. Your superego. How you write your *l* or *h* or dot your *i*, that shows what you aspire to become.

Anything in between, most of your lowercase letters, these show your ego. Whether they're crowded and spiky or spread out and loopy, these show the regular, everyday you.

Misty hands the flask to Angel and he takes a drink.

And he says, "Are you feeling anything?"

Peter's words say, ". . . it's with your blood that we preserve our world for the next generations . . ."

Your words. Your art.

Angel's fingers open around hers. They go off into the dark, and you can hear the zippers pull open on his camera bag. The brown leather smell of him steps away from her and there's the click and flash, click and flash of him taking pictures. He tilts the flask against his lips, and her reflection slides up and down the metal in his fingers.

Misty's fingers tracing the walls, the writing says: ". . . I've done my part. I found her . . ."

It says: ". . . it's not my job to kill anybody. She's the executioner . . ."

To get the look of pain just right, Misty says how the sculptor Bernini sketched his own face while he burned his leg with a candle. When Géricault painted *The Raft of the Medusa*, he went to a hospital to sketch the faces of the dying. He brought their severed heads and arms back to his studio to study how the skin changed color as it rotted.

The wall booms. It booms again, the drywall and paint shivering under her touch. The homeowner on the other side kicks the wall again with her canvas boat shoes and the framed flowers and birds rattle against the yellow wallpaper. Against the scrawls of black spray paint. She shouts, "You can tell Peter Wilmot he's going to jail for this shit."

Beyond all this, the ocean waves hiss and burst.

Her fingers still tracing your words, trying to feel how you felt, Misty says, "Have you ever heard of a local painter named Maura Kincaid?"

From behind his camera, Angel says, "Not much," and clicks the shutter. He says, "Wasn't Kincaid linked to Stendhal syndrome?"

And Misty takes another drink, a burning swallow, with tears in her eyes. She says, "Did she die from it?"

And still flashing pictures, Angel looks at her through his camera and says, "Look here." He says, "What you said about being an artist? Your anatomy stuff? Smile the way a real smile should look."

July 4

JUST SO YOU KNOW, this looks so sweet. It's Independence Day, and the hotel is full. The beach, teeming. The lobby is crowded with summer people, all of them milling around, waiting for the fireworks to launch from the mainland.

Your daughter, Tabbi, she has a strip of masking tape over each eye. Blind, she's clutching and patting her way around the lobby. From the fireplace to the reception desk, she's whispering, ". . . eight, nine, ten . . ." counting her steps from each landmark to the next.

The summer outsiders, they jump a little, startled by her little hands copping a feel. They give her tight-lipped smiles and step away. This girl in a sundress of faded pink and yellow plaid, her dark hair tied back with a yellow ribbon, she's the perfect Waytansea Island child. All pink lipstick and nail polish. Playing some lovely and old-fashioned game.

She runs her open hands along a wall, feeling across a framed picture, fingering a bookcase.

Outside the lobby windows, there's a flash and a boom. The fireworks shot from the mainland, arching up and out toward the island. As if the hotel were under attack.

Big pinwheels of yellow and orange flame. Red bursts of fire. Blue and green trails and sparks. The boom always comes late, the way thunder follows lightning. And Misty goes to her kid and says, "Honey, it's started." She says, "Open your eyes and come watch."

Her eyes still taped shut, Tabbi says, "I need to learn the room while everyone's here." Feeling her way from stranger to stranger, all of them frozen and watching the sky, Tabbi's counting her steps toward the lobby doors and the porch outside.

July 5

ON YOUR FIRST REAL DATE, you and Misty, you stretched a canvas for her.

Peter Wilmot and Misty Kleinman, on a date, sitting in the tall weeds in a big vacant lot. The summer bees and flies drifting around them. Sitting on a plaid blanket Misty brought from her apartment. Her box of paints, made of pale wood under yellowed varnish with brass corners and hinges tarnished almost black, Misty has the legs pulled out to make it an easel.

If this is stuff you already remember, skip ahead.

If you remember, the weeds were so high you had to stomp them down to make a nest in the sun.

It was spring term, and everyone on campus seemed to have the same idea. To weave a compact disc player or a computer mainframe using only native grasses and sticks. Bits of root. Seedpods. You could smell a lot of rubber cement in the air.

Nobody was stretching canvas, painting landscapes. There was nothing witty in that. But Peter sat on that blanket in the sun. He opened his jacket and pulled up the hem of his baggy sweater. And inside, against the skin of his chest and belly, there was a blank canvas stapled around a stretcher bar.

Instead of sunblock, you'd rubbed a charcoal pencil under each eye and down the bridge of your nose. A big black cross in the middle of your face.

If you're reading this now, you've been in a coma for God knows how long. The last thing this diary should do is bore you.

When Misty asked why you carried the canvas inside your clothes, tucked up under your sweater like that . . .

Peter said, "To make sure it would fit."

You said that.

If you remember, you'll know how you chewed a stalk of grass. How it tasted. Your jaw muscles big and squared, first on one side, then on the other as you chewed around and around. With one hand, you dug down between the weeds, picking out bits of gravel or clods of dirt.

All Misty's friends, they were weaving their stupid grasses. To make some appliance that looked real enough to be witty. And not unravel. Unless it had the genuine look of a real prehistoric high-technology entertainment system, the irony just wouldn't work.

Peter gave her the blank canvas and said, "Paint something."

And Misty said, "Nobody *paint* paints. Not anymore."

If anybody she knew still painted at all, they used their own blood or semen. And they painted on live dogs from the animal shelter, or on molded gelatin desserts, but never on canvas.

And Peter said, "I bet you still paint on canvas."

"Why?" Misty said. "Because I'm retarded? Because I don't know any better?"

And Peter said, "Just fucking paint."

They were supposed to be above representational art. Making pretty pictures. They were supposed to learn visual sarcasm. Misty said they were paying too much tuition not to practice the techniques of effective irony. She said a pretty picture didn't teach the world anything.

And Peter said, "We're not old enough to buy beer, what are we supposed to teach the world?" There on his back in their nest of weeds, one arm behind his head, Peter said, "All the effort in the world won't matter if you're not inspired."

In case you didn't fucking notice, you big boob, Misty really wanted you to like her. Just for the record, her dress, her sandals and floppy straw hat, she was all dressed up for you. If you'd just touch her hair you'd hear it crackle with hair spray.

She wore so much Wind Song perfume she was attracting bees.

And Peter set the blank canvas on her easel. He said, "Maura Kincaid never went to fucking art school." He spit a wad of green slobber, picked another weed stem and stuck it in his mouth. His tongue stained green, he said, "I bet if you painted what's in your heart, it could hang in a museum."

What was in her heart, Misty said, was pretty much just silly crap.

And Peter just looked at her. He said, "So what's the point of painting anything you don't love?"

What she loved, Misty told him, would never sell. People wouldn't buy it.

And Peter said, "Maybe you'd be surprised."

This was Peter's theory of self-expression. The paradox of being a professional artist. How we spend our lives trying to express ourselves well, but we have nothing to tell. We want creativity to be a system of cause and effect. Results. Marketable product. We want dedication and discipline to equal recognition and reward. We get on our art school treadmill, our graduate program for a master's in fine arts, and practice, practice, practice. With all our excellent skills, we have nothing special to document. According to Peter, nothing pisses us off more than when some strung-out drug addict, a lazy bum, or a slobbering pervert creates a masterpiece. As if by accident.

Some idiot who's not afraid to say what they really love.

"Plato," Peter says, and he turns his head to spit green slobber into the weeds. "Plato said: 'He who approaches the temple of the Muses without inspiration in the belief that craftsmanship alone suffices will remain a bungler and his presumptuous poetry will be obscured by the songs of the maniacs.' "

He stuck another weed in his mouth and chewed, saying, "So what makes Misty Kleinman a maniac?"

Her fantasy houses and cobblestone streets. Her seagulls circling the oyster boats as they came back from the shoals she'd never seen. The window boxes overflowing with snapdragons and zinnias. No way in fucking hell was she going to paint that crap.

"Maura Kincaid," Peter says, "didn't pick up a paintbrush until she was forty-one years old." He started taking paintbrushes out of the pale wood box, twisting the ends sharp. He said, "Maura got hitched to a good old Waytansea Island carpenter, and they had a couple kids." He took out her tubes of paint, setting them next to the brushes there on the blanket.

"It wasn't until her husband died," Peter said. "Then Maura got sick, really sick, with consumption or something. Back then, being forty-one made you an old lady."

It wasn't until one of her kids died, he said, that Maura Kincaid ever painted a picture. He said, "Maybe people have to really suffer before they can risk doing what they love."

You told Misty all this.

You said how Michelangelo was a manic-depressive who portrayed himself as a flayed martyr in his painting. Henri Matisse gave up being a lawyer because of appendicitis. Robert Schumann only began composing after his right hand became paralyzed and ended his career as a concert pianist.

You were digging in your pocket while you said this. You were fishing something out.

You talked about Nietzsche and his tertiary syphilis. Mozart and his uremia. Paul Klee and the scleroderma that shrank his joints and muscles to death. Frida Kahlo and the spina bifida that covered her legs with bleeding sores. Lord Byron and his clubfoot. The Brontë sisters and their tuberculosis. Mark Rothko and his suicide. Flannery O'Connor and her lupus. Inspiration needs disease, injury, madness.

"According to Thomas Mann," Peter said, " 'Great artists are great invalids.' "

And there on the blanket, you set something. There, surrounded by tubes of paint and paintbrushes, was a big rhinestone brooch. Big around as a silver dollar, the brooch was clear glass gems, tiny polished mirrors in a pinwheel of yellow and orange, all of them chipped and cloudy. There on the plaid blanket, it seemed to explode the sunlight into sparks. The metal was dull gray, gripping the rhinestones with tiny sharp teeth.

Peter said, "Are you hearing any of this?"

And Misty picked up the brooch. The sparkle reflected straight into her eyes, and she was blinded, dazzled. Disconnected from everything here, the sun and weeds.

"It's for you," Peter said, "for inspiration."

Misty, her reflection showed shattered a dozen times in every rhinestone. A thousand pieces of her face.

To the sparkling colors in her hand, Misty said, "So tell me." She said, "How did Maura Kincaid's husband die?"

And Peter, his teeth green, he spit green into the tall weeds around them. The black cross on his face. He licked his green lips with his green tongue, and Peter said, "Murder." Peter said, "They murdered him."

And Misty started to paint.

July 6

JUST FOR THE RECORD, the cruddy old library with its wallpaper peeling at every seam and dead flies inside all the milk-glass lights hanging from the ceiling, everything you can remember is still here. If you can remember it. The same shabby world globe, yellowed to the color of soup. The continents carved into places like Prussia and the Belgian Congo. They still have the framed sign that says "Anyone Caught Defacing Library Books Will Be Prosecuted."

Old Mrs. Terrymore, the librarian, she wears the same tweed suits, except now she has a lapel button as big as her face that says "Find Yourself in a New Future with Owens Landing Financial Services!"

What you don't understand, you can make mean anything.

People all over the island are wearing this same kind of button or T-shirt, selling some advertising message. They get a little prize or cash award if they're seen wearing it. Turning their bodies into billboards. Wearing baseball caps with 1-800 telephone numbers.

Misty's here with Tabbi, looking for books about horses and insects her teacher wants her to read before Tabbi starts seventh grade this fall.

No computers. No connections to the Internet or database terminals means no summer people. No lattes allowed. No videotapes or DVDs to check out. Nothing permitted above a whisper. Tabbi's off in the kids' section, and your wife's in her own personal coma: the art book section.

What they teach you in art school is that famous old masters like Rembrandt and Caravaggio and van Eyck, they just traced. They drew the way Tabbi's teacher won't let her. Hans Holbein, Diego Velázquez, they sat in a velvet tent in the murky dark and sketched the outside world that shined in through a small lens. Or bounced off a curved mirror. Or like a pinhole camera, just projected into their tiny dark room through a little hole. Projecting the outside world onto the screen of their canvas. Canaletto, Gainsborough, Vermeer, they stayed there in the dark for hours or days, tracing the building or naked model in the bright sunlight outside. Sometimes they even painted the colors straight over the projected colors, matching the shine of a fabric as it fell in projected folds. Painting an exact portrait in a single afternoon.

Just for the record, camera obscura is Latin for "dark chamber."

Where the assembly line meets the masterpiece. A camera using paint instead of silver oxide. Canvas instead of film.

They spend all morning here, and at some point Tabbi comes to stand next to her mother. Tabbi's holding a book open in her hands and says, "Mom?" Her nose still on the page, she tells Misty, "Did you know it takes a fire of at least sixteen-hundred degrees lasting seven hours to consume the average human body?"

The book's got black-and-white photos of burn victims curled into the "pugilist position," their charred arms pulled up in front of their faces. Their hands are clenched into fists, cooked by the heat of the fire. Charred black prizefighters. The book's called *Fire Forensic Investigation*.

Just for the record, today's weather is nervous disgust with tentative apprehension.

Mrs. Terrymore looks up from her desk. Misty tells Tabbi, "Put it back."

Today in the library, in the art section, your wife's touching books at random on the reference shelf. For no reason, she opens a book, and it says how when an artist used a mirror to throw an image onto canvas, the image would be reversed. This is why everyone in so many old-master paintings is left-handed. When they used a lens, the image would be upside down. Whatever way they saw the image, it was distorted. In this book, an old woodcut print shows an artist tracing a projection. Across the page, someone's written, "You can do this with your mind."

It's why birds sing, to mark their territory. It's why dogs pee.

The same as the bottom of the table in the Wood and Gold Dining Room, Maura Kincaid's life-after-death message:

"Choose any book at the library," she wrote.

Her lasting effect in pencil. Her homemade immortality.

This new message is signed *Constance Burton*.

"You can do this with your mind."

At random, Misty pulls down another book and lets it fall open. It's about the artist Charles Meryon, a brilliant French engraver who became schizophrenic and died in an asylum. In one engraving of the French Marine Ministry, a classic stone building behind a row of tall fluted columns, the work looks perfect until you notice a swarm of monsters decending from the sky.

And written across the clouds above the monsters, in pencil, it says: "We are their bait and their trap." Signed *Maura Kincaid*.

With her eyes closed, Misty walks her fingers across the spines of books on the shelf. Feeling the ridges of leather and paper and cloth, she pulls out a book without looking and lets it fall open in her hand.

Here's Francisco Goya, poisoned by the lead in his bright paints. Colors he applied with his fingers and thumbs, scooping them out of tubs until he suffered from lead encephalopathy, leading to deafness, depression, and insanity. Here on the page is a painting of the god Saturn eating his children—a murky mix of black around a bug-eyed giant biting the arms off a headless body. In the white margin of the page, someone's written: "If you've found this, you can still save yourself."

It's signed *Constance Burton*.

In the next book, the French painter Watteau shows himself as a pale, spindly guitar player, dying of tuberculosis as he was in real life. Across the blue sky of the scene, is written: "Do not paint them their pictures." Signed *Constance Burton*.

To test herself, your wife walks across the library, past the old librarian watching through little round glasses of black wire. In her arms, Misty's carrying the books on Watteau, Goya, the camera obscura, all of them open and nested one inside the next. Tabbi looks up, watching from a table heaped with kids' books. In the literature section, Misty closes her eyes again and walks, trailing her fingers across the old spines. For no reason, she stops and pulls one out.

It's a book about Jonathan Swift, about how he developed Ménière's syndrome and his life was ruined by dizziness and deafness. In his bitterness, he wrote the dark satires *Gulliver's Travels* and *A Modest Proposal*, suggesting the British could survive by eating the increasing flood of Irish children. His best work.

The book falls open to a page where someone has written: "They would have you kill all of God's children to save theirs." It's signed *Maura Kincaid*.

Your wife, she wedges this new book inside the last book, and closes her eyes again. Carrying her armload of books, she reaches out to touch another book. Misty walks her fingers from spine to spine. Her eyes closed, she steps forward—into a soft wall and the smell of talcum powder. When she looks, there's dark red lipstick in a white powdered face. A green cap across a forehead, above it a head of curly gray hair. Printed on the cap, it says, "Call 1-800-555-1785 for *Complete* Satisfaction." Below that, black-wire eye glasses. A tweed suit.

"Excuse me," a voice says, and it's Mrs. Terrymore, the librarian. She's standing there, arms folded.

And Misty takes a step back.

The dark red lipstick says, "I'd appreciate it if you didn't destroy the books by piling them together that way."

Poor Misty, she says she's sorry. Always the outsider, she goes to put them on a table.

And Mrs. Terrymore, with her hands open, clutching, she says, "Please, let me reshelve them. Please."

Misty says, not yet. She says she'd like to check them out, and while the two women wrestle over the armload, one book slips out and slams flat on the floor. Loud as a slap across your face. It flaps open to where you can read: "Do not paint them their pictures."

And Mrs. Terrymore says, "I'm afraid those are reference books."

And Misty says, No they're not. Not all of them. You can read the words: "If you've found this, you can still save yourself."

Through her black-wire glasses, the librarian sees this and

says, “Always more damage. Every year.” She looks at a tall clock in a dark walnut case, and she says, “Well, if you don’t mind, we’ve closed early today.” She checks her wristwatch against the tall clock, saying, “We closed ten minutes ago.”

Tabbi’s already checked out her books. She’s standing by the front door, waiting, and calls, “Hurry, Mom. You have to be at work.”

And with one hand, the librarian fishes in the pocket of her tweed jacket and brings out a big pink gum eraser.

July 7

THE STAINED-GLASS windows of the island church, little white trash Misty Marie Kleinman, she could draw them before she could read or write. Before she'd ever seen stained glass. She'd never been inside a church, any church. Godless little Misty Kleinman, she could draw the tombstones in the village cemetery out on Waytansea Point, drawing the dates and epitaphs before she knew they were numbers and words.

Now, sitting here in church services, it's hard for her to remember what she first imagined and what she saw for real after she'd arrived. The purple altar cloth. The thick wood beams black with varnish.

It's all what she imagined as a kid. But that's impossible.

Grace beside her in the pew, praying. Tabbi on the far side of Grace, both of them kneeling. Their hands folded.

Grace's voice, her eyes closed and her lips muttering into her hands, she says, "Please let my daughter-in-law return to the artwork she loves. Please don't let her squander the glorious talent God has given her . . ."

Every old island family around them, muttering in prayer.

Behind them, a voice is whispering, ". . . please, Lord, give Peter's wife what she needs to start her work . . ."

Another voice, Old Lady Petersen, is praying, ". . . may Misty save us before the outsiders get any worse . . ."

Even Tabbi, your own daughter, is whispering, "God, make my mom get her act together and get started on her art . . ."

All the Waytansea Island waxworks are kneeling around Misty. The Tuppers and Burtons and Niemans, they're all eyes-closed, knotting their fingers together and asking God to make her paint. All of them thinking she has some secret talent to save them.

And Misty, your poor wife, the only sane person here, she just wants to—well, all she wants is a drink.

A couple drinks. A couple aspirin. And repeat.

She wants to yell for everybody to just shut up with their goddamn prayers.

If you've reached middle age and you see how you're never going to be the big famous artist you dreamed of becoming and paint something that will touch and inspire people, really touch and move them and change their lives. You just don't have the talent. You don't have the brains or inspiration. You don't have any of what it takes to create a masterpiece. If you see how your whole portfolio of work is just grand stony houses and big pillowy flower gardens—the naked dreams of a little girl in Tecumseh Lake, Georgia—if you see how anything you could paint would just be adding more mediocre shit to a world already crammed with mediocre shit. If you realize you're forty-one years old and you've reached the end of your God-given potential, well, cheers.

Here's mud in your eye. Bottoms up.

Here's as smart as you're ever going to get.

If you realize there's no way you can give your child a better standard of living—hell, you can't even give your child the quality of life that your trailer park mom gave you—and this means no college for her, no art school, no dreams, nothing except for waiting tables like her mom . . .

Well, it's down the hatch.

This is every day in the life of Misty Marie Wilmot, queen of the slaves.

Maura Kincaid?

Constance Burton?

The Waytansea school of painters. They were different, born different. Those artists who made it look so easy. The point is some people have talent, but most people don't. Most people, we're going to top out with no glory, no perks. Folks like poor Misty Marie, they're limited, borderline dummies, but nothing enough to get a handicapped parking space. Or get any kind of Special Olympic Games. They just pay the bulk of taxes but get no special menu at the steak house. No oversized bathroom stall. No special seat at the front of the bus. No political lobby.

No, your wife's job will be to applaud other people.

In art school, one girl Misty knew, she ran a kitchen blender full of wet concrete until the motor burned out in a cloud of bitter smoke. This was her statement about life as a housewife. Right now, that girl is probably living in a loft eating organic yogurt. She's rich and can cross her legs at the knee.

Another girl Misty knew in art school, she performed a three-act play with puppets in her own mouth. These were little costumes you could slip over your tongue. You'd hold the extra costumes inside your cheek, the same as the wings to a stage. Between scene changes, you'd just close your lips as a curtain. Your teeth, the footlights and proscenium arch. You'd slip your tongue into the next costume. After doing a three-act play, she'd have stretch marks all around her mouth. Her orbicularis oris stretched all out of shape.

One night in a gallery, doing a tiny version of *The Greatest Story Ever Told*, this girl almost died when a tiny camel slipped down her throat. These days, she was probably rolling in grant money.

Peter with his praise for all of Misty's pretty houses, he was so wrong. Peter who said she should hide away on the island, paint only what she loved, his advice was so fucked.

Your advice, your praise was so very, very fucked.

According to you, Maura Kincaid washed fish in a cannery for twenty years. She potty-trained her kids, weeded her garden, then one day she sits down and paints a masterpiece. The bitch. No graduate degree, no studio time, but now she's famous forever. Loved by millions of people who will never meet her.

Just for the record, the weather today is bitter with occasional fits of jealous rage.

Just so you know, Peter, your mother's still a bitch. She's working part-time for a service that finds people pieces of china after their pattern is discontinued. She overheard some rich summer woman, just a tanned skeleton in a knit-silk pastel tank dress, sitting at lunch and saying, "What's the point of being rich here if there's nothing to buy?"

Since Grace heard this, she's been hounding your wife to paint. To give people something they can clamor to own. Like somehow Misty could pull a masterpiece out of her ass and earn the Wilmot family fortune back.

Like she could save the whole island that way.

Tabbi's birthday is coming up, the big thirteen, and there's no money for a gift. Misty's saving her tips until there's enough money for them to go live in Tecumseh Lake. They can't live in the Waytansea Hotel forever. Rich people are eating the island alive, and she doesn't want Tabbi to grow up poor, pressured by rich boys with drugs.

By the end of summer, Misty figures they can bail. About Grace, Misty doesn't know. Your mother must have friends she can live with. There's always the church that can help her. The Ladies Altar Society.

Here around them in church are the stained-glass saints, all of them pierced with arrows and hacked with knives and burning on bonfires, and now Misty pictures you. Your theory about suffering as a means to divine inspiration. Your stories about Maura Kincaid.

If misery is inspiration, Misty should be reaching her prime.

Here, with the whole island around her kneeling in prayer for her to paint. For her to be their savior.

The saints all around them, smiling and performing miracles in their moments of pain, Misty reaches out to take a hymnal. This is one book among dozens of dusty old hymnals, some without covers, some of them trailing frayed satin ribbons. She takes one at random and opens it. And, nothing.

She flips through the pages, but there's nothing. Just prayers and hymns. No special secret messages scribbled inside.

Still, when she goes to put it back, carved there in the wood of the pew where the hymnal hid it, a message says: "Leave this island before you can't."

It's signed *Constance Burton*.

July 8

ON THEIR FIFTH REAL DATE, Peter was matting and framing the picture Misty had painted.

You, Peter, you were telling Misty, "This. This picture. It will hang in a museum."

The picture, it was a landscape showing a house wrapped in porches, shaded with trees. Lace curtains hung in the windows. Roses bloomed behind a white picket fence. Blue birds flew through shafts of sunlight. A ribbon of smoke curled up from one stone chimney. Misty and Peter were in a frame shop near campus, and she was standing with her back to the shop's front window, trying to block if anybody might see in.

Misty and you.

Blocking if anybody might see her painting.

Her signature was at the bottom, below the picket fence,

Misty Marie Kleinman. The only thing missing was a smiling face. A heart dotting the *i* in Kleinman.

"Maybe a museum of kitsch," she said. This was just a better version of what she'd been painting since childhood. Her fantasy village. And seeing it felt worse than seeing the worst, most fat naked picture of yourself ever. Here it was, the trite little heart of Misty Marie Kleinman. The sugary dreams of the poor, lonely six-year-old kid she'd be for the rest of her life. Her pathetic, pretty rhinestone soul.

The trite little secret of what made her feel happy.

Misty kept peeking back over one shoulder to make sure no one was looking in. No one was seeing the most cliché, honest part of her, painted here in watercolors.

Peter, God bless him, he just cut the mat and centered the painting inside it.

You cut the mat.

Peter set up the miter saw on the shop's workbench, and he cut the lengths for each side of the frame. The painting, when Peter looked at it, half his face smiled, the zygomatic major pulling up one side of his mouth. He only lifted the eyebrow on that side. He said, "You got the porch railing perfect."

Outside, a girl from art school walked by on the sidewalk. This girl, her latest "work" was stuffing a teddy bear with dog shit. She worked with her hands inside blue rubber gloves so thick she could almost not bend her fingers. According to her, beauty was a stale concept. Superficial. A cheat. She was working a new vein. A new twist on a classic Dada theme. In her studio, she had the little teddy bear already gutted out, its fake fur spread open autopsy-style, ready to turn into art. Her rubber gloves smeared with brown stink, she could hardly hold the needle and red suture thread. Her title for all this was: *Illusions of Childhood*.

Other kids in art school, kids from rich families, the kids

who traveled and saw real art in Europe and New York, all of them did this kind of work.

Another boy in Misty's class, he was masturbating, trying to fill a piggy bank with sperm before the end of the year. He lived off dividends from a trust fund. Another girl drank different colors of egg temperas, then drank syrup of ipecac that made her vomit her masterpiece. She drove to class on a moped from Italy that cost more than the trailer where Misty grew up.

In the frame shop that morning, Peter fitted the corners of the frame together. He dabbed glue with his bare fingers and drilled holes in each corner for the screws.

Still standing between the window and the workbench, her shadow blocking the sunlight, Misty said, "You really think it's good?"

And Peter said, "If you only knew . . ."

You said that.

Peter said, "You're in my light. I can't see."

"I don't want to move," Misty told him. "People outside might see."

All the dog shit and jack-off and barf. Running the glass cutter across the glass, never taking his eyes off the little cutting wheel, a pencil tucked in the hair behind one ear, Peter said, "Just smelling super gross doesn't make their work art."

Snapping the glass into two pieces, Peter said, "Shit is an esthetic cliché." He said how the Italian painter Piero Manzoni canned his own shit, labeled "100% Pure Artist's Shit," and people bought it.

Peter was watching his hands so hard that Misty had to watch. She wasn't watching the window, and behind them they heard a bell ring. Somebody'd walked into the shop. Another shadow fell over the workbench.

Without looking up, Peter went, "Hey."

And this new guy said, "Hey."

The friend was maybe Peter's age, blond with a patch of chin hairs, but not what you'd call a beard. Another student from the art school. He was another rich kid from Waytansea Island, and he stood, his blue eyes looking down at the painting on the workbench. He smiled Peter's same half smile, the look of somebody laughing over the fact he had cancer. The look of someone facing a firing squad of clowns with real guns.

Not looking up, Peter buffed the glass and fit it into the new frame. He said, "See what I mean about the picture?"

The friend looked at the house wrapped in porches, the picket fence and blue birds. The name Misty Marie Kleinman. Half smiling, shaking his head, he said, "It's the Tupper house, all right."

It was a house Misty had just made up. Invented.

In one ear, the friend had a single earring. An old piece of junk jewelry, in the Waytansea Island style of Peter's friends. Buried in his hair, it was fancy gold filigree around a big red enamel heart, flashes of red glass, cut-glass jewels twinkled in the gold. He was chewing gum. Spearmint, from the smell.

Misty said, "Hi." She said, "I'm Misty."

And the friend, he looked at her, giving her the same doomed smile. Chewing his gum, he said, "So is this her? Is she the mythical lady?"

And slipping the picture into the frame, behind the glass, looking only at his work, Peter said, "I'm afraid so."

Still staring at Misty, his eyes jumping around every part of her, her hands and legs, her face and breasts, the friend cocked his head to one side, studying. Still chewing his gum, he said, "Are you sure she's the right one?"

Some magpie part of Misty, some little princess part, couldn't take her eyes off the guy's glittery red earring. The sparkling enamel heart. The flash of red from the cut-glass rubies.

Peter fitted a piece of backing cardboard behind the picture and sealed it around the edge with tape. Running his thumb over the tape, sealing it down, he said, "You saw the painting." He stopped and sighed, his chest getting big, then collapsing, and he said, "I'm afraid she's the real deal."

Misty, Misty's eyes were pinned inside the blond tangle of the friend's hair. The red flash of the earring there, it was Christmas lights and birthday candles. In the sunlight from the shopwindow, the earring was Fourth of July fireworks and bouquets of Valentine's Day roses. Looking at the sparkle, she forgot she had hands, a face, a name.

She forgot to breathe.

Peter said, "What'd I tell you, man?" He was looking at Misty now, watching her spellbound by the red earring, and Peter said, "She can't resist the old jewelry."

The blond guy saw Misty staring back at him, and both his blue eyes swung sideways to see where Misty's eyes were pinned.

In the earring's cut-glass sparkle, in there was the sparkle of champagne Misty had never seen. There were the sparks of beach bonfires, spiraling up to summer stars Misty could only imagine. In there was the flash of crystal chandeliers she had painted in each fantasy parlor.

All the yearning and idiot need of a poor, lonely kid. Some stupid, unenlightened part, not the artist but the idiot in her, loved that earring, the bright rich shine of it. The glitter of sugary hard candy. Candy in a cut-glass dish. A dish in a house she'd never visited. Nothing deep or profound. Just everything we're programmed to adore. Sequins and rainbows. Those bangles she should've been educated enough to ignore.

The blond, Peter's friend, he reached one hand up to touch his hair, then his ear. His mouth dropped open, so fast his gum fell out onto the floor.

Your friend.

And you said, "Careful, dude, it looks like you're stealing her away from me . . ."

And the friend, his fingers fumbled, digging in his hair, and he yanked the earring. The pop made them all wince.

When Misty opened her eyes, the blond guy was holding out his earring, his blue eyes filled with tears. His torn earlobe hung in two ragged pieces, forked, blood dripping from both points. "Here," he said, "take it." And he threw the earring toward the workbench. It landed, gold and fake rubies scattering red sparks and blood.

The screw-on back was still on the post. It was so old, the gold back had turned green. He'd yanked it off so fast the earring was tangled in blond hairs. Each hair still had the soft white bulb where it pulled out at the root.

One hand cupped over his ear, blood running from between his fingers, the guy smiled. His corrugator muscle pulling his pale eyebrows together, he said, "Sorry, Petey. It looks like you're the lucky guy."

And Peter lifted the painting, framed and finished. Misty's signature at the bottom.

Your future wife's signature. Her bourgeois little soul.

Your future wife already reaching for the bloody spot of red sparkle.

"Yeah," Peter said, "fucking lucky me."

And still bleeding, one hand clamped over his ear, the blood running down his arm to drip from his pointed elbow, Peter's friend backed up a couple steps. With his other hand, he reached for the door. He nodded at the earring and said, "Keep it. A wedding present." And he was gone.

July 9

THIS EVENING, Misty is tucking your daughter into bed when Tabbi says, "Granmy Wilmot and I have a secret."

Just for the record, Granmy Wilmot knows everybody's secrets.

Grace sits through church service and elbows Misty, telling her how the rose window the Burtons donated for their poor, sad daughter-in-law—well, the truth is Constance Burton gave up painting and drank herself to death.

Here's two centuries of Waytansea shame and misery, and your mother can repeat every detail. The cast-iron benches on Merchant Street, the ones made in England, they're in memory of Maura Kincaid, who drowned trying to swim the six miles to the mainland. The Italian fountain on Parson Street—it's in honor of Maura's husband.

The murdered husband, according to Peter.

According to you.

The whole village of Waytansea, this is their shared coma.

Just for the record, Mother Wilmot sends her love.

Not that she ever wants to visit you.

Tucked in bed, Tabbi rolls her head to look out the window and says, "Can we go on a picnic?"

We can't afford it, but the minute you die, Mother Wilmot's got a drinking fountain picked out, brass and bronze, sculpted like a naked Venus riding a conch shell sidesaddle.

Tabbi brought her pillow when Misty moved them into the Waytansea Hotel. They all brought something. Your wife brought your pillow, because it smells like you.

In Tabbi's room, Misty sits on the edge of the bed, combing her kid's hair through her fingers. Tabbi has her father's long black hair and his green eyes.

Your green eyes.

She has a little room she shares with her grandmother, next to Misty's room in the attic hallway of the hotel.

Almost every old family has rented out their house and moved into the hotel attic. The rooms papered with faded roses. The wallpaper peeling along every seam. There's a rusty sink and a little mirror bolted to the wall in each room. Two or three iron beds in every room, their paint chipped, their mattresses soft and sagging in the middle. These are the cramped rooms, under the sloping ceilings, behind their little windows, dormers like rows of little doghouses in the hotel's steep roof. The attic is a barracks, a refugee camp for nice white gentry. People to-the-manor-born now share a bathroom down the hall.

These people who've never held a job, this summer, they're waiting tables. As if everyone's money ran out at the same time, this summer every blue-blood islander is carrying luggage at the hotel. Cleaning hotel rooms. Shining shoes. Washing dishes. A service industry of blue-eyed blonds with shining hair and long legs. Polite and cheerful and eager to run fetch a fresh ashtray or decline a tip.

Your family—your wife and child and mother—they all sleep in sagging, chipped iron beds, under sloping walls with the hoarded silver and crystal relics of their former genteel life.

Go figure, but all the island families, they're smiling and whistling. As if this were some adventure. A zany lark. As if they're just slumming in the service industry. As if this tedious kind of bowing and scraping isn't going to be the rest of their lives. Their lives and their children's lives. As if the novelty won't wear off after another month. They're not stupid. It's just that none of them have ever been poor. Not like your wife, she knows about having pancakes for dinner. Eating government-surplus cheese. Powdered milk. Wearing steel-toed shoes and punching a goddamn time clock.

Sitting there with Tabbi, Misty says, "So, what's your secret?"

And Tabbi says, "I can't tell."

Misty tucks the covers in around the girl's shoulders, old hotel sheets and blankets washed until they're nothing but gray lint and the smell of bleach. The lamp beside Tabbi's bed is her pink china lamp painted with flowers. They brought it from the house. Most of her books are here, the ones that would fit. They brought her clown paintings and hung them above her bed.

Her grandmother's bed is close enough Tabbi could reach out and touch the quilt that covers it with velvet scraps from Easter dresses and Christmas clothes going a hundred years back. On the pillow, there's her diary bound in red leather with "Diary" across the cover in scrolling gold letters. All Grace Wilmot's secrets locked inside.

Misty says, "Hold still, honey," and she picks a stray eyelash off Tabbi's cheek. Misty rubs the lash between two fingers. It's long like her father's eyelashes.

Your eyelashes.

With Tabbi's bed and her grandmother's, two twin beds, there's not much room left. Mother Wilmot brought her diary. That, and her sewing basket full of embroidery thread. Her knitting needles and crochet hooks and embroidery hoops. It's something she can do while she sits in the lobby with her old lady friends or outside on the boardwalk above the beach in good weather.

Your mother's just like all the other fine old Mayflower families, getting their wagons into a circle at the Waytansea Hotel, waiting out the siege of awful strangers.

Stupid as it sounds, Misty brought her drawing tools. Her pale wood box of paints and watercolors, her paper and brushes, it's all piled in a corner of her room.

And Misty says, "Tabbi honey?" She says, "You want to maybe go live with your Grandma Kleinman over by Tecumseh Lake?"

And Tabbi rolls her head back and forth, no, against her pillow until she stops and says, "Granmy Wilmot told me why Dad was so pissed off all the time."

Misty tells her, "Don't say 'pissed off,' please."

Just for the record, Granmy Wilmot is downstairs playing bridge with her cronies in front of the big clock in the wood-paneled room off the lobby. The loudest sound in the room will be the big pendulum ticktocking back and forth. Either that or she's sitting in a big red leather wing chair next to the lobby fireplace, reading with her thick magnifying glass hovering over each page of a book in her lap.

Tabbi tucks her chin down against the satin edge of the blanket, and she says, "Granmy told me why Dad doesn't love you."

And Misty says, "Of course your daddy loves me."

And of course she's lying.

Outside the room's little dormer window, the breaking waves shimmer under the lights of the hotel. Far down the coast is the dark line of Waytansea Point, a peninsula of nothing but forest and rock jutting out into the shimmering ocean.

Misty goes to the window and puts her fingertips on the sill, saying, "You want it open or shut?" The white paint on the windowsill is blistered and peeling, and she picks at it, wedging paint chips under her fingernail.

Rolling her head back and forth on her pillow, Tabbi says, "No, Mom." She says, "Granmy Wilmot says Dad never loved you for real. He only pretended love to bring you here and make you stay."

"To bring me here?" Misty says. "To Waytansea Island?" With two fingers, she scratches off the loose flecks of white paint. The sill underneath is brown varnished wood. Misty says, "What else did your grandmother tell you?"

And Tabbi says, "Granmy says you're going to be a famous artist."

What you don't learn in art theory is how too big a compliment can hurt more than a slap in the face. Misty, a famous artist. Big fat Misty Wilmot, queen of the fucking slaves.

The white paint is flaking off in a pattern, in words. A wax candle or a finger of grease, maybe gum arabic, it makes a negative message underneath. Somebody a long time ago wrote something invisible here that new paint can't stick to.

Tabbi lifts some strands of her hair and looks at the ends, so close-up her eyes go crossed. She looks at her fingernails and says, "Granmy says we should go on a picnic out on the point."

The ocean shimmers, bright as the bad costume jewelry Peter wore in art school. Waytansea Point is nothing but black. A void. A hole in everything.

The jewelry you wore in art school.

Misty makes sure the window's locked, and she brushes the

loose paint chips into the palm of one hand. In art school, you learn the symptoms of adult lead poisoning include tiredness, sadness, weakness, stupidity—symptoms Misty has had most of her adult life.

And Tabbi says, "Granmy Wilmot says everyone will want your pictures. She says you'll do pictures the summer people will fight over."

Misty says, "Good night, honey."

And Tabbi says, "Granmy Wilmot says you'll make us a rich family again." Nodding her head, she says, "Dad brought you here to make the whole island rich again."

The paint chips cupped in one hand, Misty turns out the light.

The message on the windowsill, where the paint flaked off, underneath it said, "You'll die when they're done with you." It's signed *Constance Burton*.

Flaking off more paint, the message says, "We all do."

As she bends to turn off the pink china lamp, Misty says, "What do you want for your birthday next week?"

And a little voice in the dark, Tabbi says, "I want a picnic on the point, and I want you to start painting again."

And Misty tells the voice, "Sleep tight," and kisses it good night.

July 10

ON THEIR TENTH DATE, Misty asked Peter if he'd messed with her birth control pills.

They were in Misty's apartment. She was working on another painting. The television was on, tuned to a Spanish soap opera. Her new painting was a tall church fitted together out of cut stone. The steeple was roofed with copper tarnished dark green. The stained-glass windows were complicated as spiderwebs.

Painting the shiny blue of the church doors, Misty said, "I'm not stupid." She said, "A lot of women would notice the difference between a real birth control pill and the little pink cinnamon candies you switched them with."

Peter had her last painting, the house with the white picket fence, the picture he'd framed, and he'd stuffed it up under his baggy old sweater. Like he was pregnant with a very square baby, he waddled around Misty's apartment. His arms straight down at his sides, he was holding the picture in place with his elbows.

Then fast, he moved his arms a little and the painting dropped out. A heartbeat from the floor, from the glass breaking into a mess, Peter caught it between his hands.

You caught it. Misty's painting.

She said, "What the fuck are you doing?"

And Peter said, "I have a plan."

And Misty said, "I'm not having kids. I'm going to be an artist."

On television, a man slapped a woman to the ground and she lay there, licking her lips, her breasts heaving inside a tight sweater. She was supposed to be a police officer. Peter couldn't speak a word of Spanish. What he loved about Spanish soap operas is you could make what people say mean anything.

And stuffing the painting up under his sweater, Peter said, "When?"

And Misty said, "When what?"

The painting dropped out, and he caught it.

"When are you going to be an artist?" he said.

Another reason to love Spanish soap operas was how fast they could resolve a crisis. One day, a man and woman were hacking at each other with butcher knives. The next day, they were kneeling in church with their new baby. Their hands folded in prayer. People accepted the worst from each other, screaming and slapping. Divorce and abortion were just never a plot option.

If this was love or just inertia, Misty couldn't tell.

After she graduated, she said, then she'd be an artist. When she'd put together a body of work and found a gallery to show her. When she'd sold a few pieces. Misty wanted to be realistic. Maybe she'd teach art at the high school level. Or she'd be a technical draftsman or an illustrator. Something practical. Not everybody could be a famous painter.

Stuffing the painting inside his sweater, Peter said, "You could be famous."

And Misty told him to stop. Just stop.

"Why?" he said. "It's the truth."

Still watching the television, pregnant with the painting, Peter said, "You have such talent. You could be the most famous artist of your generation."

Watching some Spanish commercial for a plastic toy, Peter said, "With your gift, you're *doomed* to be a great artist. School for you is a waste of time."

What you don't understand, you can make mean anything.

The painting dropped out, and he caught it. He said, "All you have to do is paint."

Maybe this is why Misty loved him.

Loved you.

Because you believed in her so much more than she did. You expected more from her than she did from herself.

Painting the tiny gold of the church doorknobs, Misty said, "Maybe." She said, "But that's why I don't want kids . . ."

Just for the record, it was kind of cute. All of her birth control pills being replaced with little heart-shaped candies.

"Just marry me," Peter said. "And you'll be the next great painter of the Waytansea school."

Maura Kincaid and Constance Burton.

Misty said how only two painters didn't count as a "school."

And Peter said, "It's three, counting you."

Maura Kincaid, Constance Burton, and Misty Kleinman.

"Misty *Wilmot*," Peter said, and he stuffed the painting inside his sweater.

You said.

On television, a man shouted "*Te amo . . . Te amo . . .*" again and again to a dark-haired girl with brown eyes and feathery long eyelashes while he kicked her down a flight of stairs.

The painting dropped out of his sweater, and Peter caught it again. He stepped up beside Misty, where she was working on the details of the tall stone church, the flecks of green moss on the roof, the red of rust on the gutters. And he said, "In that church, right there, we'll get married."

And duh-duh-dumb little Misty, she said how she was making the church up. It didn't really exist.

"That's what you think," Peter said. He kissed the side of her neck and whispered, "Just marry me, the island will give you the biggest wedding anybody's seen in a hundred years."

July 11

DOWNSTAIRS, it's past midnight, and the lobby is empty except for Paulette Hyland behind the desk. Grace Wilmot would tell you how Paulette's a Hyland by marriage, but before that she was a Petersen, although her mother's a Nieman descended from the Tupper branch. That used to mean a lot of old money on both sides of her family. Now Paulette's a desk clerk.

Far across the lobby, sunk in the cushion of a red leather wing chair, is Grace, reading beside the fireplace.

The Waytansea lobby is decades of stuff, all of it layered together. A garden. A park. The wool carpet is moss green over granite tile quarried nearby. The blue carpet coming down the stairs is a waterfall flowing around landings, cascading down each step. Walnut trees, planed and polished and put back together, they make a forest of perfect square columns, straight rows of dark shining trees that hold up a forest canopy of plaster leaves and cupids.

A crystal chandelier hangs down, a solid beam of sunlight that breaks into this forest glade. The crystal doohickeys, they look tiny and twinkly so high up, but when you're on a tall ladder cleaning them, each crystal is the size of your fist.

Swags and falls of green silk almost cover the windows. Daytime, they turn the sunlight into soft green shade. The sofas and chairs are overstuffed, upholstered into flowering bushes, shaggy with long fringe along the bottom. The fireplace could be a campfire. The whole lobby, it's the island in miniature. Indoors. An Eden.

Just for the record, this is the landscape where Grace Wilmot feels most at home. Even more than her own home. Her house.

Your house.

Halfway across the lobby, Misty's edging between sofas and little tables, and Grace looks up.

She says, "Misty, come sit by the fire." She looks back into her open book and says, "How is your headache?"

Misty doesn't have a headache.

Open in Grace's lap is her diary, the red leather cover of it, and she peers at the pages and says, "What is today's date?"

Misty tells her.

The fireplace is burned down to a bed of orange coals under the grate. Grace's feet hang down in brown buckle shoes, her toes pointed, not reaching the floor. Her head of long white curls hangs forward over the book in her lap. Next to her chair, a floor lamp shines down, and the light bounces bright off the silver edge of the magnifying glass she holds over each page.

Misty says, "Mother Wilmot, we need to talk."

And Grace turns back a couple pages and says, "Oh dear. My mistake. You won't have that terrible headache until the day after tomorrow."

And Misty leans into her face and says, "How dare you set my child up to have her heart broken?"

Grace looks up from her book, her face loose and hanging with surprise. Her chin is tucked down so hard her neck is squashed into folds from ear to ear. Her superficial musculo-aponeurotic system. Her submental fat. The wrinkled platysmal bands around her neck.

Misty says, "Where do you get off telling Tabbi that I'm going to be a famous artist?" She looks around, and they're still alone, and Misty says, "I'm a waitress, and I'm keeping a roof over our heads, and that's good enough. I don't want you filling my kid with expectations that I can't fulfill." The last of her breath tight in her chest, Misty says, "Do you see how this will make me look?"

And a smooth, wide smile flows across Grace's mouth, and she says, "But Misty, the truth is you *will* be famous."

Grace's smile, it's a curtain parting. An opening night. It's Grace unveiling herself.

And Misty says, "I won't." She says, "I can't." She's just a regular person who's going to live and die ignored, obscure. Ordinary. That's not such a tragedy.

Grace shuts her eyes. Still smiling, she says, "Oh, you'll be so famous the moment—"

And Misty says, "Stop. Just stop." Misty cuts her off, saying, "It's so easy for you to build up other people's hope. Don't you see how you're ruining them?" Misty says, "I'm a darn good waitress. In case you haven't noticed, we're not the ruling class anymore. We're not the top of the heap."

Peter, your mother's problem is she's never lived in a trailer. Never stood in a grocery line with food stamps. She doesn't know how to be poor, and she's not willing to learn.

Misty says, there's worse things they can do than raise Tabbi to fit into this economy, to be able to find a job in the world she'll inherit. There's nothing wrong with waiting tables. Cleaning rooms.

And Grace lays a strip of lacy ribbon to mark her place in the diary. She looks up and says, "Then why do you drink?"

"Because I like wine," Misty says.

Grace says, "You drink and run around with men because you're afraid."

By men she must mean Angel Delaporte. The man with the leather pants who's renting the Wilmot house. Angel Delaporte with his graphology and his flask of good gin.

And Grace says, "I know *exactly* how you feel." She folds her hands on the diary in her lap and says, "You drink because you want to express yourself and you're afraid."

"No," Misty says. She rolls her head to one shoulder and looks at Grace sideways. Misty says, "No, you *do not* know how I feel."

The fire next to them, it pops and sends a spiral of sparks up the chimney. The smell of smoke drifts out past the fireplace mantel. Their campfire.

"Yesterday," Grace says, reading from the diary, "you started saving money so you could move back to your hometown. You're saving it in an envelope, and you tuck the envelope under the edge of the carpet, near the window in your room."

Grace looks up, her eyebrows lifted, the corrugator muscle pleating the spotted skin across her forehead.

And Misty says, "You've been spying on me?"

And Grace smiles. She taps her magnifying glass against the open page and says, "It's in your diary."

Misty tells her, "That's *your* diary." She says, "You can't write someone else's diary."

Just so you know, the witch is spying on Misty and writing everything down in her evil red leather record book.

And Grace smiles. She says, "I'm not *writing* it. I'm *reading* it." She turns the page and looks through her magnifying glass and says, "Oh, tomorrow looks exciting. It says you'll most likely meet a nice policeman."

Just for the record, tomorrow Misty is getting the lock on her door changed. Pronto.

Misty says, "Stop. One more time, just stop." Misty says, "The issue here is Tabbi, and the sooner she learns to live a regular life with a normal everyday job and a steady, secure, ordinary future, the happier she'll be."

"Like doing office work?" Grace says. "Grooming dogs? A nice weekly paycheck? Is that why you drink?"

Your mother.

Just for the record, she deserved this:

You deserve this:

And Misty says, "No, Grace." She says, "I drink because I married a silly, lazy, unrealistic dreamer who was raised to think he'd marry a famous artist someday and couldn't deal with his disappointment." Misty says, "You, Grace, you fucked up your own child, and I'm not letting you fuck up mine."

Leaning in so close she can see the face powder in Grace's wrinkles, her rhytides, and the red spidery lines where Grace's lipstick bleeds into the wrinkles around her mouth, Misty says, "Just stop lying to her or I swear I'll pack my bags and take Tabbi off the island tomorrow."

And Grace looks past Misty, looking at something behind her.

Not looking at Misty, Grace sighs. She says, "Oh, Misty. It's too late for *that*."

Misty turns and behind her is Paulette, the desk clerk, standing there in her white blouse and dark pleated skirt, and Paulette says, "Excuse me, Mrs. Wilmot?"

Together—both Grace and Misty—they say, Yes?

And Paulette says, “I don’t want to interupt you.” She says, “I just need to put another log on the fire.”

And Grace shuts the book in her lap and says, “Paulette, we need you to settle a disagreement for us.” Lifting her frontalis muscle to raise just one eyebrow, Grace says, “Don’t you wish Misty would hurry up and paint her masterpiece?”

The weather today is partly angry, leading to resignation and ultimatums.

And Misty turns to leave. She turns a little and stops.

The waves outside hiss and burst.

“Thank you, Paulette,” Misty says, “but it’s time everybody on the island just accepted the fact that I’m going to die a big fat nobody.”

July 12

IN CASE YOU'RE CURIOUS, your friend from art school with the long blond hair, the boy who tore his earlobe in half trying to give Misty his earring, well, he's bald now. His name's Will Tupper, and he runs the ferryboat. He's your-aged and his earlobe still hangs in two points. Scar-tissued.

On the ferry this evening coming back to the island, Misty is standing on deck. The cold wind is putting years on her face, stretching and drying her skin. The flat dead skin of her stratum corneum. She's just drinking a beer in a brown paper bag when this big dog noses up next to her. The dog's sniffing and whining. His tail's tucked, and his throat is working up and down inside his furry neck as he swallows something over and over.

She goes to pet him and the dog pulls away and pees right

there on the deck. A man comes over, holding a leash looped in one hand, and he asks her, "Are you all right?"

Just poor fat Misty in her own beer-induced coma.

As if. Like she's going to stand here in a puddle of dog pee and tell some strange man her whole fucking life story on a boat with a beer in one hand and sniffing back tears. As if Misty can just say—well, since you asked, she just spent another day in somebody's sealed-off laundry room, reading gibberish on the walls while Angel Delaporte snapped flash pictures and said her asshole husband is really loving and protective because he writes his *u*'s with the tail pointing up in a little curl, even when he's calling her an ". . . avenging evil curse of death . . ."

Angel and Misty, they were rubbing butts all afternoon, her tracing the words sprayed on the walls, the words saying: ". . . we accept the dirty flood of your money . . ."

And Angel was asking her, "Do you feel anything?"

The homeowners were bagging their family toothbrushes for laboratory analysis, for septic bacteria. For a lawsuit.

On board the ferry, the man with his dog says, "Are you wearing something from a dead person?"

Her coat's what Misty is wearing, her coat and shoes, and pinned on the lapel is one of the god-awful big costume jewelry pins Peter gave her.

Her husband gave her.

You gave her.

All afternoon in the sealed laundry room, the words written around the walls said: ". . . will not steal our world to replace the world you've ruined . . ."

And Angel said, "The handwriting is different here. It's changing." He snapped another picture and cranked to the next frame of film, saying, "Do you know what order your husband worked on these houses?"

Misty told Angel how a new owner should move in only after the full moon. According to carpenter tradition, the first to enter a new house should always be the family's favorite pet. Then should enter the family's cornmeal, the salt, the broom, the Bible, and the crucifix. Only then can the family and their furniture move in. According to superstition.

And Angel, snapping pictures, said, "What? The cornmeal's supposed to walk in by itself?"

Beverly Hills, the Upper East Side, Palm Beach, these days, Angel Delaporte says, even the best part of any city is just a deluxe luxury suite in hell. Outside your front gates, you still have to share the same gridlocked streets. You and the homeless drug addicts, you still breathe the same stinking air and hear the same police helicopters chasing criminals all night. The stars and moon erased by the lights from a million used car lots. Everyone crowds the same sidewalks, scattered with garbage, and sees the same sunrise bleary and red behind smog.

Angel says that rich people don't like to tolerate much. Money gives you permission to just walk away from everything that isn't pretty and perfect. You can't put up with anything less than lovely. You spend your life running, avoiding, escaping.

That quest for something pretty. A cheat. A cliché. Flowers and Christmas lights, it's what we're programmed to love. Someone young and lovely. The women on Spanish television with big boobs and a tiny waist like they've been twisted three times. The trophy wives eating lunch at the Waytansea Hotel.

The words on the walls say: ". . . you people with your ex-wives and stepchildren, your blended families and failed marriages, you've ruined your world and now you want to ruin mine . . ."

The trouble is, Angel says, we're running out of places to hide. It's why Will Rogers used to tell people to buy land: Nobody's making it anymore.

This is why every rich person has discovered Waytansea Island this summer.

It used to be Sun Valley, Idaho. Then it was Sedona, Arizona. Aspen, Colorado. Key West, Florida. Lahaina, Maui. All of them crowded with tourists and the natives left waiting tables. Now it's Waytansea Island, the perfect escape. For everyone except the people already living there.

The words say: ". . . you with your fast cars stuck in traffic, your rich food that makes you fat, your houses so big you always feel lonely . . ."

And Angel says, "See here, how his writing is crowded. The letters are squeezed together." He snaps a picture, cranks the film, and says, "Peter's very frightened of something."

Mr. Angel Delaporte, he's flirting, putting his hand over hers. He gives her the flask until it's empty. All this is just fine so long as he doesn't sue her like all your other clients from the mainland. All the summer people who lost bedrooms and linen closets. Everybody whose toothbrush you stuck up your butt. Half the reason why Misty gifted the house so fast to the Catholics was so nobody could put a lien against it.

Angel Delaporte says our natural instinct is to hide. As a species, we claim ground and defend it. Maybe we migrate, to follow the weather or some animal, but we know it takes land to live, and our instinct is to stake our claim.

It's why birds sing, to mark their territory. It's why dogs pee.

Sedona, Key West, Sun Valley, the paradox of a half million people going to the same place to be alone.

Misty still tracing the black paint with her index finger, she says, "What did you mean when you talked about Stendhal syndrome?"

And still snapping pictures, Angel says, "It's named after the French writer Stendhal."

The words she's tracing, they say, ". . . Misty Wilmot will send you all to hell . . ."

Your words. You fucker.

Stanislavski was right, you can find fresh pain every time you discover what you pretty much already know.

Stendhal syndrome, Angel says, is a medical term. It's when a painting, or any work of art, is so beautiful it overwhelms the viewer. It's a form of shock. When Stendhal toured the Church of Santa Croce in Florence in 1817, he reported almost fainting from joy. People feel rapid heart palpitations. They get dizzy. Looking at great art makes you forget your own name, forget even where you're at. It can bring on depression and physical exhaustion. Amnesia. Panic. Heart attack. Collapse.

Just for the record, Misty thinks Angel Delaporte is a little full of shit.

"If you read contemporary accounts," he says, "Maura Kincaid's work supposedly brought about a kind of mass hysteria."

"And now?" Misty says.

And Angel shrugs, "Search me." He says, "From what I've seen, it's okay, just some very pretty landscapes."

Looking at her finger, he says, "Do you feel anything?" He snaps another picture and says, "Funny how tastes change."

". . . we're poor," Peter's words say, "but we have what every rich person craves . . . peace, beauty, quiet . . ."

Your words.

Your life after death.

Going home tonight, it's Will Tupper who gives Misty the beer in the paper bag. He lets her drink on deck despite the rules. He asks if she's working on any paintings lately. Any landscapes, maybe?

On the ferryboat, the man with the dog, he says the dog's trained to find dead people. When somebody dies, they give off this huge stink of what the man calls epinephrine. He said it's the smell of fear.

The beer in the brown bag Misty is holding, she just drinks it and lets him talk.

The man's hair, the way it recedes above each temple, the way the skin on his exposed scalp is bright red from the cold wind, it looks like he has devil's horns. He has devil's horns, and his whole face is red and squinting into wrinkles. Dynamic wrinkling. Lateral canthal rhytides.

The dog twists his head back over one shoulder, trying to get away from her. The man's aftershave has the smell of cloves. Hooked on his belt, under the edge of his jacket, you can see a pair of chromed handcuffs.

Just for the record, the weather today is increasing turmoil with a possible physical and emotional breakdown.

Holding his dog's leash, the man says, "Are you sure you're okay?"

And Misty tells him, "Trust me, I'm not dead."

"Maybe just my skin's dead," she says.

Stendhal syndrome. Epinephrine. Graphology. The coma of details. Of education.

The man nods at her beer in the brown paper bag, and he says, "You know you're not supposed to drink in public?"

And Misty says, What? Is he a cop?

And he says, "You know? As a matter of fact, yeah, I am."

The guy flips open his wallet to flash her a badge. Engraved on the silver badge, it says: *Clark Stilton. Detective. Seaview County Hate Crimes Task Force.*

July 13—
The Full Moon

TABBI AND MISTY, they're walking through the woods. This is the tangle of land out on Waytansea Point. It's alders here, generations of trees grown and fallen and sprouting again out of their own dead. Animals, maybe deer, have cut a path that winds around the heaps of complicated trees and edges between rocks big as architecture and padded with thick moss. Above all this, the alder leaves come together in a shifting bright green sky.

Here and there, sunlight breaks through in shafts as big around as crystal chandeliers. Here's just a messier version of the lobby of the Waytansea Hotel.

Tabbi wears a single old earring, gold filigree and a haze of sparkling red rhinestones around a red enameled heart. It's pinned through her pink sweatshirt, like a brooch, but it's the earring that Peter's blond friend tore out of his ear. Will Tupper from the ferry.

Your friend.

She keeps the junk jewelry in a shoe box under her bed and wears it on special days. The chipped glass rubies pinned to her shoulder glitter with the bright green above them. The rhinestones, spotted with dirt, they reflect pink from Tabbi's sweatshirt.

Your wife and kid, they step over a rotting log that's crawling with ants, stepping around ferns that brush Misty's waist and flop on Tabbi's face. They're quiet, looking and listening for birds, but there's nothing. No birds. No little frogs. No sounds except the ocean, the hiss and burst of waves somewhere else.

They push through a thicket of green stalks, something with soft yellow leaves rotting around its base. You have to look down with every step because the ground's slippery and puddled with water. How long Misty's been walking, keeping her eyes on the ground, holding branches so they don't whip Tabbi, Misty doesn't know how long, but when she looks up, a man's standing there.

Just for the record, her levator labii muscles, the snarl muscles, the fight-or-flight muscles, all spasm, all those smooth muscles freeze into the landscape of growling, Misty's mouth squared so all her teeth show.

Her hand grabs the back of Tabbi's shirt. Tabbi, she's still looking down at the ground, walking forward, and Misty yanks her back.

And Tabbi slips and pulls her mother to the ground, saying, "Mom."

Tabbi pressed to the wet ground, the leaves and moss and beetles, Misty crouched over her, the ferns arch above them.

The man is maybe another ten steps ahead, and facing away

from them. He doesn't turn. Through the curtain of ferns, he must be seven feet tall, dark and heavy with brown leaves in his hair and mud splashed up his legs.

He doesn't turn, but he doesn't move. He must've heard them, and he stands, listening.

Just for the record, he's naked. His naked butt is right there.

Tabbi says, "Let go, Mom. There's bugs."

And Misty shushes her.

The man waits, frozen, one hand held out at waist height as if he's feeling the air for movement. No birds sing.

Misty's crouched, squatting with her hands open against the muddy ground, ready to grab Tabbi and run.

Then Tabbi slips past her, and Misty says, "No." Reaching fast, Misty clutches the air behind her kid.

It's one, maybe two seconds before Tabbi gets to the man, puts her hand in his open hand.

In that two seconds, Misty knows she's a shitty mother.

Peter, you married a coward. Misty's still here, crouched. If anything, Misty's leaning back, ready to run the other way. What they don't teach you in art school is hand-to-hand combat.

And Tabbi turns back, smiling, and says, "Mom, don't be such a spaz." She wraps both her hands around the man's one outstretched hand and pulls herself up so she can swing her legs in the air. She says, "It's just Apollo, is all."

Near the man, almost hidden in fallen leaves, is a dead body. A pale white breast with fine blue veins. A severed white arm.

And Misty's still crouched here.

Tabbi drops from the man's hand and goes to where Misty's looking. She brushes leaves off a dead white face and says, "This is Diana."

She looks at Misty crouching and rolls her eyes. "They're statues, Mom."

Statues.

Tabbi comes back to take Misty's hand. She lifts her mom's

arm and pulls her to her feet, saying, "You know? *Statues*. You're the artist."

Tabbi pulls her forward. The standing man is dark bronze, streaked with lichen and tarnish, a naked man with his feet bolted to a pedestal buried in the bushes beside the trail. His eyes have recessed irises and pupils, Roman irises, cast into them. His bare arms and legs are perfect in proportion to his torso. The golden mean of composition. Every rule of art and proportion applied.

The Greeks' formula for why we love what we love. More of that art school coma.

The woman on the ground is broken white marble. Tabbi's pink hand brushes the leaves and grass back from the long white thighs, the coy folds of the pale marble groin meet at a carved leaf. The smooth fingers and arms, the elbows without a wrinkle or crease. Her carved marble hair hangs in sculpted white curls.

Tabbi points her pink hand at an empty pedestal across the path from the bronze, and she says, "Diana fell down a long time before I met her."

The man's bronze calf muscle feels cold, but cast with every tendon defined, every muscle thick. As Misty runs her hand up the cold metal leg, she says, "You've been here before?"

"Apollo doesn't have a dick," Tabbi says. "I already looked."

And Misty yanks her hand back from the leaf cast over the statue's bronze crotch. She says, "Who brought you here?"

"Granmy," Tabbi says. "Granmy brings me here all the time."

Tabbi stoops to rub her cheek against the smooth marble cheek of the Diana.

The bronze statue, Apollo, it must be a nineteenth-century reproduction. Either that or late eighteenth century. It can't be real, not an actual Greek or Roman piece. It would be in a museum.

"Why are these here?" Misty says. "Did your grandmother tell you?"

And Tabbi shrugs. She holds out her hand toward Misty and says, "There's more." She says, "Come, and I can show you."

There is more.

Tabbi leads her through the woods that circle the point, and they find a sundial lying in the weeds, crusted a thick dark green with verdigris. They find a fountain as wide across as a swimming pool, but filled with windfall branches and acorns.

They walk past a grotto dug into a hillside, a dark mouth framed in mossy pillars and blocked with a chained iron gate. The cut stone is fitted into an arch that rises to a keystone in the middle. Fancy as a little bank building. The front of a moldy, buried state capitol building. It's cluttered with carved angels that hold stone garlands of apples, pears, and grapes. Stone wreaths of flowers. All of it streaked with dirt, it's cracked and pried apart by tree roots.

In between are plants that shouldn't be here. A climbing rose chokes an oak tree, scrambling up fifty feet to bloom above the tree's crown. Withered yellow tulip leaves are wilted in the summer heat. A towering wall of sticks and leaves turns out to be a huge lilac bush.

Tulips and lilacs aren't native to here.

None of this should be here.

In the meadow at the center of the point, they find Grace Wilmot sitting on a blanket spread over the grass. Around her bloom pink and blue bachelor buttons and little white daisies. The wicker picnic hamper is open, and flies buzz over it.

Grace rises to her knees, holding out a glass of red wine, and says, "Misty, you're back. Come take this."

Misty takes the wine and drinks some. "Tabbi showed me the statues," Misty says. "What used to be here?"

Grace gets to her feet and says, "Tabbi, get your things. It's time for us to go."

Tabbi picks up her sweater off the blanket.

And Misty says, "But we just got here."

Grace hands her a plate with a sandwich on it and says, "You're going to stay and eat. You're going to have the whole day to do your art."

The sandwich is chicken salad, and it feels warm from sitting in the sun. The flies landed on it, but it smells okay. So Misty takes a bite.

Grace nods at Tabbi and says, "It was Tabbi's idea."

Misty chews and swallows. She says, "It's a sweet idea, but I didn't bring any supplies."

And Tabbi goes to the picnic hamper and says, "Granmy did. We packed them to surprise you."

Misty drinks some wine.

Anytime some well-meaning person forces you to demonstrate you have no talent and rubs your nose in the fact you're a failure at the only dream you ever had, take another drink. That's the Misty Wilmot Drinking Game.

"Tabbi and I are going on a mission," Grace says.

And Tabbi says, "We're going to *tag sales*."

The chicken salad tastes funny. Misty chews and swallows and says, "This sandwich has a weird taste."

"That's just cilantro," Grace says. She says, "Tabbi and I have to find a sixteen-inch platter in Lenox's Silver Wheat Spray pattern." She shuts her eyes and shakes her head, saying, "Why is it that no one wants their serving pieces until their pattern is discontinued?"

Tabbi says, "And Granmy is going to buy me my birthday present. Anything I want."

Now, Misty is going to be stuck out here on Waytansea Point with two bottles of red wine and a batch of chicken salad. Her heap of paints and watercolors and brushes and paper, she hasn't touched them since her kid was a baby. The acrylics and oils have to be hard by now. The watercolors, dried up and cracked. The brushes stiff. All of it useless.

Misty included.

Grace Wilmot holds her hand out and says, "Tabbi, come along. Let's leave your mother to enjoy her afternoon."

Tabbi takes her grandmother's hand, and the two of them start back across the meadow to the dirt road where they left the car parked.

The sun's warm. The meadow's up high enough that you can look down and see the waves hiss and burst on the rocks below. Down the coastline, you can see the town. The Waytansea Hotel is a smudge of white clapboard. You can almost see the little dormer windows of the attic rooms. From here, the island looks pleasant and perfect, not crowded and busy with tourists. Ugly with billboards. It looks how the island must've looked before the rich summer people arrived. Before Misty arrived. You can see why people born here never move away. You can see why Peter was so ready to protect it.

"Mom," Tabbi calls out.

She's running back from her grandmother. Both her hands are clutching at her pink sweatshirt. Panting and smiling, she gets to where Misty is sitting on the blanket. The gold filigree earring in her hands, she says, "Hold still."

Misty holds still. A statue.

And Tabbi stoops to pin the earring through her mother's earlobe, saying, "I almost forgot until Granmy reminded me. She says you'll need this." The knees of her blue jeans are muddy and stained green from when Misty panicked and pulled them to the ground, when Misty tried to save her.

Misty says, "You want a sandwich to take with you, honey?"

And Tabbi shakes her head, saying, "Granmy told me not to eat them." Then she turns and runs away, waving one arm over her head until she's gone.

July 14

ANGEL HOLDS THE SHEET of watercolor paper, pinching the corners with the tips of his fingers. He looks at it and looks at Misty and says, "You drew a chair?"

Misty shrugs and says, "It's been years. It was the first thing that came to me."

Angel turns his back to her, holding the picture so the sunlight hits it from different angles. Still looking at it, he says, "It's good. It's very good. Where did you find the chair?"

"I drew it from my imagination," Misty says, and she tells him about being stranded out on Waytansea Point all day with just her paints and two bottles of wine.

Angel squints at the picture, holding it so close he's almost cross-eyed, and he says, "It looks like a Hershel Burke." Angel looks at her and says, "You spent the day in a grassy meadow and imagined a Hershel Burke Renaissance Revival armchair?"

This morning, a woman in Long Beach called to say she was repainting her laundry room so they'd better come see Peter's mess before she got started.

Right now, Misty and Angel are in the missing laundry room. Misty's sketching the fragments of Peter's doodles. Angel's supposed to be photographing the walls. The minute Misty opened her portfolio to take out a sketch pad, Angel saw the little watercolor and asked to see it. Sunlight comes through a window of frosted glass, and Angel holds the picture in that light.

Spray-painted across the window, it says: ". . . set foot on our island and you'll die . . ."

Angel says, "It's a Hershel Burke, I swear. From 1879 Philadelphia. Its twin is in the Vanderbilt country house, Biltmore."

It must've stuck in Misty's memory from Art History 101, or the Survey of Decorative Arts 236 or some other useless class from art school. Maybe she saw it on television, a video tour of famous houses on some public television program. Who knows where an idea comes from. Our inspiration. Why do we imagine what we imagine.

Misty says, "I'm lucky I drew anything. I got so sick. Food poisoning."

Angel's looking at the picture, turning it. The corrugator muscle between his eyebrows contracts into three deep wrinkles. His glabellar furrows. His triangularis muscle pulls his lips until marionette lines run down from each corner of his mouth.

Sketching the doodles off the walls, Misty doesn't tell Angel about the stomach cramps. That entire sucky afternoon, she tried to sketch a rock or a tree, and crumpled the paper, disgusted. She tried to sketch the town in the distance, the church steeple and clock on the library, but crumpled that. She crumpled a shitty picture of Peter she tried to draw from memory. She crumpled a picture of Tabbi. Then, a unicorn. She drank a glass of wine and looked for something new to ruin with her lack of talent. Then ate another chicken salad sandwich with its weird cilantro taste.

Even the idea of walking into the dim woods to sketch a falling, crumbling statue made the little hairs stand up behind her neck. The fallen sundial. That locked grotto. Christ. Here in the meadow, the sun was warm. The grass was humming with bugs. Somewhere beyond the woods, the ocean waves hissed and burst.

Just looking into the dark edges of the forest, Misty could imagine the towering bronze man parting the brush with his stained arms and watching her with his pitted blind eyes. As if he's killed the marble Diana and cut the body to pieces, Misty could see him stalking out of the treeline toward her.

According to the rules of the Misty Wilmot Drinking Game, when you start thinking a naked bronze statue is going to bend its metal arms around you and crush you to death with its kiss while you claw your fingernails off and beat your hands bloody against its mossy chest—well, it's time you took another drink.

When you find yourself half naked and shitting in a little hole you dig behind a bush, then wiping your ass with a linen hotel napkin, then take another drink.

The stomach cramps hit, and Misty was sweating. Her head spiked in pain with every heartbeat. Her guts shifted, and she couldn't drop her underwear fast enough. The mess splashed around her shoes and against her legs. The smell gagged her, and Misty pitched forward, her open hands against the warm grass, the little flowers. Black flies found her from miles away, crawling up and down her legs. Her chin dropped to her chest, and a double handful of pink vomit heaved out on the ground.

When you find yourself, a half hour later, with shit still running down your leg, a cloud of flies around you, take another drink.

Misty doesn't tell Angel any of that part.

Her sketching and him taking pictures here in the missing laundry room, he says, "What can you tell me about Peter's father?"

Peter's dad, Harrow. Misty loved Peter's dad. Misty says, "He's dead. Why?"

Angel snaps another picture and cranks the film forward in his camera. He nods at the writing on the wall and says, "The way a person makes their *i* means so much. The first stroke means their attachment to their mother. The second stroke, the downstroke, means their father."

Peter's dad, Harrow Wilmot, everybody called him Harry. Misty only met him the one time she came to visit before they were married. Before Misty got pregnant. Harry took her on a long tour of Waytansea Island, walking and pointing out the peeling paint and saggy roofs on the big shingled houses. Using a car key, he picked loose mortar from between the granite blocks of the church. They saw how the Merchant Street sidewalks were cracked and buckled. The storefronts streaked with growing mold. The closed hotel looked black inside, most of it gutted by a fire. The outside, shabby with its window screens rusted dark red. The shutters crooked. The gutters sagging. Harrow Wilmot kept saying, "Shirtsleeves to shirtsleeves in three generations." He said, "No matter how well we invest it, this is how long the money ever lasts."

Peter's father died after Misty went back to college.

And Angel says, "Can you get me a sample of his handwriting?"

Misty keeps sketching the doodles, and she says, "I don't know."

Just for the record, being smeared with shit and naked in the wilderness, spattered with pink vomit, this does not necessarily make you a real artist.

And neither do hallucinations. Out on Waytansea Point, with the cramps and the sweat rolling out of her hair and down the sides of her face, Misty started seeing things. With the hotel napkins she was trying to clean herself up. She rinsed her mouth with wine. Waved away the cloud of flies. The vomit still burned in her nose. It's stupid, too stupid to tell Angel, but the shadows at the edge of the forest moved.

The metal face was there in the trees. The figure took a step forward and the terrible weight of its bronze foot sunk into the soft edge of the meadow.

If you go to art school, you know a bad hallucination. You know what a flashback is. You've done plenty of chemicals that can stay in your fatty tissues, ready to flood your bloodstream with bad dreams in broad daylight.

The figure took another step, and its foot sunk into the ground. The sun made its arms bright green in places, dull brown in other places. The top of its head and its shoulders were heaped white with bird shit. The muscles in each bronze thigh stood up, tensed in high relief as each leg lifted, and the figure stepped forward. With each step, the bronze leaf shifted between its thighs.

Now, looking at the watercolor picture sitting on top of Angel's camera bag, it's more than embarrassing. Apollo, the god of love. Misty sick and drunk. The naked soul of a horny middle-aged artist.

The figure coming another step closer. A stupid hallucination. Food poisoning. It naked. Misty naked. Both of them filthy in the circle of trees around the meadow. To clear her head, to make it go away, Misty started sketching. To concentrate. It was a drawing of nothing. Her eyes closed, and Misty put the pencil to the pad of watercolor paper and felt it scratching there, laying down straight lines, rubbing with the side of her thumb to create shaded contour.

Automatic writing.

When her pencil stopped, Misty was done. The figure was gone. Her stomach felt better. The mess had dried enough she could brush the worst of it away and bury the napkins, her ruined underwear, and her crumpled drawings. Tabbi and Grace arrived. They'd found their missing teacup or cream pitcher or whatever. By then the wine was gone. Misty was dressed and smelling a little better.

Tabbi said, "Look. For my birthday," and held out her hand to show a ring shining on one finger. A square green stone, cut to sparkle. "It's a peridot," Tabbi said, and she held it above her head, making it catch the sunset.

Misty fell asleep in the car, wondering where the money came from, Grace driving them back along Division Avenue to the village.

It wasn't until later that Misty looked at the sketch pad. She was as surprised as anybody. After that, Misty just added a few colors, watercolors. It's amazing what the subconscious mind will create. Something from her growing up, some picture from art history lessons.

The predictable dreams of poor Misty Kleinman.

Angel says something.

Misty says, "Pardon?"

And Angel says, "What will you take for this?"

He means money. A price. Misty says, "Fifty?" Misty says, "Fifty *dollars*?"

This picture Misty drew with her eyes closed, naked and scared, drunk and sick to her stomach, it's the first piece of art she's ever sold. It's the best thing Misty has ever done.

Angel opens his wallet and takes out two twenties and a ten. He says, "Now what else can you tell me about Peter's father?"

For the record, walking out of the meadow, there were two deep holes next to the path. The holes were a couple of feet apart, too big to be footprints, too far apart to be a person. A trail of holes went back into the forest, too big, too far apart to be anybody walking. Misty doesn't tell Angel that. He'd think she was crazy. Crazy, like her husband.

Like you, dear sweet Peter.

Now, all that's left of her food poisoning is a pounding headache.

Angel holds the picture close to his nose and sniffs. He scrunches his nose and sniffs it again, then slips the picture into a pocket on the side of his camera bag. He catches her watching and says, "Oh, don't mind me. I thought for a second I smelled shit."

July 15

IF THE FIRST MAN who looks at your boobs in four years turns out to be a cop, take a drink. If it turns out he already knows what you look like naked, take another drink.

Make that drink a double.

Some guy sits at table eight in the Wood and Gold Room, just some your-aged guy. He's beefy with stooped shoulders. His shirt fits okay, a little tight across his gut, a white poly-cotton balloon that bumps over his belt a little. His hair, he's balding at the temples, and his recessions trail back into long triangles of scalp above each eye. Each triangle is sunburned bright red, making long pointed devil's horns that poke up from the top of his face. He's got a little spiral notebook open on the table, and he's writing in it while he watches Misty. He's wearing a striped tie and a navy blue sport coat.

Misty takes him a glass of water, her hand shaking so hard

you can hear the ice rattle. Just so you know, her headache is going on its third day. Her headache, it's the feeling of maggots rooting into the big soft pile of her brain. Worms boring. Beetles tunneling.

The guy at table eight says, "You don't get a lot of men in here, do you?"

His aftershave has the smell of cloves. He's the man from the ferry, the guy with the dog who thought Misty was dead. The cop. Detective Clark Stilton. The hate crimes guy.

Misty shrugs and gives him a menu. Misty rolls her eyes at the room around them, the gold paint and wood paneling, and says, "Where's your dog?" Misty says, "Can I get you anything to drink?"

And he says, "I need to see your husband." He says, "You're Mrs. Wilmot, aren't you?"

The name on her name tag, pinned to her pink plastic uniform—Misty Marie Wilmot.

Her headache, it's the feeling of a hammer tap, tap, tapping a long nail into the back of your head, a conceptual art piece, tapping harder and harder in one spot until you forget everything else in the world.

Detective Stilton sets his pen down on his notebook and offers his hand to shake, and he smiles. He says, "The truth is, I *am* the county's task force on hate crimes."

Misty shakes his hand and says, "Would you like some coffee?"

And he says, "Please."

Her headache is a beach ball, pumped full of too much air. More air is being forced in, but it's not air. It's blood.

Just for the record, Misty's already told the detective that Peter's in the hospital.

You're in a hospital.

On the ferry the other evening, she told Detective Stilton how you were crazy, and you left your family in debt. How you dropped out of every school and stuck jewelry through your body. You sat in the car parked in your garage with the engine running. Your graffiti, all your ranting and sealing up people's laundry rooms and kitchens, it was all just another symptom of your craziness. The vandalism. It's unfortunate, Misty told the detective, but she's been screwed on this as bad as anybody.

This is around three o'clock, the lull between lunch and dinner.

Misty says, "Yeah. Sure, go see my husband." Misty says, "Did you want coffee?"

The detective, he looks at his pad while he writes and asks, "Did you know if your husband was part of any neo-Nazi organization? Any radical hate groups?"

And Misty says, "Was he?" Misty says, "The roast beef is good here."

Just for the record, it's kinda cute. Both of them holding pads, their pens ready to write. It's a duel. A shoot-out.

If he's seen Peter's writing, this guy knows what Peter thought of her naked. Her dead fish breasts. Her legs crawling with veins. Her hands smelling like rubber gloves. Misty Wilmot, queen of the maids. What you thought of your wife.

Detective Stilton writes, saying, "So you and your husband weren't very close?"

And Misty says, "Yeah, well, I thought we were." She says, "But go figure."

He writes, saying, "Are you aware if Peter's a member of the Ku Klux Klan?"

And Misty says, "The chicken and dumplings is pretty good."

He writes, saying, "Are you aware if such a hate group exists on Waytansea Island?"

Her headache tap, tap, taps the nail into the back of her head.

Somebody at table five waves, and Misty says, "Could I get you some coffee?"

And Detective Stilton says, "Are you okay? You don't look so hot right now."

Just this morning over breakfast, Grace Wilmot said she feels terrible about the spoiled chicken salad—so terrible that she made Misty an appointment to see Dr. Touchet tomorrow. A nice gesture, but another fucking bill to pay.

When Misty shuts her eyes, she'd swear her head is glowing hot inside. Her neck is one cast-iron muscle cramp. Sweat sticks together the folds of her neck skin. Her shoulders are bound, pulled up tight around her ears. She can only turn her head a little in any direction, and her ears feel on fire.

Peter used to talk about Paganini, possibly the best violin player of all time. He was tortured by tuberculosis, syphilis, osteomyelitis in his jaw, diarrhea, hemorrhoids, and kidney stones. Paganini, not Peter. The mercury that doctors gave him for the syphilis poisoned him until his teeth fell out. His skin turned gray-white. He lost his hair. Paganini was a walking corpse, but when he played the violin, he was beyond mortal.

He had Ehlers-Danlos syndrome, a congenital disease that left his joints so flexible he could bend his thumb back far enough to touch his wrist. According to Peter, what tortured him made him a genius.

According to you.

Misty brings Detective Stilton an iced tea he didn't order, and he says, "Is there some reason why you're wearing sunglasses indoors?"

And jerking her head at the big windows, she says, "It's the light." She refills his water and says, "It hurts my eyes today." Her hand shakes so much she drops her pen. One hand clamped to the edge of the table for support, she stoops to pick it up. She sniffs and says, "Sorry."

And the detective says, "Do you know an Angel Delaporte?"

And Misty sniffs and says, "Want to order now?"

Stilton's handwriting, Angel Delaporte should see it. His letters are tall, soaring up, ambitious, idealistic. The writing slants hard to the right, aggressive, stubborn. His heavy pressure against the page shows a strong libido. That's what Angel would tell you. The tails of his letters, the lowercase *y*'s and *g*'s, hang straight down. This means determination and strong leadership.

Detective Stilton looks at Misty and says, "Would you describe your neighbors as hostile to outsiders?"

Just for the record, if you have masturbation down to less than three minutes because you share a bathtub with fourteen people, take another drink.

In art theory, you learn that women look for men with prominent brows and large, square chins. This was some study a sociologist did at West Point Academy. It proved that rectangular faces, deep-set eyes, and ears that lie close to their heads, this is what makes men attractive.

This is how Detective Stilton looks, plus a few extra pounds. He's not smiling now, but the wrinkles that crease his cheeks and his crow's-feet prove he smiles a lot. He smiles more than he frowns. The scars of happiness. It could be his extra weight, but the corrugator wrinkles between his eyes and the brow-lift wrinkles across his forehead, his worry lines, are almost invisible.

All that, and the bright red horns on his forehead.

These are all little visual cues you respond to. The code of attraction. This is why we love who we love. Whether or not you're consciously aware of them, this is the reason we do what we do.

This is how we know what we don't know.

Wrinkles as handwriting analysis. Graphology. Angel would be impressed.

Dear sweet Peter, he grew his black hair so long because his ears stuck out.

Your ears stick out.

Tabbi's ears are her father's. Tabbi's long dark hair is his.

Yours.

Stilton says, "Life's changing around here and plenty of people won't like that. If your husband isn't acting alone, we could see assault. Arson. Murder."

All Misty has to do is look down, and she starts to fall. If she turns her head, her vision blurs, the whole room smears for a moment.

Misty tears the detective's check out of her pad and lays it on the table, saying, "Will there be anything else?"

"Just one more question, Mrs. Wilmot," he says. He sips his glass of iced tea, watching her over the rim. And he says, "I'd like to talk to your in-laws—your husband's parents—if that's possible."

Peter's mother, Grace Wilmot, is staying here in the hotel, Misty tells him. Peter's father, Harrow Wilmot, is dead. Since about thirteen or fourteen years ago.

Detective Stilton makes another note. He says, "How did your father-in-law die?"

It was a heart attack, Misty thinks. She's not sure.

And Stilton says, "It sounds like you don't know any of your in-laws very well."

Her headache tap, tap, tapping the back of her skull, Misty says, "Did you say if you wanted some coffee?"

July 16

DR. TOUCHET SHINES a light into Misty's eyes and tells her to blink. He looks into her ears. He looks up her nose. He turns out the office lights while he makes her point a flashlight into her mouth. The same way Angel Delaporte's flashlight looked into the hole in his dining room wall. This is an old doctor's trick to illuminate the sinuses, they spread out, glowing red under the skin around your nose, and you can check for shadows that mean blockage, infections. Sinus headaches. He tilts Misty's head back and peers down her throat.

He says, "Why do you say it was food poisoning?"

So Misty tells him about the diarrhea, the cramps, the headaches. Misty tells him everything except the hallucination.

He pumps up the blood pressure cuff around her arm and releases the pressure. With her every heartbeat, they both watch the pressure spike on the dial. The pain in her head, the throb matches every pulse.

Then her blouse is off, and Dr. Touchet's holding one of her arms up while he feels inside the armpit. He's wearing glasses and stares at the wall beside them while his fingers work. In a mirror on one wall, Misty can watch them. Her bra looks stretched so tight the straps cut into her shoulders. Her skin rolls over the waistband of her slacks. Her necklace of junk jewelry pearls, as it wraps around the back of her neck, the pearls disappear into a deep fold of fat.

Dr. Touchet, his fingers root, tunnel, bore into her armpit.

The windows of the examining room are frosted glass, and her blouse hangs on a hook on the back of the door. This is the same room where Misty had Tabbi. Pale green tiled walls and a white tiled floor. It's the same examination table. Peter was born here. So was Paulette. Will Tupper. Matt Hyland. Brett Petersen. So was everyone on the island under the age of fifty. The island's so small, Dr. Touchet is also the mortician. He prepared Peter's father, Harrow, before his funeral. His cremation.

Your father.

Harrow Wilmot was everything Misty wanted Peter to become. The way men want to meet their prospective mother-in-law so they can judge how their fiancée will look in another twenty years, that's what Misty did. Harry would be the man Misty would be married to in her middle age. Tall with gray sideburns, a straight nose, and a long cleft chin.

Now when Misty closes her eyes and tries to picture Harrow Wilmot, what she sees is his ashes being scattered from the rocks on Waytansea Point. A long gray cloud.

If Dr. Touchet uses this same room for embalming, Misty doesn't know. If he lives long enough, he'll prepare Grace Wilmot. Dr. Touchet was the physician on the scene when they found Peter.

When they found you.

If they ever pull the plug, he'll probably prepare the body.

Your body.

Dr. Touchet feels underneath each arm. Rooting around for nodes. For cancer. He knows just where to press your spine to make your head tilt back. The fake pearls folded deep in the back of her neck. His eyes, the irises are too far apart for him to be looking at you. He hums a tune. Focusing somewhere else. You can tell he's used to working with dead people.

Sitting on the examination table, watching them both in the mirror, Misty says, "What used to be out on the point?"

And Dr. Touchet jumps, startled. He looks up, eyebrows arched with surprise.

As if some dead body just spoke.

"Out on Waytansea Point," Misty says. "There's statues, like it used to be a park. What was it?"

His finger probes deep between the tendons on the back of her neck, and he says, "Before we had a crematorium in this area, that was our cemetery." This would feel good except his fingers are so cold.

But Misty didn't see any tombstones.

His fingers probing for lymph nodes under her jaw, he says, "There's a mausoleum dug into the hill out there." His eyes staring at the wall, he frowns and says, "At least a couple centuries ago. Grace could tell you more than I could."

The grotto. The little stone bank building. The state capitol with its fancy columns and carved archway, all of it crumbling and held together with tree roots. The locked iron gate, the darkness inside.

Her headache tap, tap, taps the nail in deeper.

The diplomas on the examining room's green tiled wall are yellowed, cloudy under glass. Water-stained. Flyspecked. Daniel Touchet, M.D. Holding her wrist between two fingers, Dr. Touchet checks her pulse against his wristwatch.

His triangularis pulling both corners of his mouth down in a frown, he puts his cold stethoscope between her shoulder blades. He says, "Misty, I need you to take a deep breath and hold it."

The cold stab of the stethoscope moves around her back.

"Now let it out," he says. "And take another breath."

Misty says, "Did you know, did Peter ever have a vasectomy?" She breathes again, deep, and says, "Peter told me that Tabbi was a miracle from God so I wouldn't abort."

And Dr. Touchet says, "Misty, how much are you drinking these days?"

This is such a small fucking town. And poor Misty Marie, she's the town drunk.

"A police detective came into the hotel," Misty says. "He was asking if we had the Ku Klux Klan out here on the island."

And Dr. Touchet says, "Killing yourself is not going to save your daughter."

He sounds like her husband.

Like you, dear sweet Peter.

And Misty says, "Save my daughter from *what*?" Misty turns to meet his eyes and says, "Do we have Nazis out here?"

And looking at her, Dr. Touchet smiles and says, "Of course not." He goes to his desk and picks up a folder with a few sheets of paper in it. Inside the folder, he writes something. He looks at a calendar on the wall above the desk. He looks at his watch and writes inside the folder. His handwriting, the tail of every letter hanging low, below the line, subconscious, impulsive. Greedy, hungry, evil, Angel Delaporte would say.

Dr. Touchet says, "So, are you doing anything different lately?"

And Misty tells him yes. She's drawing. For the first time since college, Misty's drawing, painting a little, mostly watercolors. In her attic room. In her spare time. She's put up her easel so she can see out the window, down the coastline to

Waytansea Point. She works on a picture every day. Working from her imagination. The wish list of a white trash girl: big houses, church weddings, picnics on the beach.

Yesterday Misty worked until she saw it was dark outside. Five or six hours had just disappeared. Vanished like a missing laundry room in Seaview. Bermuda triangulated.

Misty tells Dr. Touchet, "My head always hurts, but I don't feel as much pain when I'm painting."

His desk is painted metal, the kind of steel desk you'd see in the office of an engineer or accountant. The kind with drawers that slide open on smooth rollers and close with thunder and a loud boom. The blotter is green felt. Above it on the wall are the calendar, the old diplomas.

Dr. Touchet with his spotted, balding head and a few long brittle hairs combed from one ear to the other, he could be an engineer. With his thick round glasses in their steel frames, his thick wristwatch on a stretch-metal band, he could be an accountant. He says, "You went to college, didn't you?"

Art school, Misty tells him. She didn't graduate. She quit. They moved here when Harrow died, to look after Peter's mother. Then Tabbi came along. Then Misty fell asleep and woke up fat and tired and middle-aged.

The doctor doesn't laugh. You can't blame him.

"When you studied history," he says, "did you cover the Jains? The Jain Buddhists?"

Not in art history, Misty tells him.

He pulls open one of the desk drawers and takes out a yellow bottle of pills. "I can't warn you enough," he says. "Don't let Tabbi within ten feet of these." He pops open the bottle and shakes a couple into his hand. They're clear gelatin capsules, the kind that pull apart into two halves. Inside each one is some loose, shifting dark green powder.

The peeling message on Tabbi's windowsill: *You'll die when they're done with you.*

Dr. Touchet holds the bottle in her face and says, “Only take these when you have pain.” There isn’t a label. “It’s an herbal compound. It should help you focus.”

Misty says, “Has anybody ever died from Stendhal syndrome?”

And the doctor says, “These are green algae mostly, some white willow bark, a little bee pollen.” He puts the capsules back in the bottle and snaps it shut. He sets the bottle on the table, next to her thigh. “You can still drink,” he says, “but only in moderation.”

Misty says, “I only drink in moderation.”

And turning back to his desk, he says, “If you say so.”

Fucking small towns.

Misty says, “How did Peter’s dad die?”

And Dr. Touchet says, “What did Grace Wilmot tell you?”

She didn’t. She’s never mentioned it. When they scattered the ashes, Peter told Misty it was a heart attack. Misty says, “Grace said it was a brain tumor.”

And Dr. Touchet says, “Yes, yes it was.” He closes his metal desk drawer with a boom. He says, “Grace tells me you demonstrate a very promising talent.”

Just for the record, the weather today is calm and sunny, but the air is full of bullshit.

Misty askes about those Buddhists he mentioned.

“Jain Buddhists,” he says. He takes the blouse off the back of the door and hands it to her. Under each sleeve, the fabric is ringed with dark sweat stains. Dr. Touchet moves around beside Misty, holding the blouse for her to slip each arm inside.

He says, “What I mean is sometimes, for an artist, chronic pain can be a gift.”

July 17

WHEN THEY WERE in school, Peter used to say that everything you do is a self-portrait. It might look like *Saint George and the Dragon* or *The Rape of the Sabine Women*, but the angle you use, the lighting, the composition, the technique, they're all you. Even the reason why you chose this scene, it's you. You are every color and brushstroke.

Peter used to say, "The only thing an artist can do is describe his own face."

You're doomed to being you.

This, he says, leaves us free to draw anything, since we're only drawing ourselves.

Your handwriting. The way you walk. Which china pattern you choose. It's all giving you away. Everything you do shows your hand.

Everything is a self-portrait.

Everything is a diary.

With the fifty dollars from Angel Delaporte, Misty buys a round ox-hair number 5 watercolor brush. She buys a puffy number 4 squirrel brush for painting washes. A round number 2 camel-hair brush. A pointed number 6 cat's-tongue brush made of sable. And a wide, flat number 12 sky brush.

Misty buys a watercolor palette, a round aluminum tray with ten shallow cups, like a pan for baking muffins. She buys a few tubes of gouache watercolors. Cyprus green, viridian lake green, sap green, and Winsor green. She buys Prussian blue, and a tube of madder carmine. She buys Havannah Lake black and ivory black.

Misty buys milky white art masking fluid for covering her mistakes. And piss-yellow lifting preparation for painting on early so mistakes will wipe off. She buys gum arabic, the amber color of weak beer, to keep her colors from bleeding together on the paper. And clear granulation medium to give the colors a grainy look.

She buys a pad of watercolor paper, fine-grained cold-press paper, 19 by 24 inches. The trade name for this size is a "Royal." A 23-by-28-inch paper is an "Elephant." Paper 26.5 by 40 inches is called a "Double Elephant." This is acid-free, 140-pound paper. She buys art boards, canvas stretched and glued over cardboard. She buys boards sized "Super-Royal" and "Imperial" and "Antiquarian."

She gets all this to the cash register, and it's so far beyond fifty dollars she has to put it on a credit card.

When you're tempted to shoplift a tube of burnt sienna, it's time to take one of Dr. Touchet's little green algae pills.

Peter used to say that an artist's job is to make order out of chaos. You collect details, look for a pattern, and organize. You make sense out of senseless facts. You puzzle together bits of everything. You shuffle and reorganize. Collage. Montage. Assemble.

If you're at work and every table in your section is waiting for something, but you're still hiding out in the kitchen sketching on scraps of paper, it's time to take a pill.

When you present people with their dinner check and on the back you've drawn a little study in light and shadow—you don't even know where it's supposed to be, this image just came into your mind. It's nothing, but you're terrified of losing it. Then it's time to take a pill.

"These useless details," Peter used to say, "they're only useless until you connect them all together."

Peter used to say, "Everything is nothing by itself."

Just for the record, today in the dining room, Grace Wilmot was standing with Tabbi in front of the glass cabinet that covers most of one wall. Inside it, china plates sit on stands under soft lights. Cups sit on saucers. Grace Wilmot points to them one at a time. And Tabbi points with her index finger and says, "Fitz and Floyd . . . Wedgwood . . . Noritake . . . Lenox . . ."

And shaking her head, Tabbi folds her arms and says, "No, that's not right." She says, "The Oracle Grove pattern has a border of fourteen-carat gold. Venus Grove has twenty-four carat."

Your baby daughter, an expert in extinct china patterns.

Your baby daughter, a teenager now.

Grace Wilmot reaches over and loops a few stray hairs behind Tabbi's ear, and she says, "I swear, this child is a natural."

With a tray of lunches on her shoulder, Misty stops long enough to ask Grace, "How did Harrow die?"

And Grace looks away from the china. Her orbicularis oculi muscle making her eyes wide, she says, "Why do you ask?"

Misty mentions her doctor's appointment. Dr. Touchet. And how Angel Delaporte thinks Peter's handwriting says something about his relationship with his dad. All the details that look like nothing standing alone.

And Grace says, "Did the doctor give you any pills to take?"

The tray is heavy and the food's getting cold, but Misty says, "The doc says Harrow had liver cancer."

Tabbi points and says, "Gorham . . . Dansk . . ."

And Grace smiles. "Of course. Liver cancer," she says. "Why are you asking me?" She says, "I thought Peter told you."

Just for the record, the weather today is foggy with widely conflicting stories about your father's cause of death. No detail is anything by itself.

And Misty says, she can't talk. Too busy. It's the lunch rush. Maybe later.

In art school, Peter used to talk about the painter James McNeill Whistler, and how Whistler worked for the U.S. Army Corps of Engineers, sketching the coastline settings for proposed lighthouses. The problem was, Whistler wouldn't stop doodling little figure studies in the margins. He drew old women, babies, beggars, anything he saw on the street. He did his job, documenting land for the government, but he couldn't ignore everything else. He couldn't let anything slip away. Men smoking pipes. Children rolling hoops. He collected all of it in doodles around the margin of his official work. Of course, the government canned him for it.

"Those doodles," Peter used to say, "they're worth millions today."

You used to say.

In the Wood and Gold Room, they serve butter in little crocks, only now each pad has a little picture carved in it. A little figure study.

Maybe it's a picture of a tree or the particular way a hillside in Misty's imagination slopes, right to left. There's a cliff, and a waterfall from a hanging canyon, and a small ravine full of shade and mossy boulders and vines around the thick trunks of trees, and by the time she's imagined it all and sketched it on a paper napkin, people are coming to the bus station to refill their own cups of coffee. People tap their glasses with forks to get her attention. They snap their fingers. These summer people.

They don't tip.

A hillside. A mountain stream. A cave in a riverbank. A tendril of ivy. All these details come to her, and Misty just can't let them go. By the end of her dinner shift, she has shreds of napkins and paper towels and credit card receipts, each one with some detail drawn on it.

In her attic room, in the heap of paper scraps, she's collected the patterns of leaves and flowers she's never seen. In another heap, she has abstract shapes that look like rocks and mountaintops on the horizon. There are the branching shapes of trees, the cluster of bushes. What could be briers. Birds.

What you don't understand you can make mean anything.

When you sit on the toilet for hours, sketching nonsense on a sheet of toilet paper until your ass is ready to fall out—take a pill.

When you just stop going down to work altogether, you just stay in your room and phone for room service. You tell everyone you're sick so you can stay up all night and day sketching landscapes you've never seen, then it's time to take a pill.

When your daughter knocks and begs you for a good-night kiss, and you keep telling her to go to bed, that you'll be there in a minute, and finally her grandmother takes her away from the door, and you can hear her crying as they go down the hallway—take two pills.

When you find the rhinestone bracelet she's pushed under the door, take another.

When nobody seems to notice your bad behavior, they just smile and say, "So, Misty, how's the painting coming along?" it's pill time.

When the headaches won't let you eat. Your pants fall down

because your ass is gone. You pass a mirror and don't recognize the thin, sagging ghost you see. Your hands only stop shaking when you're holding a paintbrush or a pencil. Then take a pill. And before you're half through the bottle, Dr. Touchet leaves another bottle at the front desk with your name on it.

When you just cannot stop working. When completing this one project is all you can imagine. Then take a pill.

Because Peter's right.

You're right.

Because everything is important. Every detail. We just don't know why yet.

Everything is a self-portrait. A diary. Your whole drug history's in a strand of your hair. Your fingernails. The forensic details. The lining of your stomach is a document. The calluses on your hand tell all your secrets. Your teeth give you away. Your accent. The wrinkles around your mouth and eyes.

Everything you do shows your hand.

Peter used to say, an artist's job is to pay attention, collect, organize, archive, preserve, then write a report. Document. Make your presentation. The job of an artist is just not to forget.

July 21—
The Third-Quarter Moon

ANGEL DELAPORTE holds up one painting, then another, all of them watercolors. They're different subjects, some just the outline of a strange horizon, some of them are landscapes of sunny fields. Pine forests. The shape of a house or a village in the middle distance. In his face, only Angel's eyes move, jumping back and forth on every sheet of paper.

"Incredible," he says. "You look terrible, but your work . . . my God."

Just for the record, Angel and Misty, they're in Oysterville. This is somebody's missing family room. They've crawled in through another hole to take pictures and see the graffiti.

Your graffiti.

The way Misty looks, how she can't get warm, even wearing two sweaters, her teeth chatter. How her hand shakes when she holds a picture out to Angel, she makes the stiff watercolor paper flap. It's some intestinal bug lingering from her case of food poisoning. Even here in a dim sealed room with only the light filtered through the drapes, she's wearing sunglasses.

Angel drags along his camera bag. Misty brings her portfolio. It's her old black plastic one from school, a thin suitcase with a zipper that goes around three sides so you can open it and lay it flat. Thin straps of elastic hold watercolor paintings to one side of the portfolio. On the other side, sketches are tucked in pockets of different sizes.

Angel's snapping pictures while Misty opens the portfolio on the sofa. When she takes out her pill bottle, her hand's shaking so much you can hear the capsules rattle inside. Pinching a capsule out of the bottle, she tells Angel, "Green algae. It's for headaches." Misty puts the capsule in her mouth and says, "Come look at some pictures and tell me what you think."

Across the sofa, Peter's spray-painted something. His black words scrawl across framed family photos on the wall. Across needlepoint pillows. Silk lampshades. He's pulled the pleated drapes shut and spray-painted his words across the inside of them.

You have.

Angel takes the bottle of pills out of her hand and holds it up to light from the window. He shakes the bottle, the capsules inside. He says, "These are huge."

The gelatin capsule in her mouth is getting soft, and inside you can taste salt and tinfoil, the taste of blood.

Angel hands her the flask of gin from his camera bag, and Misty gulps her bitter mouthful. Just for the record, she drank his booze. What you learn in art school is there's an etiquette to drugs. You have to share.

Misty says, "Help yourself. Take one."

And Angel pops the bottle open and shakes out two. He

slips one in his pocket, saying, "For later." He swallows the other with gin and makes a terrible gagging face, leaning forward with his red and white tongue stuck out. His eyes squeezed shut.

Immanuel Kant and his gout. Karen Blixen and her syphilis. Peter would tell Angel Delaporte that suffering is his key to inspiration.

Getting the sketches and watercolors spread out across the sofa, Misty says, "What do you think?"

Angel sets each picture down and lifts the next. Shaking his head no. Just a hair side to side, a kind of palsy. He says, "Simply unbelievable." He lifts another picture and says, "What kind of software are you using?"

Her brush? "Sable," Misty says. "Sometimes squirrel or oxtail."

"No, silly," he says, "on your computer, for the drafting. You can't be doing this with hand tools." He taps his finger on the castle in one painting, then taps on the cottage in another.

Hand tools?

"You don't use just a straightedge and a compass, do you?" Angel says. "And a protractor? Your angles are identical, perfect. You're using a stencil or a template, right?"

Misty says, "What's a compass?"

"You know, like in geometry, in high school," Angel says, spreading his thumb and forefinger to demonstrate. "It has a point on one leg, and you put a pencil in the other leg and use it to draw perfect curves and circles."

He holds up a picture of a house on a hillside above the beach, the ocean and trees just different shades of blue and green. The only warm color is a dot of yellow, a light in one window. "I could look at this one forever," he says.

Stendhal syndrome.

He says, "I'll give you five hundred dollars for it."

And Misty says, "I can't."

He takes another from the portfolio and says, "Then how about this one?"

She can't sell any of them.

"How about a thousand?" he says. "I'll give you a thousand just for this one."

A thousand bucks. But still, Misty says, "No."

Looking at her, Angel says, "Then I'll give you ten thousand for the whole batch. Ten thousand dollars. Cash."

Misty starts to say no, but—

Angel says, "Twenty thousand."

Misty sighs, and—

Angel says, "Fifty thousand dollars."

Misty looks at the floor.

"Why," Angel says, "do I get the feeling that you'd say no to a million dollars?"

Because the pictures aren't done. They're not perfect. People can't see them, not yet. There are more she hasn't even started. Misty can't sell them because she needs them as studies for something bigger. They're all parts of something she can't see yet. They're clues.

Who knows why we do what we do.

Misty says, "Why are you offering me so much money? Is this some kind of test?"

And Angel zippers open his camera bag and says, "I want you to see something." He takes out some shiny tools made of metal. One is two sharp rods that join at one end to make a V. The other is a half circle of metal, shaped like a D and marked with inches along the straight side.

Angel holds the metal D against a sketch of a farmhouse and says, "All your straight lines are absolutely straight." He sets the D flat against a watercolor of a cottage, and her lines are all perfect. "This is a protractor," he says. "You use it to measure angles."

Angel sets the protractor against picture after picture and

says, "Your angles are all perfect. Perfect ninty-degree angles. Perfect forty-five-degree angles." He says, "I noticed this on the chair painting."

He picks up the V-shaped tool and says, "This is a compass. You use it to draw perfect curves and circles." He stabs one pointed leg of the compass in the center of a charcoal sketch. He spins the other leg around the first leg and says, "Every circle is perfect. Every sunflower and birdbath. Every curve, perfect."

Angel points at her pictures spread across the green sofa, and he says, "You're drafting perfect figures. It isn't possible."

Just for the record, the weather today is getting really, *really* pissy right about now.

The only person who doesn't expect Misty to be a great painter, he's telling her it's impossible. When your only friend says no way can you be a great artist, a naturally talented, skilled artist, then take a pill.

Misty says, "Listen, my husband and I both went to art school." She says, "We were *trained* to draw."

And Angel asks, was she tracing a photograph? Was Misty using an opaque projector? A camera obscura?

The message from Constance Burton: "You can do this with your mind."

And Angel takes a felt-tipped pen from his camera bag and gives it to her, saying, "Here." He points at the wall and says, "Right there, draw me a circle with a four-inch diameter."

With the pen, without even looking, Misty draws him a circle.

And Angel sets the straight edge of the protractor, the edge marked in inches, against the circle. And it's four inches. He says, "Draw me a thirty-seven-degree angle."

Slash, slash, and Misty marks two intersecting lines on the wall.

He sets on the protractor and it's exactly thirty-seven degrees.

He asks for an eight-inch circle. A six-inch line. A seventy-degree angle. A perfect S curve. An equilateral triangle. A square. And Misty sketches them all in an instant.

According to the straightedge, the protractor, the compass, they're all perfect.

"Do you see what I mean?" he says. He pokes the point of his compass in her face and says, "Something's wrong. First it was wrong with Peter, and now it's wrong with you."

Just for the record, it seems Angel Delaporte liked her loads better when she was just the fat fucking slob. A maid at the Waytansea Hotel. A sidekick he could lecture about Stanislavski or graphology. First she's Peter's student. Then Angel's.

Misty says, "The only thing I see is how you can't deal with my maybe having this incredible natural gift."

And Angel jumps, startled. He looks up, eyebrows arched with surprise.

As if some dead body just spoke.

He says, "Misty Wilmot, would you just listen to yourself?"

Angel shakes his compass point at her and says, "This isn't just talent." He points his finger at the perfect circles and angles doodled on the wall and says, "The police need to see this."

Stuffing the paintings and sketches back in her portfolio, Misty says, "How come?" Zippering it shut, she says, "So they can arrest me for being *too good an artist*?"

Angel takes his camera out and cranks to the next frame of film. He snaps a flash attachment to the top. Watching her through the viewfinder, he says, "We need more proof." He says, "Draw me a hexagon. Draw me a pentagram. Draw me a perfect spiral."

And with the felt-tipped pen, Misty does one, then the next. The only time her hands don't shake is when she draws or paints.

On the wall in front of her, Peter's scrawled: ". . . we will destroy you with your own neediness and greed . . ."

You scrawled.

The hexagon. The pentagram. The perfect spiral. Angel snaps a picture of each.

With the flash blinding them, they don't see the homeowner stick her head through the hole. She looks at Angel standing there, snapping photos. Misty, drawing on the wall. And the homeowner clutches her own head in both hands and says, "What the *hell* are you doing? Stop!" She says, "Has this become an ongoing art project for you people?"

July 24

JUST SO YOU KNOW, Detective Stilton phoned Misty today. He wants to pay Peter a little visit.

He wants to pay you a little visit.

On the phone, he says, "When did your father-in-law die?"

The floor around Misty, the bed, her whole room, it's cluttered with wet balls of watercolor paper. The crumpled wads of azure blue and Winsor green, they fill the brown shopping bag she brought her art supplies home in. Her graphite pencils, her colored pencils, her oils and acrylics and gouache watercolors, she's wasted them all to make trash. Her greasy oil pastels and chalky soft pastels, they're worn down to just nubs so small you can't hold them anymore. Her paper's almost gone.

What they don't teach you in art school is how to hold a telephone conversation and still paint. Holding the phone in one hand and a brush in her other, Misty says, "Peter's dad? Fourteen years ago, right?"

Smearing the paints with the side of her hand, blending with the pad of her thumb, Misty's as bad as Goya, setting herself up for lead encephalopathy. Deafness. Depression. Topical poisoning.

Detective Stilton, he says, "There's no record that Harrow Wilmot ever died."

To give her brush a sharp point, Misty twists it in her mouth. Misty says, "We scattered his ashes." She says, "It was a heart attack. Maybe a brain tumor." Against her tongue, the paint tastes sour. The color feels gritty between her back teeth.

And Detective Stilton says, "There's no death certificate."

Misty says, "Maybe they faked his death." She's all out of guesses. Grace Wilmot and Dr. Touchet, this whole island is about image control.

And Stilton says, "Who do you mean, *they*?"

The Nazis. The Klan.

With a number 12 camel-hair sky brush, she's putting a perfect wash of blue above the trees on a perfect jagged horizon of perfect mountains. With a number 2 sable brush, she's putting sunlight on the top of each perfect wave. Perfect curves and straight lines and exact angles, so fuck Angel Delaporte.

Just for the record, on paper, the weather is what Misty says it will be. Perfect.

Just for the record, Detective Stilton says, "Why do you think your father-in-law would fake his death?"

Misty says she's just joking. Of course Harry Wilmot's dead.

With a number 4 squirrel brush, she's dabbing shadows into the forest. Days she's wasted locked up here in this room, and nothing she's done is half as good as the sketch of a chair she did while shitting her pants. Out on Waytansea Point. Being menaced by a hallucination. With her eyes shut, food-poisoned.

That only sketch, she's sold it for a lousy fifty bucks.

On the phone, Detective Stilton says, "Are you still there?"

Misty says, "Define *there*."

She says, "Go. See Peter." She's putting perfect flowers in a perfect meadow with a number 2 nylon brush. Where Tabbi is, Misty doesn't know. If Misty's supposed to be at work right now, she doesn't care. The only fact she's sure about is she's working. Her head doesn't hurt. Her hands don't shake.

"The problem is," Stilton says, "the hospital wants you to be present when I see your husband."

And Misty says she can't. She has to paint. She has a thirteen-year-old kid to raise. She's on the second week of a migraine headache. With a number 4 sable brush, she's wiping a band of gray-white across the meadow. Paving over the grass. She's excavating a pit. Sinking in a foundation.

On the paper in front of her, the paintbrush kills trees and hauls them away. With brown paint, Misty cuts into the slope of the meadow. Misty regrades. The brush plows under the grass. The flowers are gone. White stone walls rise out of the pit. Windows open in the walls. A tower goes up. A dome swells over the center of the building. Stairs run down from the doorways. A railing runs along the terraces. Another tower shoots up. Another wing spreads out to cover more of the meadow and push the forest back.

It's Xanadu. San Simeon. Biltmore. Mar a Lago. It's what people with money build to be protected and alone. The places people think will make them happy. This new building is just the naked soul of a rich person. It's the alternate heaven for people too rich to get into the real thing.

You can paint anything because the only thing you ever reveal is yourself.

And on the phone, a voice says, "Can we say three o'clock tomorrow, Mrs. Wilmot?"

Statues appear along the perfect roofline of one wing. A

pool opens in one perfect terrace. The meadow is almost gone as a new flight of steps runs down to the edge of the perfect woods.

Everything is a self-portrait.

Everything is a diary.

And the voice on the phone says, "Mrs. Wilmot?"

Vines scramble up the walls. Chimneys sprout from the slates on the roof.

And the voice on the phone says, "Misty?" The voice says, "Did you ever request the medical examiner's records for your husband's suicide attempt?" Detective Stilton says, "Do you know where your husband might have gotten sleeping pills?"

Just for the record, the problem with art school is that it can teach you technique and craft, but it can't give you talent. You can't buy inspiration. You can't reason your way to an epiphany. Develop a formula. A road map to enlightenment.

"Your husband's blood," Stilton says, "was loaded with sodium phenobarbital."

And there's no evidence of drugs at the scene, he says. No pill bottle or water. No record of Peter ever having a prescription.

Still painting, Misty asks where this is going.

And Stilton says, "You might think about who'd want to kill him."

"Only me," Misty says. Then she wishes she hadn't.

The picture is finished, perfect, beautiful. It's no place Misty's ever seen. Where it came from, she has no idea. Then, with a number 12 cat's-tongue brush full of ivory black, she wipes out everything in sight.

July 25

ALL THE HOUSES along Gum Street and Larch Street, they look so grand the first time you see them. All of them three or four stories tall with white columns, they all date from the last economic boom, eighty years ago. A century. House after house, they sit back among branching trees as big as green storm clouds, walnuts and oaks. They line Cedar Street, facing each other across rolled lawns. The first time you see them, they look so rich.

"Temple fronts," Harrow Wilmot told Misty. Starting in about 1798, Americans built simple but massive Greek Revival façades. By 1824, he says, when William Strickland designed the Second Bank of the United States in Philadelphia, there was no going back. After that, houses large and small had to have a row of fluted columns and a looming pediment roof across the front.

People called them "end houses" because all this fancy detail was confined to one end. The rest of the house was plain.

That could describe almost any house on the island. All façade. Your first impression.

From the Capitol building in Washington, D.C., to the smallest cottage, what architects called "the Greek cancer" was everywhere.

"For architecture," Harrow said, "it was the end of progress and the beginning of recycling." He met Misty and Peter at the bus station in Long Beach and drove them down to the ferry.

The island houses, they're all so grand until you see how the paint's peeled and heaping around the base of each column. On the roof, the flashing is rusted and hangs off the edge in bent red strips. Brown cardboard patches windows where the glass is gone.

Shirtsleeves to shirtsleeves in three generations.

No investment is yours forever. Harry Wilmot told her that. The money was already running out.

"One generation makes the money," Harrow told her once. "The next generation protects the money. The third runs out of it. People always forget what it takes to build a family fortune."

Peter's scrawled words: ". . . your blood is our gold . . ."

Just for the record, while Misty drives to meet Detective Stilton, the whole three-hour drive to Peter's warehousing facility, she puts together everything she can remember about Harrow Wilmot.

The first time Misty saw Waytansea Island was while visiting with Peter, when his father drove them around in the old family Buick. All the cars in Waytansea were old, clean and polished, but their seats were patched with clear strapping tape so the stuffing stayed inside. The padded dashboard was cracked from too much sun. The chrome trim and the bumpers were spotted and pimpled with rust from the salt air. The paint colors were dull under a thin layer of white oxide.

Harrow had thick white hair combed into a crown over his forehead. His eyes were blue or gray. His teeth were more yellow than white. His chin and nose, sharp and jutting out. The rest of him, skinny, pale. Plain. You could smell his breath. An old island house with his own rotting interior.

"This car's ten years old," he said. "That's a lifetime for a car at the shore." He drove them down to the ferry and they waited at the dock, looking across the water at the dark green of the island. Peter and Misty, they were out of school for the summer, looking for jobs, dreaming of living in a city, any city. They'd talked about dropping out and moving to New York or Los Angeles. Waiting for the ferry, they said they might study art in Chicago or Seattle. Someplace they could each start a career. Misty remembers she had to slam her car door three times before it would stay shut.

This was the car where Peter tried to kill himself.

The car you tried to kill yourself in. Where you took those sleeping pills.

The same car she's driving now.

Stenciled down the side now, the bright yellow words say, "Bonner & Mills—When You're Ready to Stop Starting Over."

What you don't understand you can make mean anything.

On the ferry that first day, Misty sat in the car while Harrow and Peter stood at the railing.

Harrow leaned close to Peter and said, "Are you sure she's the one?"

Leaned close to you. Father and son.

And Peter said, "I've seen her paintings. She's the real deal . . ."

Harrow raised his eyebrows, his corrugator muscle gathering the skin of his forehead into long wrinkles, and he said, "You know what this means."

And Peter smiled, but only by lifting his levator labii, his sneer muscle, and he said, "Yeah, sure. *Fucking lucky me*."

And his father nodded. He said, "That means we'll be rebuilding the hotel finally."

Misty's hippie mom, she used to say it's the American dream to be so rich you can escape from everyone. Look at Howard Hughes in his penthouse. William Randolph Hearst in San Simeon. Look at Biltmore. All those lush country homes where rich folks exile themselves. Those homemade Edens where we retreat. When that breaks down, and it always does, the dreamer returns to the world.

"Scratch any fortune," Misty's mom used to say, "and you'll find blood only a generation or two back." Saying this was supposed to make their trailer lifestyle better.

Child labor in mines or mills, she'd say. Slavery. Drugs. Stock swindles. Wasting nature with clear-cuts, pollution, harvesting to extinction. Monopolies. Disease. War. Every fortune comes out of something unpleasant.

Despite her mom, Misty thought her whole future was ahead of her.

At the coma center, Misty parks for a minute, looking up at the third row of windows. Peter's window.

Your window.

These days, Misty's clutching the edge of everything she walks past, doorframes, countertops, tables, chair backs. To steady herself. Misty can't carry her head more than halfway off her chest. Anytime she leaves her room, she has to wear sunglasses because the light hurts so much. Her clothes hang loose, billowing as if there's nothing inside. Her hair . . . there's more of it in the brush than her scalp. Any of her belts can wrap twice around her new waist.

Spanish soap opera skinny.

Her eyes shrunken and bloodshot in the rearview mirror, Misty could be Paganini's dead body.

Before she gets out of the car, Misty takes another green algae pill, and her headache spikes when she swallows it with a can of beer.

Just inside the glass lobby doors, Detective Stilton waits, watching her cross the parking lot. Her hand clutching every car for balance.

While Misty climbs the front steps, one hand grips the rail and pulls her forward.

Detective Stilton holds the door open for her, saying, "You don't look so hot."

It's the headache, Misty tells him. It could be her paints. Cadmium red. Titanium white. Some oil paints are loaded with lead or copper or iron oxide. It doesn't help that most artists will twist the brush in their mouth to make a finer point. In art school, they're always warning you about Vincent van Gogh and Toulouse-Lautrec. All those painters who went insane and suffered so much nerve damage they painted with a brush tied to their dead hand. Toxic paints, absinthe, syphilis.

Weakness in your wrists and ankles, a sure sign of lead poisoning.

Everything is a self-portrait. Including your autopsied brain. Your urine.

Poisons, drugs, disease. Inspiration.

Everything is a diary.

Just for the record, Detective Stilton is scribbling all this down. Documenting her every slurred word.

Misty needs to shut up before they put Tabbi in state custody.

They check in with the woman at the front desk. They sign the day's log and get plastic badges to clip on their coats. Misty's wearing one of Peter's favorite brooches, a big pinwheel of yellow rhinestones, the jewels all chipped and cloudy.

The silver foil has flaked off the back of some stones so they don't sparkle. They could be broken bottles off the street.

Misty clips the plastic security badge next to the brooch.

And the detective says, "That looks old."

And Misty says, "My husband gave it to me when we were dating."

They're waiting for the elevator when Detective Stilton says, "I'll need proof that your husband has been here for the past forty-eight hours." He looks from the blinking elevator floor numbers to her and says, "And you might want to document your whereabouts for that same period."

The elevator opens and they step inside. The doors close. Misty presses the button for the third floor.

Both of them looking at the doors from the inside, Stilton says, "I have a warrant to arrest him." He pats the front of his sport coat, just over the inside pocket.

The elevator stops. The doors open. They step out.

Detective Stilton flips open his notebook and reads it, saying, "Do you know the people at 346 Western Bayshore Drive?"

Misty leads him down the hallway, saying, "Should I?"

"Your husband did some remodeling work for them last year," he says.

The missing laundry room.

"And how about the people at 7856 Northern Pine Road?" he says.

The missing linen closet.

And Misty says yeah. Yes. She saw what Peter did there, but no, she didn't know the people.

Detective Stilton flips his notebook shut and says, "Both houses burned last night. Five days ago, another house burned. Before that, another house your husband remodeled was destroyed."

All of them arson, he says. Every house that Peter sealed his hate graffiti inside for someone to find, they're all catching fire. Yesterday the police got a letter from some group claiming responsibility. The Ocean Alliance for Freedom. OAFF for short. They want a stop to all coastline development.

Following her down the long linoleum hallway, Stilton says, "The white supremacy movement and the Green Party have connections going way back." He says, "It's not a long stretch from protecting nature to preserving racial purity."

They get to Peter's room and Stilton says, "Unless your husband can prove he's been here the night of every fire, I'm here to arrest him." And he pats the warrant in his jacket pocket.

The curtain is pulled shut around Peter's bed. Inside it, you can hear the rushing sound of the respirator pumping air. You can hear the soft blip of his heart monitor. You can hear the faint tinkle of something Mozart from his earphones.

Misty throws back the curtain around the bed.

An unveiling. An opening night.

And Misty says, "Be my guest. Ask him anything."

In the middle of the bed, a skeleton's curled on its side, papier-mâchéd in waxy skin. Mummified in blue-white with dark lightning bolts of veins branching just under the surface. The knees are pulled up to the chest. The back arches so the head almost touches the withered buttocks. The feet point, sharp as whittled sticks. The toenails long and dark yellow. The hands knot under so tight the fingernails cut into bandages wrapped to protect each wrist. The thin knit blanket is pushed to the bottom of the mattress. Tubes of clear and yellow loop to and from the arms, the belly, the dark wilted penis, the skull. So little muscle is left that the knees and elbows, the bony feet and hands look huge.

The lips—shiny with petroleum jelly—pull back to show the black holes of missing teeth.

With the curtain open, there's the smell of it all, the alcohol swabs, the urine, the bedsores and sweet skin cream. The smell of warm plastic. The hot smell of bleach and the powdery smell of latex gloves.

The diary of you.

The respirator's ribbed blue plastic tube hooks into a hole halfway down the throat. Strips of white surgical tape hold the eyes shut. The head is shaved for the brain pressure monitor, but black scruffy hair bristles on the ribs and in the hammock of loose skin between the hipbones.

The same as Tabbi's black hair.

Your black hair.

Holding the curtain back, Misty says, "As you can see, my husband doesn't get out much."

Everything you do shows your hand.

Detective Stilton swallows, hard. The levator labii superioris pulls his top lip up to his nostrils, and his face goes down into his notebook. His pen gets busy writing.

In the little cabinet next to the bed, Misty finds the alcohol swabs and rips the plastic cover off one. Coma patients are graded according to what's called the Glasgow Coma Scale, she tells the detective. The scale runs from fully awake to unconscious and unresponsive. You give the patient verbal commands and see if he can respond by moving. Or by speaking. Or by blinking his eyes.

Detective Stilton says, "What can you tell me about Peter's father?"

"Well," Misty says, "he's a drinking fountain."

The detective gives her a look. Both eyebrows squeezed together. The corrugator muscles doing their job.

Grace Wilmot dropped a wad of money on a fancy brass drinking fountain in Harrow's memory. It's on Alder Street where it meets Division Avenue, near the hotel, Misty tells him. Harrow's ashes, she scattered them in a ceremony out on Waytansea Point.

Detective Stilton is scribbling all this in his notebook.

With the alcohol swab, Misty wipes the skin clean around Peter's nipple.

Misty lifts the earphones off his head and takes the face in both her hands, settling it in the pillow so he looks up at the ceiling. Misty unhooks the yellow pinwheel brooch from her coat.

The lowest score you can get on the Glasgow Coma Scale is a three. This means you never move, you never speak, you never blink. No matter what people say or do to you. You don't react.

The brooch opens into a steel pin as long as her little finger, and Misty polishes the pin with the alcohol swab.

Detective Stilton's pen stops, still on the page of his notebook, and he says, "Does your daughter ever visit?"

And Misty shakes her head.

"Does his mother?"

And Misty says, "My daughter spends most of her time with her grandmother." Misty looks at the pin, polished silver and clean. "They go to tag sales," Misty says. "My mother-in-law works for a service that finds pieces of china for people in discontinued patterns."

Misty peels the tape off Peter's eyes.

Off your eyes.

Misty holds his eyes open with her thumbs and leans close to his face, shouting, "Peter!"

Misty shouts, "How did your father really die?"

Her spit dotting his eyes, his pupils two different sizes, Misty shouts, "Are you part of some neo-Nazi ecoterrorist gang?"

Turning to look at Detective Stilton, Misty shouts, "Are you sneaking out every night to burn down houses?"

Misty shouts, "Are you an oaf?"

The Ocean Alliance for Freedom.

Stilton folds his arms and drops his chin to his chest, watching her out of the tops of his eyes. The orbicularis oris muscles around his lips clamp his mouth into a thin straight line. The frontalis muscle lifts his eyebrows so his forehead folds into three wrinkles from temple to temple. Wrinkles that weren't there before now.

With one hand, Misty pinches Peter's nipple and pulls it up, stretching it out to a long point.

With the other hand, Misty drives the pin through. Then she pulls the pin out.

The heart monitor blips every moment, not one beat more fast or slow.

Misty says, "Peter darling? Can you feel this?" And again Misty drives the pin through.

So you can feel fresh pain every time. The Stanislavski Method.

Just so you know, there's so much scar tissue this is tough as pushing a pin through a tractor tire. The nipple skin stretches forever before the pin pops out the other side.

Misty shouts, "Why did you kill yourself?"

Peter's pupils stare up at the ceiling, one wide open and the other a pinhole.

Then two arms come around her from behind. Detective Stilton. They pull her away. Her shouting, "Why the fuck did you bring me here?"

Stilton pulls her away until the pin Misty's holding pulls out, little by little, until it pulls free. Her shouting, "Why the fuck did you get me pregnant?"

July 28—
The New Moon

MISTY'S FIRST BATCH of birth control pills, Peter monkeyed with. He replaced them with little cinnamon candies. The next batch he just flushed down the toilet.

You flushed down the toilet. By accident, you said.

After that, student health services wouldn't refill her prescription for another thirty days. They got her fitted for a diaphragm, and a week later Misty found a little hole poked through the center of it. She held it up to the window to show Peter, and he said, "Those things don't last forever."

Misty said she just got it.

"They wear out," he said.

Misty said his penis wasn't so big it hit her cervix and punched a hole in her diaphragm.

Your penis isn't that big.

After that, Misty kept running out of spermicidal foam.

This was costing her a fortune. Each can, Misty used maybe one time and then she'd find it empty. After a few cans, Misty came out of the bathroom one day and asked Peter, was he messing with her foam?

Peter was watching his Spanish soap operas, where all the women had waists so small they could be wet rags wrung dry. They lugged around giant breasts behind spaghetti straps. Their eyes smeared with glitter makeup, they were supposed to be doctors and lawyers.

Peter said, "Here," and he reached around behind his neck with both hands. He pulled something from inside the collar of his black T-shirt and held it out. This was a shimmering necklace of pink rhinestones, strands of ice-cold pink, all pink flash and sparkle. And he said, "You want this?"

And Misty was struck stupid as his Spanish bimbos. All she could do was reach out and take one end of the necklace in each hand. In the bathroom mirror, it sparkled against her skin. Looking at the necklace in the mirror, touching it, Misty heard the prattle of Spanish from the other room.

Misty yelled, "Just don't touch my foam anymore. Okay?"

All Misty heard was Spanish.

Of course, her next period never came. After the first couple days, Peter brought her a box of pregnancy test sticks. These were the kind you pee on. They'd show a yes or no if you're knocked up. The sticks weren't sealed in any paper wrappers. They all smelled like pee. They already showed a "no" for not pregnant.

Then Misty saw how the bottom of the box had been pulled open and then taped shut. To Peter, standing, waiting outside the bathroom door, Misty said, "You just bought these today?"

Peter said, "What?"

Misty could hear Spanish.

When they'd fuck, Peter kept his eyes shut, panting and

heaving. When he came, his eyes squeezed shut, he'd shout, *"Te amo!"*

Through the bathroom door, Misty shouted, "Did you pee on these?"

The doorknob turned, but Misty had it locked. Then, through the door, Peter's voice said, "You don't need those. You're not pregnant."

And Misty asked, so where was her monthly visit from dot?

"Right here," his voice said. Then fingers poked through the crack under the door. They were shoving something white and soft. "You dropped these on the floor," he said. "Take a good look at them."

It was her panties, spotted with fresh blood.

July 29—
The New Moon

JUST FOR THE RECORD, the weather today is heavy and scratchy and it hurts every time your wife tries to move.

Dr. Touchet's just left. He's spent the past two hours wrapping her leg in strips of sterile cloth and clear acrylic resin. Her leg, from the ankle to the crotch, is one straight fiberglass cast. It's her knee, the doctor said.

Peter, your wife is a klutz.

Misty is the klutz.

She's carrying a tray of Waldorf salads from the kitchen into the dining room when she trips. Right in the kitchen doorway, her feet go out from under her, and Misty, the tray, the plates of Waldorf salad, it all goes headfirst onto table eight.

Of course, the whole dining room gets up to come look at her covered in mayonnaise. Her knee looks fine, and Raymon comes out of the kitchen and helps her to her feet. Still, the knee is sprained, says Dr. Touchet. He comes an hour later, after Raymon and Paulette help her up the stairs to her room. The doctor holds an ice pack on the knee, then offers Misty a cast in neon yellow, neon pink, or plain white.

Dr. Touchet's squatting at her feet while Misty sits in a straight chair with her leg propped on a footstool. He's moving the ice pack, looking for signs of swelling.

And Misty asks him, did he fill out Harrow's death certificate?

Misty asks, did he prescribe sleeping pills for Peter?

The doctor looks at her for a moment, then goes back to icing her leg. He says, "If you don't relax, you may never walk again."

Her leg, it already feels fine. It looks fine. Just for the record, her knee doesn't even hurt.

"You're in shock," Touchet says. He brings a briefcase, not a black doctor's bag. It's the kind of briefcase a lawyer would carry. Or a banker. "For you, a cast would be prophylactic," he says. "Without it, you'll be running around with that police detective, and your leg will never heal."

Such a small town, the whole Waytansea Island wax museum is spying on her.

Somebody knocks at the door, and then Grace and Tabbi come into the room. Tabbi says, "Mom, we brought you more paints," and she holds a plastic shopping bag in each hand.

Grace says, "How is she?"

And Dr. Touchet says, "If she stays in this room the next three weeks, she'll be fine." He starts winding gauze around the knee, layers and layers of gauze, thicker and thicker.

Just so you know, the moment Misty found herself on the floor, when people came to help her, as they carried her upstairs, even while the doctor squeezed and flexed her knee, Misty kept saying, "What did I trip over?"

There's nothing there. There's really nothing near that doorway to trip over.

After that, Misty thanked God this happened at work. No way could the hotel beef about her missing work.

Grace says, "Can you wiggle your toes?"

Yes, Misty can. She just can't reach them.

Next, the doctor wraps the leg in strips of fiberglass.

Tabbi comes over and touches the huge fiberglass log with her mother's leg lost somewhere inside it, and she says, "Can I sign my name on it?"

"Give it a day to dry," the doctor says.

Misty's leg straight out in front of her, it must weigh eighty pounds. She feels fossilized. Embedded in amber. An ancient mummy. This is going to be a real ball and chain.

It's funny, the way your mind tries to make sense out of chaos. Misty feels terrible about it now, but the moment Raymon came out of the kitchen, as he put his arm under her and lifted, she said, "Did you just trip me?"

He brushed the Waldorf salad, the apple chunks and chopped walnuts, out of her hair, and he said, "*Cómo?*"

What you don't understand you can make mean anything.

Even then, the kitchen door was propped open and the floor there was clean and dry.

Misty said, "How did I fall?"

And Raymon shrugged and said, "On your *culo*."

All the kitchen guys standing around, they laughed.

Now, up in her room, her leg cocooned in a heavy white piñata, Grace and Dr. Touchet lift Misty under each arm and steer her over to the bed. Tabbi gets her green algae pills out of her purse and sets them on the bedside table. Grace unplugs the telephone and loops the cord, saying, "You need peace and quiet." Grace says, "There's nothing wrong with you that a little art therapy won't cure," and she starts taking things out of the shopping bags, tubes of paint and brushes, and setting them in piles on the dresser.

Out of his briefcase, the doctor takes a syringe. He wipes Misty's arm with cold alcohol. Better her arm than her nipple.

Can you feel this?

The doctor fills the syringe from a bottle and sticks the needle in her arm. He pulls it out and gives her a wad of cotton to stop any blood. "It's to help you sleep," he says.

Tabbi sits on the edge of the bed and says, "Does it hurt?"

No, not a bit. Her leg feels fine. The shot hurt more.

The ring on Tabbi's finger, the sparkling green peridot, it catches light from the window. The rug edges along the bottom of the window, and under the rug's where Misty's hidden her tip money. Their ticket home to Tecumseh Lake.

Grace puts the phone into an empty shopping bag and holds her hand out to Tabbi. She says, "Come. Let's give your mother a rest."

Dr. Touchet stands in the open door and says, "Grace? If I could talk to you, in private?"

Tabbi gets off the bed, and Grace leans down to whisper in her ear. Then Tabbi nods her head, fast. She's wearing the heavy pink necklace of shimmering rhinestones. It's so wide it must feel as heavy around her neck as the cast does around her mother's leg. A sparkling millstone. A junk jewelry ball and chain. Tabbi undoes the clasp and brings it to the bed, saying, "Hold up your head."

She reaches a hand past each of Misty's shoulders and snaps the necklace around her mother's neck.

Just for the record, Misty's not an idiot. Poor Misty Marie Kleinman knew the blood on her panties was Peter's. But right now, at this moment, she's so glad she didn't abort her child.

Your blood.

Why Misty said yes to marrying you—she doesn't know.

Why does anyone do anything? Already she's melting into the bed. Every breath is slower than the last. Her levator palpebrae muscles have to work hard to keep her eyes open.

Tabbi goes to the easel and takes down a tablet of drawing paper. She brings the paper and a charcoal pencil and puts them on the blankets beside her mother, saying, "For in case you get inspiration."

And Misty gives her a slow-motion kiss on the forehead.

Between the cast and the necklace, Misty feels pinned to the bed. Staked out. A sacrifice. An anchoress.

Then Grace takes Tabbi's hand and they go out to Dr. Touchet in the hallway. The door closes. It's so quiet, Misty's not sure if she hears right. But there's an extra little click.

And Misty calls, "Grace?" Misty calls, "Tabbi?" In slow motion, Misty says, "Hey there? Hello?" Just for the record, they've locked her in.

July 30

THE FIRST TIME Misty wakes up after her accident, her pubic hair's gone and a catheter is inside her, snaking down her good leg to a clear plastic bag hooked to the bedpost. Bands of white surgical tape strap the tube to her leg skin.

Dear sweet Peter, nobody has to tell you how *that* feels.

Dr. Touchet's been at work again.

Just for the record, waking up on drugs with your pubic hair shaved and something plastic stuck in your vagina doesn't necessarily make you a real artist.

If it did, Misty would be painting the Sistine Chapel. Instead she's wadding up another wet sheet of 140-pound watercolor paper. Outside her little dormer window, the sun's baking the sand on the beach. The waves hiss and burst. Seagulls tremble, hanging in the wind, hovering white kites, while kids make sand castles and splash in the rising tide.

It would be one thing to trade all her sunny days for a masterpiece, but this . . . her day's been just one shitty smeared mistake after another. Even with her full-leg cast and her little bag of piss, Misty wants to be outside. As an artist, you organize your life so you get a chance to paint, a window of time, but that's no guarantee you'll create anything worth all your effort. You're always haunted by the idea you're wasting your life.

The truth is, if Misty were on the beach, she'd be looking up at this window, dreaming of being a painter.

The truth is, wherever you choose to be, it's the wrong place.

Misty's half standing at her easel, balanced on a tall stool, looking out the window toward Waytansea Point, Tabbi's sitting in the patch of sunlight at her feet, coloring her cast with felt-tipped pens. That's what hurts. It's bad enough Misty spent most of her childhood hiding indoors, coloring in books, dreaming of being an artist. Now she's modeling this bad behavior for her kid. All the mud pies Misty missed baking, now Tabbi's going to miss. Whatever it is teenagers do. All the kites Misty didn't fly, the games of tag Misty skipped, all the dandelions Misty didn't pick, Tabbi is making her same mistake.

The only flowers Tabbi's seen, she found with her grandmother, painted around the rim of a teacup.

School starts in a few weeks, and Tabbi's still so pale from staying inside.

Misty's brush making another mess on the page in front of her, Misty says, "Tabbi honey?"

Tabbi sits, rubbing a red pen on the cast. The resin and cloth is so thick, Misty can't feel a thing.

Misty's smock is one of Peter's old blue work shirts with a rusted fur clip of fake rubies on the front pocket. Fake rubies and glass diamonds. Tabbi's brought the box of dress-up jewelry, all the junk brooches and bracelets and single earrings that Peter gave Misty in school.

That you gave your wife.

Misty's wearing your shirt, and she tells Tabbi, "Why don't you run outside for a few hours?"

Tabbi switches the red pen for a yellow one, and she says, "Granmy Wilmot said for me not to." Coloring, Tabbi says, "She told me to stay with you as long as you're awake."

This morning, Angel Delaporte's brown sports car pulled into the hotel's gravel parking lot. Wearing a wide straw beach hat, Angel got out and walked up to the front porch. Misty kept expecting Paulette to come up from the front desk and say she had a visitor, but no. A half hour later, Angel came out the hotel's front doors and walked down the porch steps. With one hand, he held his hat in place as he tilted his head back and scanned the hotel windows, the clutter of signs and logos. Corporate graffiti. Competing immortalities. Then Angel put on his sunglasses, slipped into his sports car, and drove away.

In front of her is another painted mess. Her perspective is all wrong.

Tabbi says, "Granmy told me to help you get inspired."

Instead of painting, Misty should be teaching her child some skill—bookkeeping or cost analysis or television repair. Some realistic way she can pay her bills.

Sometime after Angel Delaporte drove away, Detective Stilton drove up in a plain beige county government car. He walked into the hotel, then went back to his car a few minutes later. He stood in the parking lot, shading his eyes with one hand, staring up at the hotel, looking from window to window, but not seeing her. Then he drove away.

The mess in front of her, the colors are running and smudged. The trees could be microwave relay towers. The ocean could be volcano lava or cold chocolate pudding or just six bucks' worth of gouache watercolors, wasted. Misty tears off the sheet and wads it into a ball. Her hands are almost black with wadding up her failures all day. Her head aches. Misty closes her eyes and presses a hand to her forehead, where she feels it stick with wet paint.

Misty drops the wadded painting on the floor.

And Tabbi says, "Mom?"

Misty opens her eyes.

Tabbi's colored birds and flowers down the length of her cast. Blue birds and red robins and red roses.

When Paulette brings up their lunch on a room service cart, Misty asks if anyone has tried to phone from the front desk. Paulette shakes out the cloth napkin and tucks it into the collar of the blue work shirt. She says, "Sorry, nobody." She takes the warming cover off a plate of fish and says, "Why do you ask?"

And Misty says, "No reason."

Now, sitting here with Tabbi, with flowers and birds crayoned on her leg, Misty knows she'll never be an artist. The picture she sold Angel, it was a fluke. An accident. Instead of crying, Misty just pees a few drips into her plastic tube.

And Tabbi says, "Close your eyes, Mom." She says, "Color with your eyes closed, like you did on my birthday picnic."

Like she did when she was little Misty Marie Kleinman. Her eyes closed on the shag carpet in the trailer.

Tabbi leans close and whispers, "We were hiding in the trees and peeking at you." She says, "Granmy said we had to let you get inspiration."

Tabbi goes to the dresser and gets the roll of masking tape that Misty uses to hold paper on the easel. She tears off two strips and says, "Now close your eyes."

Misty has nothing to lose. She can indulge her kid. Her work couldn't get any worse. Misty closes her eyes.

And Tabbi's little fingers press a strip of tape over each eyelid.

The way her father's eyes are taped shut. To keep them from drying out.

Your eyes are taped shut.

In the dark, Tabbi's fingers put a pencil in Misty's hand. You can hear as she sets a drawing pad on the easel and lifts the cover sheet. Then her hands take Misty's and carry the pencil until it touches the paper.

The sun from the window feels warm. Tabbi's hand lets go, and her voice in the dark says, "Now draw your picture."

And Misty's drawing, the perfect circles and angles, the straight lines Angel Delaporte says are impossible. Just by the feeling, it's perfect and right. What it is, Misty has no idea. The way a stylus moves itself across a Ouija board, the pencil takes her hand back and forth across the paper so fast Misty has to grip it tight. Her automatic writing.

Misty's just able to hold on, and she says, "Tabbi?"

The tape tight over her eyes, Misty says, "Tabbi? Are you still there?"

August 2

THERE'S A LITTLE TUG between Misty's legs, a little pull deep inside her when Tabbi snaps the bag off the end of Misty's catheter and takes it down the hall to the bathroom. She empties the bag into the toilet and washes it. Tabbi brings it back and snaps it onto the long plastic tube.

She does all this so Misty can keep working in the pitch dark. Her eyes taped. Blind.

There's just the feel of warm sunshine from the window. The moment the paintbrush stops, Misty says, "This is done."

And Tabbi slips the drawing off the easel and clips on a new sheet of paper. She takes the pencil when it looks dull and gives Misty a sharp one. She holds out a tray of pastel crayons, and Misty feels them blind, greasy piano keys of color, and picks one.

Just for the record, every color Misty picks, every mark she makes, is perfect because she's stopped caring.

For breakfast, Paulette brings up a room service tray, and Tabbi cuts everything into single bites. While Misty works, Tabbi puts the fork into her mother's mouth. With the tape over her face, Misty can only open her mouth so far. Just wide enough to suck her paintbrush into a sharp point. To poison herself. Still working, Misty doesn't taste. Misty doesn't smell. After a few bites of breakfast, she's had enough.

Except for the scratch of the pencil on paper, the room is quiet. Outside, five floors down, the ocean waves hiss and burst.

For lunch, Paulette brings up more food Misty doesn't eat. Already the leg cast feels loose from all the weight she's lost. Too much solid food would mean a trip to the toilet. It would mean a break in her work. Almost no white is left on the cast, Tabbi has covered it with so many flowers and birds. The fabric of her smock is stiff with slopped paint. Stiff and sticking to her arms and breasts. Her hands are crusted with dried paint. Poisoned.

Her shoulders ache and pop, and her wrist grinds inside. Her fingers are numb around a charcoal pencil. Her neck spasms, cramping up along each side of her spine. Her neck feels the way Peter's neck looks, arched back and touching his butt. Her wrists feel the way Peter's look, twisted and knotted.

Her eyes taped shut, her face is relaxed so it won't fight the two strips of masking tape that run from her forehead down across each eye, down her cheeks to her jaw, then down to her neck. The tape keeps the orbicularis oculi muscle around her eye, the zygomatic major at the corner of her mouth, it keeps all her facial muscles relaxed. With the tape, Misty can open her lips just a sliver. She can only talk in a whisper.

Tabbi puts a drinking straw in her mouth and Misty sucks

some water. Tabbi's voice says, "No matter what happens, Granmy says you have to keep doing your art."

Tabbi wipes around her mother's mouth, saying, "I need to go pretty soon." She says, "Please don't stop, no matter how much you miss me." She says, "Do you promise?"

And still working, Misty whispers, "Yes."

"No matter how long I'm gone?" Tabbi says.

And Misty whispers, "I promise."

August 5

BEING TIRED doesn't make you done. Being hungry or sore doesn't either. Needing to pee doesn't have to stop you. A picture is done when the pencil and paint are done. The telephone doesn't interrupt. Nothing else gets your attention. While the inspiration comes, you keep going.

All day Misty's working blind, and then the pencil stops and she waits for Tabbi to take the picture and give her a blank sheet of paper. Then nothing happens.

And Misty says, "Tabbi?"

This morning, Tabbi pinned a big cluster brooch of green and red glass to her mother's smock. Then Tabbi stood still as Misty put the shimmering necklace of fat pink rhinestones around her daughter's neck. A statue. In the sunlight from the window, they sparkled bright as forget-me-nots and all the other flowers Tabbi has missed this summer. Then Tabbi taped her mother's eyes shut. That was the last time Misty saw her.

Again, Misty says, "Tabbi honey?"

And there's no sound, nothing. Just the hiss and burst of each wave on the beach. With her fingers spread, Misty reaches out and feels the air around her. For the first time in days, she's been left alone.

The two strips of masking tape, they each start at her hairline and run down across her eyes to curve under her jaw. With the thumb and forefinger of each hand, Misty pinches the tape at the top and pulls each strip off, slow, until they both peel away. Her eyes flutter open. The sunlight is too bright for her to focus. The picture on the easel is blurred for a minute while her eyes adjust.

The pencil lines come into focus, black against the white paper.

It's a drawing of the ocean, just offshore from the beach. Something floating. A person floating facedown in the water, a young girl with her long black hair spread out around her on the water.

Her father's black hair.

Your black hair.

Everything is a self-portrait.

Everything is a diary.

Outside the window, down on the beach, a mob of people wait at the edge of the water. Two people wade toward shore, carrying something between them. Something shiny flashes bright pink in the sunlight.

A rhinestone. A necklace. It's Tabbi they have by the ankles and under the arms, her hair hanging straight and wet into the waves that hiss and burst on the beach.

The crowd steps back.

And loud footsteps come down the hallway outside the bedroom door. A voice in the hallway says, "I have it ready."

Two people carry Tabbi up the beach toward the hotel porch.

The lock on the bedroom door, it goes click, and the door swings open, and Grace is there with Dr. Touchet. Flashing bright in his hand is a dripping hypodermic needle.

And Misty tries to stand, her leg cast dragging behind her. Her ball and chain.

The doctor rushes forward.

And Misty says, "It's Tabbi. Something's wrong." Misty says, "On the beach. I've got to get down there."

The cast tips and its weight pulls her to the floor. The easel crashing over beside her, the glass jar of murky rinse water, it's broken all around them. Grace comes to kneel, to take her arm. The catheter's pulled out of the bag and you can smell her piss leaking out on the rug. Grace is rolling up the sleeve on her smock.

Your old blue work shirt. Stiff with dried paint.

"You can't go down there in this state," the doctor says. He's holding the syringe and taps the air bubbles to the top, saying, "Really, Misty, there's nothing you can do."

Grace forces Misty's arm straight out, and the doctor drives in the needle.

Can you feel this?

Grace holds her by both arms, pinning her down. The brooch of fake rubies has come open and the pin is sunk into Misty's breast, her blood red on the wet rubies. The broken jar. Grace and the doctor holding her to the rug, her piss spreads under them. It wicks up the blue shirt and stings her skin where the pin is stuck in.

Grace, half on top of her, Grace says, "Misty wants to go downstairs now." Grace isn't crying.

Her own voice deep with slow-motion effort, Misty says, "How the fuck do you know what I want?"

And Grace says, "It's in your diary."

The needle pulls out of her arm and Misty feels someone rubbing the skin around the shot. The cold feel of alcohol. Hands come under her arms and pull her until she's sitting upright.

Grace's face, her levator labii superioris muscle, the sneer muscle, pulls her face in tight around her nose, and she says, "It's blood. Oh, and urine, all over her. We can't take her downstairs like this. Not in front of everyone."

The stink on Misty, it's the smell of the old Buick's front seat. The stink of your piss.

Someone's stripping the shirt off her, wiping her skin with paper towels. From across the room, the doctor's voice says, "This is excellent work. Very impressive." He's leafing through her stack of finished drawings and paintings.

"Of course they're good," Grace says. "Just don't get them out of order. They're all numbered."

Just for the record, no one mentions Tabbi.

They're tucking her arms into a clean shirt. Grace pulls a brush through her hair.

The drawing on the easel, the girl drowned in the ocean, it's fallen onto the floor and blood and piss is soaked through it from underneath. It's ruined. The image gone.

Misty can't make a fist. Her eyes keep falling shut. The wet slip of drool slides out the corner of her mouth, and the stab in her breast fades away.

Grace and the doctor, they heave her onto her feet. Outside in the hallway, more people wait. More arms come around her from both sides, and they're flying her down the stairs in slow motion. They're flying past the sad faces that watch from every landing. Paulette and Raymon and someone else, Peter's blond friend from college. Will Tupper. His earlobe still in two sharp points. The whole Waytansea Island wax museum.

It's all so quiet, except her cast drags, thudding against every step.

A crowd of people fill the lobby's gloomy forest of polished trees and mossy carpet, but they fall back as she's carried toward the dining room. Here's all the old island families, the Burtons and Hylands and Petersens and Perrys. There's not a summer face among them.

Then the doors to the Wood and Gold Room swing open.

On table six, a four-top near the windows, there's something covered with a blanket. The profile of a little face, a little girl's flat chest. And Grace's voice says, "Hurry while she's still conscious. Let her see. Lift the blanket."

An unveiling. A curtain going up.

And behind Misty, all her neighbors crowd around to watch.

August 7

IN ART SCHOOL, Peter once asked Misty to name a color. Any color.

He told her to shut her eyes and hold still. You could feel him step up, close. The heat of him. You could smell his unraveling sweater, the way his skin had the bitter smell of semisweet baker's chocolate. His own self-portrait. His hands pinched the fabric of her shirt and a cold pin scratched across her skin underneath. He said, "Don't move or I'll stick you by accident."

And Misty held her breath.

Can you feel this?

Every time they met, Peter would give her another piece of his junk jewelry. Brooches, bracelets, rings, and necklaces.

Her eyes closed, waiting. Misty said, "Gold. The color, gold."

His fingers working the pin through the fabric, Peter said, "Now tell me three words that describe gold."

This was an old form of psychoanalysis, he told her. Invented by Carl Jung. It was based on universal archetypes. A kind of insightful party game. Carl Jung. Archetypes. The vast common subconscious of all humanity. Jains and yogis and ascetics, this was the culture Peter grew up with on Waytansea Island.

Her eyes closed, Misty said, "Shiny. Rich. Soft." Her three words that described gold.

Peter's fingers clicked the brooch's tiny clasp shut, and his voice said, "Good."

In that previous life, in art school, Peter told her to name an animal. Any animal.

Just for the record, the brooch was a gilded turtle with a big, cracked green gem for a shell. The head and legs moved, but one leg was gone. The metal was so tarnished it had already rubbed black on her shirt.

And Misty pulled it out from her chest, looking at it, loving it for no good reason. She said, "A pigeon."

Peter stepped away and waved for her to walk along with him. They were walking through the campus, between brick buildings shaggy with ivy, and Peter said, "Now tell me three words that describe a pigeon."

Walking next to him, Misty tried to put her hand in his, but he clasped his together behind his back.

Walking, Misty said, "Dirty." Misty said, "Stupid. Ugly."

Her three words that described a pigeon.

And Peter looked at her, his bottom lip curled in between his teeth, and his corrugator muscle squeezing his eyebrows together.

That previous life, in art school, Peter asked her to name a body of water.

Walking next to him, Misty said, "The St. Lawrence Seaway."

He turned to look at her. He'd stopped walking. "Name three adjectives describing it," he said.

And Misty rolled her eyes and said, "Busy, fast, and crowded."

And Peter's levator labii superioris muscle pulled his top lip into a sneer.

Walking with Peter, he asked her just one last thing. Peter said to imagine you're in a room. All the walls are white, and there are no windows or doors. He said, "In three words, tell me how that room feels to you."

Misty had never dated anyone this long. For all she knew, this was the kind of veiled way that lovers interview each other. The way Misty knew Peter's favorite flavor of ice cream was pumpkin pie, she didn't think his questions meant anything.

Misty said, "Temporary. Transitory." She paused and said, "Confusing."

Her three words to describe a sealed white room.

In her previous life, still walking with Peter, not holding hands, he told her how Carl Jung's test worked. Each question was a conscious way to access the subconscious.

A color. An animal. A body of water. An all-white room.

Each of these, Peter said was an archetype according to Carl Jung. Each image represented some aspect of a person.

The color Misty had mentioned, gold, that's how she saw herself.

She'd described herself as "Shiny. Rich. Soft," Peter said.

The animal was how we perceived other people.

She perceived people as "Dirty. Stupid. Ugly," Peter said.

The body of water represented her sex life.

Busy, fast, and crowded. According to Carl Jung.

Everything we say shows our hand. Our diary.

Not looking at her, Peter said, "I wasn't thrilled to hear your answer."

Peter's last question, about the all-white room, he says that room with no windows or doors, it represents death.

For her, death will be temporary, transitory, confusing.

August 12—
The Full Moon

THE JAINS WERE a sect of Buddhists who claimed they could fly. They could walk on water. They could understand all languages. It's said they could turn junk metal into gold. They could heal cripples and cure the blind.

Her eyes shut, Misty listens while the doctor tells her all this. She listens and paints. Before dawn, she gets up so Grace can tape her face. The tape comes off after sunset.

"Supposedly," the doctor's voice says, "the Jains could raise the dead."

They could do all this because they tortured themselves. They starved and lived without sex. This life of hardship and pain is what gave them their magic power.

"People call this idea 'asceticism,' " the doctor says.

Him talking, Misty just draws. Misty works while he holds

the paint she needs, the brushes and pencils. When she's done he changes the page. He does what Tabbi used to.

The Jain Buddhists were famous throughout the kingdoms of the Middle East. In the courts of Syria and Egypt, Epirus and Macedonia, as early as four hundred years before the birth of Christ, they worked their miracles. These miracles inspired the Essene Jews and early Christians. They astonished Alexander the Great.

Doctor Touchet talking on and on, he says Christian martyrs were offshoots of the Jains. Every day, Saint Catherine of Siena would whip herself three times. The first whipping was for her own sins. Her second whipping was for the sins of the living. The third was for the sins of all dead people.

Saint Simeon was canonized after he stood on a pillar, exposed to the elements, until he rotted alive.

Misty says, "This is done." And she waits for a new sheet of paper, a new canvas.

You can hear the doctor lift the new picture. He says, "Marvelous. Absolutely inspired," his voice fading as he carries it across the room. There's a scratching sound as he pencils a number on the back. The ocean outside, the waves hiss and burst. He sets the picture beside the door, then his doctor's voice comes back, close and loud, and he says, "Do you want paper again or a canvas?"

It doesn't matter. "Canvas," Misty says.

Misty hasn't seen one of her pictures since Tabbi died. She says, "Where do you take them?"

"Someplace safe," he says.

Her period is almost a week late. From starvation. She doesn't need to pee on any pregnancy test sticks. Peter's done his job, getting her here.

And the doctor says, "You can start." His hand closes around hers, and pulls it forward to touch the rough, tight cloth already prepped with a coat of rabbit-skin glue.

The Jewish Essenes, he says, were originally a band of Persian anchorites that worshiped the sun.

Anchorites. This is what they called the women sealed alive in the basements of cathedrals. Sealed in to give the building a soul. The crazy history of building contractors. Sealing whiskey and women and cats inside walls. Her husband included.

You.

Misty, trapped in her attic room, her heavy cast keeping her here. The door kept locked from the outside. The doctor always ready with a syringe of something if she gets uppity. Oh, Misty could write a book about anchorites.

The Essenes, Dr. Touchet says, lived away from the regular world. They trained themselves by enduring sickness and torture. They abandoned their families and property. They suffered in the belief that immortal souls from heaven were baited to come down and take a physical form in order to have sex, drink, take drugs, overeat.

Essenes taught the young Jesus Christ. They taught John the Baptist.

They called themselves healers and performed all of Christ's miracles—curing the sick, reviving the dead, casting out demons—for centuries before Lazarus. The Jains turned water into wine centuries before the Essenes, who did it centuries before Jesus.

"You can repeat the same miracles over and over as long as no one remembers the last time," the doctor says. "You remember that."

The same way Christ called himself a stone rejected by masons, the Jain hermits had called themselves logs rejected by all carpenters.

"Their idea," the doctor says, "is that the visionary must live apart from the normal world, and reject pleasure and comfort and conformity in order to connect with the divine."

Paulette brings lunch on a tray, but Misty doesn't want food. Behind her closed eyelids, she hears the doctor eating. The scrape of the knife and fork on the china plate. The ice rattling in the glass of water.

He says, "Paulette?" His voice full of food, he says, "Can you take those pictures there, by the door, and put them in the dining room with the others?"

Someplace safe.

You can smell ham and garlic. There's something chocolate, too, pudding or cake. You can hear the doctor chew, and the wet sound of each swallow.

"The interesting part," the doctor says, "is when you look at pain as a spiritual tool."

Pain and deprivation. The Buddhist monks sit on roofs, fasting and sleepless until they reach enlightenment. Isolated and exposed to the wind and sun. Compare them to Saint Simeon, who rotted on his pillar. Or the centuries of standing yogis. Or Native Americans who wandered on vision quests. Or the starving girls in nineteenth-century America who fasted to death out of piety. Or Saint Veronica, whose only food was five orange seeds, chewed in memory of the five wounds of Christ. Or Lord Byron, who fasted and purged and made his heroic swim of the Hellespont. A romantic anorexic. Moses and Elijah, who fasted to receive visions in the Old Testament. English witches of the seventeenth century who fasted to cast their spells. Or whirling dervishes, exhausting themselves for enlightenment.

The doctor just goes on and on and on.

All these mystics, throughout history, all over the world, they all found their way to enlightenment by physical suffering.

And Misty just keeps on painting.

"Here's where it gets interesting," the doctor's voice says. "According to split-brain physiology, your brain is divided like a walnut into two halves."

The left half of your brain deals with logic, language, calculation, and reason, he says. This is the half people perceive as their personal identity. This is the conscious, rational, everyday basis of our reality.

The right side of your brain, the doctor tells her, is the center of your intuition, emotion, insight, and pattern recognition skills. Your subconscious.

"Your left brain is a scientist," the doctor says. "Your right brain is an artist."

He says people live their lives out of the left half of their brains. It's only when someone is in extreme pain, or upset or sick, that their subconscious can slip into their conscious. When someone's injured or sick or mourning or depressed, the right brain can take over for a flash, just an instant, and give them access to divine inspiration.

A flash of inspiration. A moment of insight.

The French psychologist Pierre Janet called this condition "the lowering of the mental threshold."

Dr. Touchet says, "*Abaissement du niveau mental.*"

When we're tired or depressed or hungry or hurting.

According to the German philosopher Carl Jung, this lets us connect to a universal body of knowledge. The wisdom of all people over all time.

Carl Jung, what Peter told Misty about herself. Gold. Pigeons. The St. Lawrence Seaway.

Frida Kahlo and her bleeding sores. All great artists are invalids.

According to Plato, we don't learn anything. Our soul has lived so many lives that we know everything. Teachers and education can only remind us of what we already know.

Our misery. This suppression of our rational mind is the source of inspiration. The muse. Our guardian angel. Suffering takes us out of our rational self-control and lets the divine channel through us.

"Enough of any stress," the doctor says, "good or bad, love or pain, can cripple our reason and bring us ideas and talents we can achieve in no other way."

All this could be Angel Delaporte talking. Stanislavski's method of physical actions. A reliable formula for creating on-demand miracles.

As he hovers close to her, the doctor's breath is warm against the side of Misty's face. The smell of ham and garlic.

Her paintbrush stops, and Misty says, "This is done."

Someone knocks at the door. The lock clicks. Then Grace, her voice says, "How is she, Doctor?"

"She's working," he says. "Here, number this one—eighty-four. Then, put it with the others."

And Grace says, "Misty dear, we thought you might like to know, but we've been trying to reach your family. About Tabbi."

You can hear someone lift the canvas off the easel. Footsteps carry it across the room. How it looks, Misty doesn't know.

They can't bring Tabbi back. Maybe Jesus could or the Jain Buddhists, but nobody else could. Misty's leg crippled, her daughter dead, her husband in a coma, Misty herself trapped and wasting away, poisoned with headaches, if the doctor is right she could be walking on water. She could raise the dead.

A soft hand closes over her shoulder and Grace's voice comes in close to her ear. "We'll be dispersing Tabbi's ashes this afternoon," she says. "At four o'clock, out on the point."

The whole island, everybody will be there. The way they were for Harrow Wilmot's funeral. Dr. Touchet embalming the body in his green-tiled examining room, with his steel accountant's desk and the flyspecked diplomas on the wall.

Ashes to ashes. Her baby in an urn.

Leonardo's Mona Lisa is just a thousand thousand smears of paint. Michelangelo's David is just a million hits with a hammer. We're all of us a million bits put together the right way.

The tape tight over each eye, keeping her face relaxed, a mask, Misty says, "Has anyone gone to tell Peter?"

Someone sighs, one long breath in, then out. And Grace says, "What would that accomplish?"

He's her father.

You're her father.

The gray cloud of Tabbi will drift off on the wind. Drifting back down the coastline toward the town, the hotel, the houses and church. The neon signs and billboards and corporate logos and trademarked names.

Dear sweet Peter, consider yourself told.

August 15

JUST FOR THE RECORD, one problem with art school is it makes you so much less of a romantic. All that garbage about painters and garrets, it disappears under the load you have to learn about chemistry, about geometry and anatomy. What they teach you explains the world. Your education leaves everything so neat and tidy.

So resolved and sensible.

Her whole time dating Peter Wilmot, Misty knew it wasn't him she loved. Women just look for the best physical specimen to father their children. A healthy woman is wired to seek out the triangle of smooth muscle inside Peter's open collar because humans evolved hairless in order to sweat and stay cool while outrunning some hot and exhausted form of furry animal protein.

Men with less body hair are also less likely to harbor lice, fleas, and mites.

Before their dates, Peter would take a painting of hers. It would be framed and matted. And Peter would press two long strips of extrastrong double-sided mounting tape onto the back of the frame. Careful of the sticky tape, he'd tuck the painting up inside the hem of his baggy sweater.

Any woman would love how Peter ran his hands through her hair. It's simple science. Physical touch mimics early parent-child grooming practices. It stimulates your release of growth hormone and ornithine decarboxylase enzymes. Inversely, Peter's fingers rubbing the back of her neck would naturally lower her levels of stress hormones. This has been proved in a laboratory, rubbing baby rats with a paintbrush.

After you know about biology, you don't have to be used by it.

On their dates, Peter and Misty, they'd go to art museums and galleries. Just the two of them, walking and talking, Peter looking a little square in front, a little pregnant with her painting.

There is nothing special in the world. Nothing magic. Just physics.

Idiot people like Angel Delaporte who look for a supernatural reason for ordinary events, those people drive Misty nuts.

Walking the galleries looking for a blank wall space, Peter was a living example of the golden section, the formula used by ancient Greek sculptors for perfect proportion. His legs were 1.6 times longer than his torso. His torso is 1.6 times longer than his head.

Look at your fingers, how the first joint is longer than the second, then the second is longer than the end joint. The ratio is called Phi, after the sculptor Phidias.

The architecture of you.

Walking, Misty told Peter about the chemistry of painting. How physical beauty turns out to be chemistry and geometry and anatomy. Art is really science. Discovering why people like something is so you can replicate it. Copy it. It's a paradox, "creating" a real smile. Rehearsing again and again a spontaneous moment of horror. All the sweat and boring effort that goes into creating what looks easy and instant.

When people look at the ceiling of the Sistine Chapel, they need to know that carbon black paint is the soot from natural gas. The color rose madder is the ground root of the madder plant. Emerald green is copper acetoarsenite, also called Paris green and used as an insecticide. A poison. Tyrian purple is made from clams.

And Peter, he slid the painting out from under his sweater. Alone in the gallery with no one around to see, the painting of a stone house behind a picket fence, he pressed it to the wall. And there it was, the signature of Misty Marie Kleinman. And Peter said, "I told you someday your work would hang in a museum."

His eyes are deep Egyptian brown, the paint made from ground-up mummies, bone ash and asphalt, and used until the nineteenth century, when artists discovered that icky reality. After twisting years of brushes between their lips.

Peter kissing the back of her neck, Misty said how when you look at the Mona Lisa, you need to remember that burnt sienna is just clay colored with iron and manganese and cooked in an oven. Sepia brown is the ink sacs from cuttlefish. Dutch pink is crushed buckhorn berries.

Peter's perfect tongue licked the back of her ear. Something, but not a painting, felt stiff inside his clothes.

And Misty whispered, "Indian yellow is the urine of cattle fed mango leaves."

Peter wrapped one arm around her shoulders. With his

other arm, he pressed the back of her knee so it buckled. He lowered her to the gallery's marble floor, and Peter said, "*Te amo*, Misty."

Just for the record, this came as a little surprise.

His weight on top of her, Peter said, "You think you know so much," and he kissed her.

Art, inspiration, love, they're all so easy to dissect. To explain away.

The paint colors iris green and sap green are the juice of flowers. The color of Cappagh brown is Irish dirt, Misty whispered. Cinnabar is vermilion ore shot from high Spanish cliffs with arrows. Bistre is the yellowy brown soot of burnt beech wood. Every masterpiece is just dirt and ash put together in some perfect way.

Ashes to ashes. Dust to dust.

Even while they kissed, you closed your eyes.

And Misty kept hers open, not watching you, but the earring in your ear. Silver tarnished almost brown, holding a knot of square-cut glass diamonds, twinkling and buried in the black hair falling over your shoulders—that's what Misty loved.

That first time, Misty kept telling you, "The paint color Davy's gray is powdered slate. Bremen blue is copper hydroxide and copper carbonate—a deadly poison." Misty said, "Brilliant scarlet is iodine and mercury. The color bone black is charred bones . . ."

August 16

THE COLOR BONE BLACK is charred bones.

Shellac is the shit aphids leave on leaves and twigs. Drop black is burnt grapevines. Oil paints use the oil of crushed walnuts or poppy seeds. The more you know about art, the more it sounds like witchcraft. Everything crushed and mixed and baked, the more it could be cooking.

Misty was still talking, talking, talking, but this was days later, in gallery after gallery. This was in a museum, with her painting of a tall stone church pasted to the wall between a Monet and a Renoir. With Misty sitting on the cold floor straddling Peter between her legs. It was late afternoon, and the museum was deserted. Peter's perfect head of black hair pressed hard on the floor, he was reaching up, both his hands inside her sweater, thumbing her nipples.

Both your hands.

Behavioral psychologists say that humans copulate face-to-face because of breasts. Females with larger breasts attracted more partners, who insisted on breast play during intercourse. More sex bred more females, who inherited the larger breasts. That begat more face-to-face sex.

Now, here on the floor, Peter's hands, his breast play, his erection sliding around inside his pants, Misty's thighs spread above him, she said how when William Turner painted his masterpiece of Hannibal crossing the Alps to slaughter the Salassian army, Turner based it on a hike he took in the Yorkshire countryside.

Another example of everything being a self-portrait.

Misty told Peter what you learn in art history. That Rembrandt slopped his paint on so thick that people joked you could lift each portrait by its nose.

Her hair hung heavy with sweat down over her face. Her chubby legs trembled, exhausted but still holding her up. Dry-humping the lump in his pants.

Peter's fingers clutched her breasts tighter. His hips pushed up, and his face, his orbicularis oculi, squeezed his eyes shut. His triangularis pulled the corners of his mouth down so his bottom teeth showed. His coffee-yellowed teeth bit at the air.

A hot wetness pulsed out of Misty, and Peter's erection was pulsing inside his pants, and everything else stopped. They both stopped breathing for one, two, three, four, five, six, seven long moments.

Then they both wilted. Withering. Peter's body relaxed onto the wet floor. Misty's flattened onto him. Both of them, their clothes were pasted together with sweat.

The painting of the tall church looked down from the wall.

And right then, a museum guard walked up.

August 20—
The Third-Quarter Moon

GRACE'S VOICE, in the dark, it tells Misty, "The work you're doing will buy your family freedom." It says, "No summer people will come back here for decades."

Unless Peter wakes up someday, Grace and Misty are the only Wilmots left.

Unless you wake up, there won't be any more Wilmots.

You can hear the slow, measured sound of Grace cutting something with scissors.

Shirtsleeves to shirtsleeves in three generations. There's no point rebuilding the family fortune. Let the house go to the Catholics. Let the summer people swarm over the island. With Tabbi dead, the Wilmots have no stake in the future. No investment.

Grace says, "Your work is a gift to the future, and anyone who tries to stop you will be cursed by history."

While Misty paints, Grace's hands circle her waist with something, then her arms, her neck. It's something that rubs her skin, light and soft.

"Misty dear, you have a seventeen-inch waist," Grace says.

It's a tape measure.

Something smooth slips between her lips, and Grace's voice says, "It's time you took another pill." A drinking straw pokes into her mouth, and Misty sips enough water to swallow the capsule.

In 1819, Théodore Géricault painted his masterpiece, *The Raft of the Medusa*. It showed the ten castaways that survived out of one hundred and forty-seven people left adrift on a raft for two weeks after their ship sank. At the time, Géricault had just abandoned his pregnant mistress. To punish himself, he shaved his head. He saw no friends for almost two years, never going out in public. He was twenty-seven and lived in isolation, painting. Surrounded by the dying people and cadavers he studied for his masterpiece. After several suicide attempts, he died at thirty-two.

Grace says, "We all die." She says, "The goal isn't to live forever, the goal is to create something that will."

She runs the tape measure down the length of Misty's legs.

Something cold and smooth slides against Misty's cheek, and Grace's voice tells her, "Feel." Grace says, "It's satin. I'm sewing your gown for the opening."

Instead of "gown," Misty hears *shroud*.

Just from the feel, Misty knows it's white satin. Grace is cutting down Misty's wedding dress. Remaking it. Making it last forever. Born again. Reborn. Misty's Wind Song perfume still on it, Misty recognizes herself.

Grace says, "We've invited everyone. All the summer people. Your opening will be the biggest social event in a hundred years."

The same as her wedding. Our wedding.

Instead of "opening," Misty hears *offering*.

Grace says, "You're almost done. Only eighteen more paintings to complete."

To make an even one hundred.

Instead of "done," Misty hears *dead*.

August 21

TODAY IN THE DARKNESS behind Misty's eyelids, the hotel's fire alarm goes off. One long ringing bell in the hallway, it comes through the door so loud Grace has to shout, "Oh, what is it now?" She puts a hand on Misty's shoulder and says, "Keep working."

The hand squeezes, and Grace says, "Just finish this last picture. That's all we need."

Her footsteps go away, and the door to the hall opens. The alarm is louder for a moment, ringing, shrill as the recess bell at Tabbi's school. At her own grade school, growing up. The ringing is soft, again, as Grace shuts the door behind her. She doesn't lock it.

But Misty keeps painting.

Her mom in Tecumseh Lake, when Misty told her about

maybe marrying Peter Wilmot and moving to Waytansea Island, her mom told Misty that all big-money fortunes are based on fooling people and pain. The bigger the fortune, she said, the more people got hurt. For rich people, she said, the first marriage was just about reproduction. She asked, did Misty really want to spent the rest of her life surrounded by that kind of person?

Her mom asked, "Don't you want to be an artist anymore?"

Just for the record, Misty told her, Yeah, sure.

It wasn't even that Misty was so in love with Peter. Misty didn't know what it was. She just couldn't go home to that trailer park, not anymore.

Maybe it's just a daughter's job to piss off her mother.

They don't teach you that in art school.

The fire alarm keeps ringing.

The week Peter and Misty eloped, it was over Christmas break. That whole week, Misty let her mom worry. The minister looked at Peter and said, "Smile, son. You look as though you're facing a firing squad."

Her mom, she called the college. She called the hospitals. One emergency room had the body of a dead woman, a young woman found naked in a ditch and stabbed a hundred times in the stomach. Misty's mom, she spent Christmas Day driving across three counties to look at the mutilated dead body of this Jane Doe. While Peter and Misty marched down the main aisle of the Waytansea church, her mom held her breath and watched a police detective pull down the zipper on a body bag.

Back in that previous life, Misty called her mom a couple days after Christmas. Sitting in the Wilmot house behind a locked door, Misty fingered the junk jewelry Peter had given her during their dating, the rhinestones and fake pearls. On her answering machine, Misty listened to a dozen panicked messages from her mom. When Misty finally got around to dialing their number in Tecumseh Lake, her mom just hung up.

It was no big deal. After a little cry, Misty never called her mom again.

Already Waytansea Island felt more like home than the trailer ever had.

The hotel fire alarm keeps ringing, and through the door someone says, "Misty? Misty Marie?" There's a knock. It's a man's voice.

And Misty says, Yes?

The alarm is loud with the door opening, then quiet. A man says, "Christ, it stinks in here!" And it's Angel Delaporte come to her rescue.

Just for the record, the weather today is frantic, panicked, and slightly rushed with Angel pulling the tape off her face. He takes the paintbrush out of her hand. Angel slaps her one time, hard on each cheek, and says, "Wake up. We don't have much time."

Angel Delaporte slaps her the way you'd slap a bimbo on Spanish television. Misty all skin and bones.

The hotel fire alarm just keeps ringing and ringing.

Squinting against the sunlight from her one tiny window, Misty says, Stop. Misty says he doesn't understand. She has to paint. It's all she has left.

The picture in front of her is a square of sky, smudged blue and white, nothing complete, but it fills the whole sheet of paper. Stacked against the wall near the doorway are other pictures, their faces to the wall. A number penciled on the back of each. Ninety-seven on one. Ninety-eight. Another is ninety-nine.

The alarm just ringing and ringing.

"Misty," Angel says. "Whatever this little experiment is, you are done." He goes to her closet and gets out a bathrobe and sandals. He comes back and sticks each of her feet in one, saying, "It's going to take about two minutes for people to find out this is a false alarm."

Angel slips a hand under each of her arms and heaves Misty to her feet. He makes a fist and knocks it against her cast, saying, "What is *this* all about?"

Misty asks, What is he here for?

"That pill you gave me," Angel says, "it gave me the worst migraine of my life." He's throwing the bathrobe over her shoulders and says, "I had a chemist analyze it." Dropping each of her tired arms into a bathrobe sleeve, he says, "I don't know what kind of doctor you have, but those capsules contain powdered lead with trace amounts of arsenic and mercury."

The toxic parts of oil paints: Vandyke red, ferrocyanide; iodine scarlet, mercuric iodide; flake white, lead carbonate; cobalt violet, arsenic—all those beautiful compounds and pigments that artists treasure but turn out to be deadly. How your dream to create a masterpiece will drive you nuts and then kill you.

Her, Misty Marie Wilmot, the poisoned drug addict possessed by the devil, Carl Jung, and Stanislavski, painting perfect curves and angles.

Misty says he doesn't understand. Misty says, Tabbi, her daughter. Tabbi's dead.

And Angel stops. His eyebrows up in surprise, he says, "How?"

A few days ago, or weeks. Misty doesn't know. Tabbi drowned.

"Are you sure?" he says. "It wasn't in the newspaper."

Just for the record, Misty's not sure of anything.

Angel says, "I smell urine."

It's her catheter. It's pulled out. They're leaving a trail of pee from her easel, out the room, and down the hallway carpet. Pee, and her cast dragging.

"My bet," Angel says, "is you don't even need that leg in a cast." He says, "You know that chair in the picture you sold me?"

Misty says, "Tell me."

His arms around her, he's dragging Misty through a door, into the stairwell. "That chair was made by the cabinetmaker Hershel Burke in 1879," he says, "and shipped to Waytansea Island for the Burton family."

Her cast thuds on every step. Her ribs hurt from Angel's fingers holding too tight, rooting and digging under her arms, and Misty tells him, "A police detective." Misty says, "He said some ecology club is burning down all those houses Peter wrote inside."

"Burned," Angel says. "Mine included. They're all gone."

The Ocean Alliance for Freedom. OAFF for short.

Angel's hands still in their leather driving gloves, he drags her down another flight of stairs, saying, "You know this means something paranormal is happening, don't you?"

First, Angel Delaporte says, it's impossible she could draw so well. Now it's some evil spirit just using her as a human Etch A Sketch. She's only good enough to be some demonic drafting tool.

Misty says, "I thought you'd say that."

Oh, Misty, she *knows* what's happening.

Misty says, "Stop." She says, "Just why are you here?"

Why since the start of all this has he been her friend? What is it that keeps Angel Delaporte pestering her? Until Peter wrecked his kitchen, until Misty rented him her house, they were strangers. Now he's pulling fire alarms and dragging her down a stairway. Her with a dead kid and a comatose husband.

Her shoulders twist. Her elbows jerk up, hitting him around the face, smack in his missing eyebrows. To make him drop her. To make him leave her alone. Misty says, "Just stop."

There on the stairs, the fire alarm stops. It's quiet. Only her ears still ring.

You can hear voices from the hallway on each floor. A voice from the attic says, “Misty’s gone. She’s not in her room.”

It’s Dr. Touchet.

Before they go another step, Misty waves her fists at Angel. Misty whispers, “Tell me.” Collapsed on the stairs, she whispers, “Why are you fucking with me?”

August 21 . . . and One-Half

ALL THE THINGS Misty loved about Peter, Angel loved them first. In art school, it was Angel and Peter, until Misty came along. They'd planned out their whole future. Not as artists, but as actors. It didn't matter if they made money, Peter had told him. Told Angel Delaporte. Someone in Peter's generation would marry a woman who'd make the Wilmot family and his whole community wealthy enough that none of them would have to work. He never explained the details of this system.

You never did.

But Peter said every four generations, a boy from the island would meet a woman he'd have to marry. A young art student. Like an old fairy tale. He'd bring her home, and she'd paint so well it would make Waytansea Island rich for another hundred years. He'd sacrifice his life, but it was just one life. Just once every four generations.

Peter had shown Angel Delaporte his junk jewelry. He'd told Angel the old custom, how the woman who responded to the jewelry, who was attracted and trapped by it, that would be the fairy-tale woman. Every boy in his generation had to enroll in art school. He had to wear a piece of the jewelry, scratched and rusted and tarnished. He had to meet as many women as possible.

You had to.

Dear sweet closeted bisexual Peter.

The "walking peter" Misty's friends tried to warn her about.

The brooches, they pinned through their foreheads, their nipples. Navels and cheekbones. The necklaces, they'd thread through holes in their noses. They calculated to be revolting. To disgust. To prevent any woman from admiring them, and they each prayed another boy would meet the rumored woman. Because the day one unlucky boy married this woman, the rest of his generation would be free to live their own lives. And so would the next three generations.

Shirtsleeves to shirtsleeves.

Instead of progress, the island was stuck in this repeating loop. Recycling the same ancient success. Period revival. This same ritual.

It was Misty the unlucky boy would meet. Misty was their fairy-tale woman.

There on the hotel stairs, Angel told her this. Because he could never understand why Peter had left and gone off to marry her. Because Peter could never tell him. Because Peter never loved her, Angel Delaporte says.

You never loved her.

You shit sack.

And what you can't understand you can make mean anything.

Because Peter was only fulfilling some fabled destiny. A superstition. An island legend, and no matter how hard Angel tried to talk him out of it, Peter insisted that Misty was his destiny.

Your destiny.

Peter insisted that his life should be wasted, married to a woman he never loved, because he'd be saving his family, his future children, his entire community from poverty. From losing control of their small, beautiful world. Their island. Because their system had worked for hundreds of years.

Collapsed there on the stairs, Angel says, "That's why I hired him to work on my house. That's why I've followed him here." Misty and him on the stairs, her cast stretched out between them, Angel Delaporte leans in close, his breath full of red wine, and says, "I just want you to tell me why he sealed those rooms. And why the room here—room 313—here in this hotel?"

Why did Peter sacrifice his life to marry her? His graffiti, it wasn't a threat. Angel says it was a warning. Why was Peter trying to warn everyone?

A door opens into the stairwell above them, and a voice says, "There she is." It's Paulette, the desk clerk. It's Grace Wilmot and Dr. Touchet. It's Brian Gilmore, who runs the post office. And old Mrs. Terrymore from the library. Brett Petersen, the hotel manager. Matt Hyland from the grocery store. It's the whole village council coming down the stairs toward them.

Angel leans close, clutching her arm, and says, "Peter didn't kill himself." He points up the stairs and says, "They did. They murdered him."

And Grace Wilmot says, "Misty dear. You need to get back to work." She shakes her head, clucking her tongue, and says, "We're so, so close to being done."

And Angel's hands, his leather driving gloves let go. He backs off, now a step lower, and says, "Peter warned me."

Glancing from the crowd above them to Misty, to the crowd, he backs off, saying, "I just want to know what's happening."

From behind her, the hands are closing around her shoulders, her arms, and lifting.

And Misty, all she can say is, "*Peter was gay?*"

You're gay?

But Angel Delaporte is stumbling backward, down the stairs. He stumbles to the next floor lower, still shouting up the stairwell, "I'm going to the police!" He shouts, "The truth is, Peter was trying to save people from *you*!"

August 23

HER ARMS ARE NOTHING but loose ropes of skin. Across the back of her neck, the bones feel bundled together with dried tendons. Inflamed. Sore and tired. Her shoulders hanging from the spine at the base of her skull. Her brain could be a baked black stone inside her head. Her pubic hair's growing back, scratchy and pimpled around her catheter. With a new piece of paper in front of her, a blank canvas, Misty picks up a brush or a pencil, and nothing will happen. When Misty sketches, forcing her hand to make something, it's a stone house. A rose garden. Just her own face. Her self-portrait diary.

Fast as her inspiration came, it's gone.

Someone slips the blindfold off her head, and the sunlight from the dormer window makes her squint. It's so blinding bright. It's Dr. Touchet here with her, and he says, "Congratulations, Misty. It's all over."

It's what he said when Tabbi was born.

Her homemade immortality.

He says, "It might take a few days before you can stand," and he slips an arm around her back, hooked under her arms, and lifts Misty to her feet.

On the windowsill, someone's left Tabbi's shoe box full of junk jewelry. The glittering, cheap bits of mirror, cut into diamond shapes. Every angle reflecting light in a different direction. Dazzling. A little bonfire, there in the sun bouncing off the ocean.

"By the window?" the doctor says. "Or would you rather be in bed?"

Instead of "in bed," Misty hears *dead*.

The room is just how Misty remembers it. Peter's pillow on the bed, the smell of him. The paintings are, all of them, gone. Misty says, "What have you done with them?"

The smell of you.

And Dr. Touchet steers her to a chair by the window. He lowers her into a blanket spread over the chair and says, "You've done another perfect job. We couldn't ask for better." He pulls the curtains back to show the ocean, the beach. The summer people crowding each other down to the water's edge. The trash along the tide line. A beach tractor chugs along, dragging a roller. The steel drum rolls, imprinting the wet sand with a lopsided triangle. Some corporate logo.

Next to the logo stamped in the sand, you can read the words: "Using your past mistakes to build a better future."

Somebody's vague mission statement.

"In another week," the doctor says, "that company will pay a fortune to erase its name from this island."

What you don't understand you can make mean anything.

The tractor drags the roller, printing its message again and again until the waves wash it away.

The doctor says, "When an airliner crashes, all the airlines pay to cancel their newspaper and television advertisements. Did you know that? None of them want to risk any association with that kind of disaster." He says, "In another week, there won't be a corporate sign on this island. They'll pay anything it takes to buy their names back."

The doctor folds Misty's dead hands in her lap. Embalming her. He says, "Now rest. Paulette will be up soon for your dinner order."

Just for the record, he goes to her night table and picks up the bottle of capsules. As he leaves, he slips the bottle into the side pocket of his suit jacket and doesn't mention it. "Another week," he says, "and the entire world will fear this place—but they'll leave us alone." Going out, he doesn't lock the door.

In her previous life, Peter and Misty, they'd sublet a place in New York when Grace called to say Harrow was dead. Peter's father was dead and his mother was alone in their big house on Birch Street. Four stories tall with its mountain range of roofs, its towers and bay windows. And Peter said they had to go take care of her. To settle Harrow's estate. Peter was the executor of the will. Just for a few months, he said. Then Misty was pregnant.

They kept telling each other New York was still the plan. Then they were parents.

Just for the record, Misty couldn't complain. There was a little window of time, the first few years after Tabbi was born, when Misty could curl on the bed with her and not want anything else in the world. Having Tabbi made Misty part of something, of the Wilmot clan, of the island. Misty felt complete and more peaceful than she'd ever thought possible. The waves on the beach outside the bedroom window, the quiet streets, the island was far enough removed from the world that you stopped wanting. You stopped needing. Worrying. Wishing. Always expecting something more.

She quit painting and smoking dope.

She didn't need to accomplish or become or escape. Just being here was enough.

The quiet rituals of washing the dishes or folding clothes. Peter would come home, and they'd sit on the porch with Grace. They'd read to Tabbi until her bedtime. They'd creak in the old wicker furniture, the moths swarming the porch light. Deep inside the house, a clock would strike the hour. From the woods beyond the village, they might hear an owl.

Across the water, the mainland towns were crowded, plastered with signs selling city products. People ate cheap food in the streets and dropped litter on the beach. The reason the island never hurt is—there was nothing there to do. There were no rooms to rent. No hotel. No summer houses. No parties. You couldn't buy food because there was no restaurant. Nobody sold hand-painted seashells with "Waytansea Island" written on them in gold script. The beaches were rocky on the ocean side . . . muddy with oyster flats on the side that faced the mainland.

About that time, the village council started work to reopen the closed hotel. It was crazy, using the last bit of everyone's trust money, all the island families chipping in to rebuild the burned-out, crumbling old ruin that rose on the hillside above the harbor. Wasting the last of their resources to attract reams of tourists. Dooming their next generation to waiting tables, cleaning rooms, painting souvenir crap on seashells.

It's so hard to forget pain, but it's even harder to remember sweetness.

We have no scar to show for happiness. We learn so little from peace.

Curled on the quilt, a part of every person for generations, Misty could put her arms around her daughter. Misty could hold her baby, her body cupped around Tabbi, as if she were still inside. Still part of Misty. Immortal.

The sour milk smell of Tabbi, of her breath. The sweet smell of baby powder, almost powdered sugar. Misty's nose tucked against the warm skin of her baby's neck.

Inside those years, they had no reason to hurry. They were young. Their world was clean. It was church on Sunday. It was reading books, soaking in the bathtub. Picking wild berries and making jelly at night, when the white kitchen was cool with a breeze, the windows up. They always knew the phase of the moon, but seldom the day of the week.

Just for that little window of years, Misty could see how her life wasn't an end. She was a means to the future.

They'd stand Tabbi against the front doorframe. Against all the forgotten names still there. Those children, now dead. They'd mark her height with a felt-tipped pen.

Tabbi, age four.

Tabbi, age eight.

Just for the record, the weather today is slightly maudlin.

Here, sitting at the dormer window of her attic room in the Waytansea Hotel, the island is spread out under her, filthy with strangers and messages. Billboards and neon. Logos. Trademarks.

The bed where Misty curled around Tabbi, trying to keep her inside. Angel Delaporte sleeps there now. Some crazy man. A stalker. In her room, in her bed, under the window with the hiss and burst of ocean waves breaking outside. Peter's house.

Our house. Our bed.

Until Tabbi turned ten years old, the Waytansea Hotel was sealed, empty. The windows shuttered, with plywood bolted into each window frame. The doors boarded over.

The summer Tabbi turned ten, the hotel opened. The village became an army of bellhops and waiters, maids and desk clerks. That was the year Peter started working off the island, doing drywall. Little remodeling jobs for summer people with too many houses to look after. With the hotel open, the ferry started to run all day, every day, cramming the island with tourists and traffic.

After that, the paper cups and fast food wrappers arrived. The car alarms and long lines hunting for a place to park. The used diapers people left in the sand. The island went downhill until this year, until Tabbi turned thirteen, until Misty walked out to the garage to find Peter asleep in the car and the gas tank empty. Until people started calling to say their laundry room was gone, their guest bedroom missing. Until Angel Delaporte is exactly where he's always wanted to be. In her husband's bed.

In your bed.

Angel lying in her bed. Angel sleeping with her painting of the antique chair.

Misty, with nothing. Tabbi, gone. Her inspiration, gone.

Just for the record, Misty never told anyone, but Peter had packed a suitcase and hidden it in the car's trunk. A suitcase to take along, a change of clothes for hell. It never made sense. Nothing Peter did in the past three years has made much sense.

Outside her little attic window, down on the beach, kids are splashing in the waves. One boy wears a frilly white shirt and black pants. He's talking to another boy, wearing just soccer shorts. They pass a cigarette back and forth, taking turns smoking it. The one boy in the frilly white shirt has black hair, just long enough to tuck behind his ears.

On the windowsill is Tabbi's shoe box of junk jewelry. The bracelets, the orphaned earrings and chipped old brooches. Peter's jewelry. Rattling around in the box with the loose plastic pearls and glass diamonds.

From her window, Misty looks down on the beach where

she saw Tabbi for the last time. Where it happened. The boy with short dark hair is wearing an earring, something glittering gold and red. And with nobody to hear it, Misty says, "Tabbi."

Misty's fingers gripping the windowsill, she pushes her head and shoulders out and shouts, "Tabbi?" Misty must be half out the window, ready to fall five stories to the hotel porch, and she yells, "Tabbi!"

And it is. It's Tabbi. With her hair cut. Flirting with some kid. Smoking.

The boy just puffs on the cigarette and hands it back. He flips his hair and laughs with one hand over his mouth. His hair in the ocean wind, a flickering black flag.

The waves hiss and burst.

Her hair. Your hair.

Misty twists through the little window, and the shoe box spills out. The box slides down the shingled roof. It hits the gutter and flips, and the jewelry flies. It falls, flashing red and yellow and green, flashing bright as fireworks and falling the way Misty's about to, down to shatter on the concrete floor of the hotel porch.

Only the hundred pounds of her cast, her leg embedded in fiberglass, keeps her from pitching out the window. Then two arms come around her, and a voice says, "Misty, don't." Someone pulls her back, and it's Paulette. A room service menu is dropped on the floor. Paulette's arms come around her from behind. Paulette's hands lock together, and she swings Misty, spinning her around the solid weight of the full-leg cast, planting her facedown on the paint-stained carpet.

Panting, panting and dragging her huge fiberglass leg, her ball and chain, back toward the window, Misty says, "It was Tabbi." Misty says, "Outside."

Her catheter is pulled out again, pee squirted everywhere.

Paulette gets to her feet. She's making a nasty face, her risorius muscles cinching her face tight around her nose while she dries her hands on her dark skirt. She tucks her blouse back tight into her waistband and says, "No, Misty. No it wasn't." And she picks up the room service menu.

Misty has to get downstairs. To get outside. She's got to find Tabbi. Paulette has to help lift the cast. They've got to get Dr. Touchet to cut it off.

And Paulette shakes her head and says, "If they take off that cast, you'll be crippled for life." She goes to the window and shuts it. She locks it and pulls the curtains.

And from the floor, Misty says, "Please. Paulette, help me up."

But Paulette taps her foot. She fishes an order pad out of the side pocket in her skirt and says, "The kitchen is out of the whitefish."

And just for the record, Misty's still trapped.

Misty's trapped, but her kid could be alive.

Your kid.

"A steak," Misty says.

Misty wants the thickest piece of beef they can find. Cooked well done.

August 24

WHAT MISTY REALLY WANTS is a steak knife. She wants a serrated knife to cut through the side of this leg cast, and she wants Paulette not to notice when the knife's missing from her tray after dinner. Paulette doesn't notice, and she doesn't lock the door from the outside, either. Why bother when Misty's hobbled by a ton of fucking fiberglass.

All night, Misty's in bed, picking and hacking. Misty's sawing at the cast. Digging with the knife blade and scooping the fiberglass shavings into her hand, throwing them under the bed.

Misty's a convict digging herself out of a very small prison, a prison felt-tip-penned with Tabbi's flowers and birds.

It takes until midnight to cut from her waist, halfway down her thigh. The knife keeps slipping, stabbing and lancing into her side. By the time she gets to her knee, Misty's falling asleep. Scabbed and crusted in dried blood. Glued to the sheets. By three in the morning, she's only partway down her calf. She's almost free, but she falls asleep.

Something wakes her up, the knife still in her hand.

It's another longest day of the year. Again.

The noise, it's a car door slamming shut in the parking lot. If Misty holds the split cast closed, she can hobble to the window and look. It's the beige county government car of Detective Stilton. He's not outside, so he must be in the hotel lobby. Maybe looking for her.

Maybe this time he'll find her.

With the steak knife, Misty starts hacking again. Hacking and half asleep, she stabs her calf muscle. The blood floods out, dark red against her white, white skin, her leg sealed inside too long. Misty hacks again and stabs her shin, the blade going through thin skin, stuck into the bone.

Still hacking, the knife throws blood and splinters of fiberglass. Fragments of Tabbi's flowers and birds. Bits of her hair and skin. With both hands, Misty grabs the edge on each side of the split. She pries the cast open until her leg is half out. The ragged edges pinch her, biting into the hacked skin, the needles of fiberglass digging.

Oh, dear sweet Peter, nobody has to tell you how this hurts.

Can you feel this?

Her fingers stuck with splinters of fiberglass, Misty grips the ragged edges and pulls them apart. Misty bends her knee, forcing it up out of the straight cast. First her pale kneecap, smeared with blood. The way a baby's head appears. Crowning. A bird breaking out of its eggshell. Then her thigh. Her child being born. Finally her shin breaks up, out of the shattered cast. With one shake, her foot is free, and the cast slips, rolls, slumps, and crashes to the floor.

A chrysalis. A butterfly emerging, bloody and tired. Reborn.

The cast hitting the floor is so loud the curtains shake. A framed hotel picture flaps against the wall. With her hands pressed over her ears, Misty waits for someone to come investigate. To find her free and lock her door from the outside.

Misty waits for her heart to beat three hundred times, fast. Counting. Then, nothing. Nothing happens. Nobody comes.

Slow and smooth, Misty makes her leg straight. Misty bends her knee. Testing. It doesn't hurt. Holding on to the night table, Misty swings her legs off the bed and flexes them. With the bloody steak knife, she cuts the loops of surgical tape that hold her catheter to her good leg. Pulling the tube out of her, she loops it in one hand and sets it aside.

It's one, three, five careful steps to the closet, where she takes out a blouse. A pair of jeans. Hanging there, inside a plastic wrapper, is the white satin dress Grace has sewn for her art show. Misty's wedding dress, born again. When she steps into the jeans and works the button and the zipper, when she reaches for the blouse, the jeans fall to the floor. That's how much weight she's lost. Her hips are gone. Her ass is two empty sacks of skin. The jeans sit around her ankles, smeared with the blood from the steak knife cuts in each leg.

There's a skirt that fits, but not one of her own. It's Tabbi's, a plaid, pleated wool skirt that Grace must've picked out.

Even her shoes feel loose, and Misty has to ball her toes into a knot to keep her feet inside.

Misty listens until the hall outside her door sounds empty. She heads for the stairs, the skirt sticking to the blood on her legs, her shaved pubic hair snagging on her panties. With her toes clenched, Misty walks down the four flights to the lobby. There, people wait at the front desk, standing in the middle of their luggage.

Out through the lobby doors, you can still see the beige county government car in the parking lot.

A woman's voice says, "Oh my God." It's some summer woman, standing near the fireplace. With the pastel fingernails of one hand hooked inside her mouth, she stares at Misty and says, "My God, your legs."

In one hand, Misty still holds the bloody steak knife.

Now the people at the front desk turn and look. A clerk behind the desk, a Burton or a Seymour or a Kincaid, he turns and whispers behind his hand to the other clerk and she picks up the house phone.

Misty heads for the dining room, past the pale looks, people wincing and looking away. Summer women peeking from between their spidery fingers. Past the hostess. Past tables three, seven, ten, and four, there's Detective Stilton, sitting at table six with Grace Wilmot and Dr. Touchet.

It's raspberry scones. Coffee. Quiche. Grapefruit halved in bowls. They're having breakfast.

Misty gets to them, clutching the bloody knife, and says, "Detective Stilton, it's my daughter. My daughter, Tabbi." Misty says, "I think she's still alive."

His grapefruit spoon halfway to his mouth, Stilton says, "Your daughter died?"

She drowned, Misty tells him. He has to listen. A week, three weeks ago, Misty doesn't know. She's not sure. She's been locked in the attic. They put this big cast on her leg so she couldn't escape.

Her legs under the plaid wool, they're coated and running with blood.

By now the whole dining room's watching. Listening.

"It's a plot," Misty says. With both hands, she reaches out to calm the spooked look on Stilton's face. Misty says, "Ask Angel Delaporte. Something terrible is about to happen."

The blood dried on her hands. Her blood. The blood from her legs soaking through her plaid skirt.

Tabbi's skirt.

A voice says, "You've ruined it!"

Misty turns, and it's Tabbi. In the dining room doorway, she's wearing a frilly blouse and tailored black slacks. Her haircut pageboy short, she has an earring in one ear, the red enameled heart Misty saw Will Tupper rip out of his earlobe a hundred years ago.

Dr. Touchet says, "Misty, have you been drinking again?"

Tabbi says, "Mom . . . my skirt."

And Misty says, "You're not dead."

Detective Stilton dabs his mouth with his napkin. He says, "Well, that makes one person who's not dead."

Grace spoons sugar into her coffee. She pours milk and stirs it, saying, "So you really think it's these OAFF people who committed the murder?"

"Killed Tabbi?" Misty says.

Tabbi comes to the table and leans against her grandmother's chair. There's some nicotine yellow between her fingers as she lifts a saucer, studying the painted border. It's gold with a repeating wreath of dolphins and mermaids. Tabbi shows it to Grace and says, "Fitz and Floyd. The Sea Wreath pattern."

She turns it over, reads the bottom, and smiles.

Grace smiles up at her, saying, "You're getting so I can't praise you enough, Tabitha."

Just for the record, Misty wants to hug and kiss her kid. Misty wants to hug her and run to the car and drive straight to her mom's trailer in Tecumseh Lake. Misty wants to wave good-bye with her middle finger to this whole fucking island of genteel lunatics.

Grace pats an empty chair next to her and says, "Misty, come sit down. You look distraught."

Misty says, "Who did OAFF kill?"

The Ocean Alliance for Freedom. Who burned Peter's graffiti in all the beach houses.

Your graffiti.

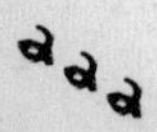

"That's what I'm here about," the detective says. He takes the notebook out of his inside jacket pocket. He flips it open on the table and gets his pen ready to write. Looking at Misty, he says, "If you wouldn't mind answering a few questions?"

About Peter's vandalism?

"Angel Delaporte was murdered last night," he says. "It could be a burglary, but we're not ruling anything out. All's we know is he was stabbed to death in his sleep."

In her bed.

Our bed.

Tabbi's dead, then she's alive. The last time Misty saw her kid, Tabbi was on this very table, under a sheet and not breathing. Misty's knee is broken, then it's fine. One day Misty can paint, and then she can't. Maybe Angel Delaporte was her husband's boyfriend, but now he's dead.

Your boyfriend.

Tabbi takes her mother's hand. She leads Misty to the empty seat. She pulls out the chair, and Misty sits.

"Before we start . . ." Grace says. She leans across the table to tap Detective Stilton on his shirt cuff, and she says, "Misty's art show opens three days from now, and we're counting on you being there."

My paintings. They're here somewhere.

Tabbi smiles up at Misty, and slips a hand into her grandmother's hand. The peridot ring, sparkling green against the white linen tablecloth.

Grace's eyes flicker toward Misty, and she winces like someone walking into a spiderweb, her chin tucked and her hands touching the air. Grace says, "So much has been *unpleasant* on the island lately." She inhales, her pearls rising, then sighs and says, "I'm hoping the art show will give us all a fresh start."

August 24 . . . and One-Half

IN AN ATTIC BATHROOM, Grace runs water into the tub, then goes out to wait in the hallway. Tabbi stays in the room to watch Misty. To guard her own mother.

Just for the record, just this summer, it feels as if years have gone by. Years and years. The girl Misty saw from her window, flirting. This girl, she could be a stranger with yellow fingers.

Misty says, "You really shouldn't smoke. Even if you're already dead." What they don't teach you in art school is how to react when you find out your only child has connived to break your heart. For now, with just Tabbi and her mother in the bathroom, maybe it's a daughter's job to piss off her mother.

Tabbi looks at her face in the bathroom mirror. She licks her index finger and uses it to fix the edge of her lipstick. Not looking at Misty, she says, "You might be more careful, Mother. We don't need you anymore."

She picks a cigarette out of a pack from her pocket. Right in front of Misty, she flicks a lighter and takes a puff.

Her panties loose and baggy on her stick legs, Misty slips them off under the skirt and kicks them free of her shoes, saying, "I loved you a lot more when you were dead."

On her cigarette hand, the ring from her grandmother, the peridot flashes green in the light from above the sink. Tabbi stoops to lift the bloody plaid skirt off the floor. She holds it between two fingers and says, "Granmy Wilmot needs me to get ready for the art show." Saying as she leaves, "For *your show*, Mother."

In the bathtub, the cuts and scratches from the steak knife, they fill with soap and sting until Misty grits her teeth. The dried blood turns the bathwater milky pink. The hot water gets the bleeding started again, and Misty ruins a white towel, staining it with red smears while she tries to dry off.

According to Detective Stilton, a man called the police station on the mainland this morning. He wouldn't give his name, but he said Angel Delaporte was dead. He said the Ocean Alliance for Freedom would keep killing tourists until the crowds quit stressing the local environment.

The silverware as big as garden tools. The ancient bottles of wine. The old Wilmot paintings, none of it was taken.

In her attic bedroom, Misty dials her mom's phone number in Tecumseh Lake, but the hotel operator comes on the line. A cable is broken, the operator says, but it should be fixed soon. The house phone still works. Misty just can't call the mainland.

When she checks under the edge of the carpet, her envelope of tip money is gone.

Tabbi's peridot ring. The birthday gift from her grandmother.

The warning Misty ignored: "Get off the island before you can't."

All the hidden messages people leave so they won't be forgotten. The ways we all try to talk to the future. Maura and Constance.

"You'll die when they're done with you."

It's easy enough to get into room 313. Misty's been a maid, Misty Wilmot, queen of the fucking slaves. She knows where to find the passkey. The room's a double, a queen-size bed with a view of the ocean. It's the same furniture as in every guest room. A desk. A chair. A chest of drawers. On the luggage stand is an open suitcase of some summer person. Slacks and flowered silk hangs in the closet. A damp bikini is flopped over the shower curtain rod.

Just for the record, it's the best job of wallpapering Misty's ever seen. Plus, it's not bad paper, the wallpaper in room 313, pastel green stripes alternating with rows of pink cabbage roses. A design that looked ancient the day it was printed. It's stained with tea to look yellowed with age.

What gives it away is the paper's too perfect. Too seamless and even and straight, up and down. They've matched the seams too well. It's definitely not Peter's work.

Not your work. Dear sweet lazy Peter, who never took any art very serious.

Whatever Peter left here for people to find, sealed inside this room, when he drywalled over the door, it's gone now. Peter's little time capsule or time bomb, the people of Waytansea Island have erased it. The way Mrs. Terrymore erased the library books. The same way the mainland houses have all been burned. The work of OAFF.

The way Angel Delaporte is dead. Stabbed in bed, in his sleep.

In Misty's bed. Your bed. With nothing taken, and no sign of a break-in.

Just for the record, the summer people could walk in at any

time. To find Misty hiding here, clutching a bloody knife in one hand.

With the serrated blade, Misty picks at a seam and peels away a strip of wallpaper. Using the sharp tip, Misty peels off another strip. Peeling away a third long, slow strip of wallpaper, Misty can read:

". . . in love with Angel Delaporte, and I'm sorry but I will not die for . . ."

And just for the record, this is not what she really wanted to find.

August 24 . . .
and Three-Quarters

WITH THE WHOLE WALL shredded, all the old cabbage roses and pale green stripes peeled away in long strips, here's what Peter left for people to find.

What you left.

"I'm in love with Angel Delaporte, and I'm sorry but I will not die for our cause." Written around and around the walls, it says, "I won't let you kill me the way you've killed all the painters' husbands since Gordon Kincaid."

The room's littered with curls and shreds of wallpaper. Dusty with the dried glue. You hear voices in the hallway, and Misty waits frozen in the wrecked room. Waiting for the summer people to open their door.

Across the wall, it's written, "I don't care about our traditions anymore."

It says, "I don't love Misty Marie," it says, "but she doesn't deserve to be tortured. I love our island, but we have to find a new way to save our way of life. We can't keep harvesting people."

It's written, "This is ritual mass murder, and I won't condone it."

The summer people, their stuff is buried, the luggage and cosmetics and sunglasses. Buried in shredded trash.

"By the time you find this," the writing says, "I'll be gone. I'm leaving with Angel tonight. If you're reading this, then I'm sorry, but it's already too late. Tabbi will have a better future if her generation has to fend for itself."

Written under the strips of wallpaper, it says, "I'm genuinely sorry for Misty."

You've written, "It's true I never loved her, but I don't hate her enough to complete our plan."

It's written, "Misty deserves better than this. Dad, it's time we set her free."

The sleeping pills Detective Stilton said Peter had taken. The prescription Peter didn't have. The suitcase he'd packed and put in the trunk. He was planning to leave us. To leave with Angel.

You were planning to leave.

Somebody drugged him and left him in the car with the engine running, shut in the garage for Misty to find. Somebody didn't know about the suitcase, packed and ready in the trunk for his getaway. They didn't know the gas tank was half empty.

"Dad," meaning Harrow Wilmot. Peter's father, who's supposed to already be dead. Since before Tabbi was born.

Around the room, it's written, "Don't unveil the devil's work."

Written there, it says, "Destroy all her paintings."

What they don't teach you in art school is how to make sense of a nightmare.

It's signed *Peter Wilmot*.

August 25

IN THE HOTEL dining room, a crew of island people are hanging Misty's work, all her paintings. But not separate, they fit together, paper and canvas, to form a long mural. A collage. The crew keeps the mural covered as they assemble it, only letting one edge show, just enough to attach the next row of paintings. What it is, you can't tell. What could be a tree, could really be a hand. What looks like a face, might be a cloud. It's a crowd scene or a landscape or a still life of flowers and fruit. The moment they add a piece to the mural, the crew moves a drape to cover it.

All you can tell is it's huge, filling the longest wall of the dining room.

Grace is with them, directing. Tabbi and Dr. Touchet, watching.

When Misty goes to look, Grace stops her with one blue,

lumpy hand and says, “Have you tried on that dress I made you?”

Misty just wants to look at her painting. It’s her work. Because of the blindfold, she has no idea what she’s done. What part of herself she’s showing to strangers.

And Dr. Touchet says, “That wouldn’t be a very good idea.” He says, “You’ll see it opening night, with the rest of the crowd.”

Just for the record, Grace says, “We’re moving back into the house this afternoon.”

Where Angel Delaporte was killed.

Grace says, “Detective Stilton gave his all clear.” She says, “If you’ll pack, we can take your things for you.”

Peter’s pillow. Her art supplies in their pale wood box.

“It’s almost over, my dear,” Grace says. “I know exactly how you feel.”

According to the diary. Grace’s diary.

With everyone busy, Misty goes to the attic, to the room Grace and Tabbi share. Just for the record, Misty’s already packed, and stealing the diary from Grace’s room. She’s carrying her suitcase down to the car. Misty, she’s still dusted with dried wallpaper glue. Paper shreds of pale green stripes and pink roses in her hair.

The book that Grace is always reading, studying, with its red cover and gold script across the front, it’s supposed to be the diary of a woman who lived on the island a hundred years ago. The woman in Grace’s diary, she was forty-one years old and a failed art student. She’d got pregnant and dropped out of art school to get married on Waytansea Island. She didn’t love her new husband as much as she loved his old jewelry and the dream of living in a big stone house.

Here was a ready-made life for her, an instant role to step into. Waytansea Island, with all its tradition and ritual. All of it worked out. The answers for everything.

The woman was happy enough, but even a hundred years ago the island was filling up with wealthy tourists from the city. Pushy, needy strangers with enough money to take over. Just as her family money was running out, her husband shot himself while cleaning a gun.

The woman was sick with migraine headaches, exhausted and throwing up everything she ate. She worked as a maid in the hotel until she tripped on the stairs and became bedridden, one of her legs splinted inside a massive plaster cast. Trapped with nothing to do, she started to paint.

Just like Misty, but not Misty. This imitation Misty.

Then, her ten-year-old son drowns.

After one hundred paintings, her talent and ideas seemed to disappear. Her inspiration dwindles away.

Her handwriting, wide and long, she's what Angel Delaporte would call a giving, caring person.

What you don't learn in art school is how Grace Wilmot will follow you around and write down everything you do. Turn your life into this kind of sick fiction. Here it is. Grace Wilmot is writing a novel patterned after Misty's life. Oh, she's changed a few bits. She gave the woman three kids. Grace made her a maid instead of a dining room server. Oh, it's all very coincidental.

Just for the record, Misty's waiting in line at the ferry, reading this shit in Harrow's old Buick.

The book says how most of the village has moved into the Waytansea Hotel, turning it into a barracks. A refugee camp for island families. The Hylands do everyone's laundry. The Burtons do all the cooking. The Petersens, all the cleaning.

There doesn't look like one original thought in any of it.

Just by reading this shit, Misty's probably going to make it come true. Self-fulfill the prophecy. She'll start living into someone's idea for how her life should go. But sitting here, she can't stop reading.

Within Grace's novel, the woman narrator finds a diary. The diary she finds seems to follow her own life. She reads how her artwork is hung in a huge show. On the night it opens, the hotel is crowded with summer tourists.

Just for the record, dear sweet Peter, if you've recovered from your coma, this might put you right back there. The simple fact is Grace, your mother, is writing about your wife, making her out to be some drunken slut.

This has got to be how Judy Garland felt when she read *Valley of the Dolls*.

Here in line at the ferry dock, Misty's waiting for a ride to the mainland. Sitting here in the car where Peter almost died, or almost ran off and left her, Misty's sitting here in a hot line of summer people. Her suitcase packed and in the trunk. The white satin dress included.

The same way your suitcase was in the trunk.

That's where the diary ends. The last entry is just before the art show. After that . . . there's nothing.

Just so you don't feel bad about yourself, Misty's leaving your kid the way you were abandoning them both. You're still married to a coward. The same way she was ready to run away when she thought the bronze statue would kill Tabbi—the only person on the island Misty gives a shit for. Not Grace. Not the summer people. There's nobody here Misty needs to save.

Except Tabbi.

August 26

JUST FOR THE RECORD, you're *still* one chickenshit piece of work. You're a selfish, half-assed, lazy, spineless piece of crap. Yeah, sure, you were planning to save your wife, but you were also going to dump her. Stupid brain-damaged fuck that you are. Dear sweet stupid you.

But now, Misty knows just how you felt.

Today is your 157th day as a vegetable. And her first.

Today, Misty drives the three hours to see you and sit by your bedside.

Just for the record, Misty asks you, "Is it okay to kill strangers to prop up a way of life just because the people who live it are the people you love?"

Well, *thought* you loved.

The way people are coming to the island, more and more

every summer, you see more litter. The fresh water is in shorter and shorter supply. But of course, you can't cap growth. It's anti-American. Selfish. It's tyrannical. Evil. Every child has the right to a life. Every person has the right to live where they can afford. We're entitled to pursue happiness wherever we can drive to, fly to, sail to, to hunt it down. Too many people rushing to one place, sure, they ruin it—but that's the system of checks and balances, the way the market adjusts itself.

This way, wrecking a place is the only way to save it. You have to make it look horrible to the outside world.

There is no OAFF. There's only people fighting to preserve their world from more people.

Part of Misty hates these people who come here, invaders, infidels, crowding in to wreck her way of life, her daughter's childhood. All these outsiders, trailing their failed marriages and stepchildren and drug habits and sleazy ethics and phony status symbols, these aren't the kind of friends Misty wants to give her kid.

Your kid.

Their kid.

To save Tabbi, Misty could let happen what always happens, Misty could just let it happen again. The art show. Whatever it is, she could let the island myth run its course. And maybe Waytansea would be saved.

"We will kill every one of God's children to save our own."

Or maybe they can give Tabbi something better than a future of no challenges, a calm, secure life of peace.

Sitting here with you now, Misty leans over and kisses your puffy red forehead.

It's okay that you never loved her, Peter. Misty loved you.

At least for believing she could be a great artist, a savior. Something more than a technical illustrator or commercial artist. More than human, even. Misty loves you for that.

Can you feel this?

Just for the record, she's sorry about Angel Delaporte. Misty's sorry you were raised inside such a fucked-up legend. She's sorry she ever met you.

August 27—
The New Moon

GRACE TWIRLS HER HAND in the air between them, her fingernails ridged and yellow under clear polish, and she says, "Misty dear, turn around so I can see how the back hangs."

Misty's first time to confront Grace, the evening of the art show, the first thing Grace says is, "I *knew* that dress would look wonderful on you."

This is in the old Wilmot house on Birch Street. There, the doorway to her old bedroom is sealed behind a sheet of clear plastic and yellow police tape. A time capsule. A gift to the future. Through the plastic, you can see the mattress is gone. The shade is gone from the bedside lamp. A spray of something dark ruins the wallpaper above the headboard. The handwriting of blood pressure. The doorframe and windowsill, the white paint is smudged with black fingerprint powder.

Deep, fresh tracks from a vacuum cleaner crisscross the rug. The invisible dust of Angel Delaporte's dead skin, it's all been sucked up for DNA testing.

Your old bedroom.

On the wall above the empty bed is the painting Misty did of the antique chair. Her eyes closed out on Waytansea Point. The hallucination of the statue coming to kill her. Blood sprayed across it.

With Grace now, in her bedroom across the hallway, Misty says not to try anything funny. The mainland police are parked right outside, waiting for them. If Misty's not out there in ten minutes, they'll come in, guns blazing.

Grace, she sits on the shiny pink-padded stool in front of her huge vanity table, her perfume bottles and jewelry spread out around her on the glass top. Her silver hand mirror and hairbrushes.

The souvenirs of wealth.

And Grace says, "*Tu es ravissante ce soir.*" She says, "You look pretty this evening."

Misty has cheekbones now. And collarbones. Her shoulders are bony and white and stick out, coat-hanger-straight, from the dress that was her wedding dress in its previous life. The dress falls from a shred over one shoulder, white stain draped in folds, already loose and billowing since Grace measured her only a few days ago. Or weeks. Her bra and panties, they're so big Misty's done without. Misty's almost as thin as her husband, the withered skeleton with machines pumping air and vitamins through him.

Thin as you.

Her hair is longer than before her knee accident. Her skin is blanched pale from so much time inside. Misty has a waist and sunken cheeks. Misty has a single chin, and her neck looks long and stringy with muscle.

She's starved until her teeth and eyes look huge.

Before the showing tonight, Misty called the police. Not just Detective Stilton, Misty called the state patrol and the Federal Bureau of Investigation. Misty said that OAFF would be attacking the art show tonight, at the hotel on Waytansea Island. After them, Misty called the fire department. Misty told them, seven or seven-thirtyish tonight, there would be a disaster on the island. Bring ambulances, she told them. Then she called the television news and told them to bring a crew with the biggest, strongest relay truck they had. Misty called the radio stations. She called everybody but the Boy Scouts.

In Grace Wilmot's bedroom, in that house with the legacy of names and ages written just inside the front door, Misty tells Grace how tonight, her plan is ruined. The firemen and police. The television cameras. Misty's invited the whole world, and they'll all be at the hotel for the unveiling.

And clipping an earring on one ear, Grace looks at Misty reflected in the vanity mirror and says, "Of course you did, but you called them the last time."

Misty says, What does Grace mean by *last* time?

"And we really wish you wouldn't," Grace says. She's smoothing her hair with the palms of her lumpy hands, saying, "You only make the final death toll higher than it needs to be."

Misty says there won't be a death toll. Misty says how she stole the diary.

From behind her, a voice says, "Misty dear, you can't steal what's already yours."

The voice behind her. A man's voice. It's Harrow, Harry, Peter's father.

Your father.

He's wearing a tuxedo, his white hair combed into a crown on his square head, his nose and chin sharp and jutting out. The man Peter was supposed to become. You can still smell his breath. The hands that stabbed Angel Delaporte to death in her bed. That burned the houses Peter wrote inside, trying to warn people away from the island.

The man who tried to kill Peter. To kill you. His son.

He's standing in the hallway, holding Tabbi's hand. Your daughter's hand.

Just for the record, it seems like a lifetime ago that Tabbi left her. Ran out of her grip to grab the cold hand of a man Misty thought was a killer. The statue in the woods. The old cemetery on Waytansea Point.

Grace has both elbows in the air, her hands behind her neck fastening a strand of pearls, and she says, "Misty dear, you remember your father-in-law, don't you?"

Harrow leans down to kiss Grace's cheek. Standing, he says, "Of course she remembers."

The smell of his breath.

Grace holds her hands out, clutching the air, and says, "Tabbi, come give me a kiss. It's time the grown-ups went to their party."

First Tabbi. Then Harrow. Another thing they don't teach you in art school is what to say when people come back from the dead.

To Harrow, Misty says, "Aren't you supposed to be cremated?"

And Harrow lifts his hand to look at his wristwatch. He says, "Actually, not for another four hours."

He shoots his shirt cuff to hide the watch and says, "We'd like to introduce you to the crowd tonight. We're counting on you to say a few words of welcome."

Still, Misty says, he knows what she'll tell everyone. To run. To leave the island and not come back. What Peter tried to tell them. Misty will tell them one man is dead and another is in a coma because of some crazy island curse. The second they get her onstage, she'll shout "Fire." She'll do her damnedest to clear the room.

Tabbi steps up beside Grace, sitting on the vanity stool. And Grace says, "Nothing would make us happier."

Harrow says, "Misty dear, give your mother-in-law a kiss." He says, "And please, forgive us. We won't bother you again after tonight."

August 27 . . . and One-Half

THE WAY HARROW told Misty. The way he explained the island legend is she can't *not* succeed as an artist.

She's doomed to fame. Cursed with talent. Life after life.

She's been Giotto di Bondone, then Michelangelo, then Jan Vermeer.

Or Misty was Jan van Eyck and Leonardo da Vinci and Diego Velázquez.

Then Maura Kincaid and Constance Burton.

And now she's Misty Marie Wilmot, but only her name changes. She has always been an artist. She will always be an artist.

What they don't teach you in art school is how your whole life is about discovering who you already were.

Just for the record, this is Harrow Wilmot talking. Peter's crazy killer father. The Harry Wilmot who's been hiding out since before Peter and Misty got married. Before Tabbi was born.

Your crazy father.

If you believe Harry Wilmot, Misty's the finest artists who've ever lived.

Two hundred years ago, Misty was Maura Kincaid. A hundred years ago, she was Constance Burton. In that previous life, Constance saw some jewelry worn by one of the island sons while he was on tour in Europe. It was a ring that had been Maura's. By accident, he found her and brought her back. After Constance died, people saw how her diary matched Maura's. Their lives were identical, and Constance had saved the island the way Maura had saved it.

How her diary matched her earlier diary. How her every diary will match the diary before. How Misty will always save the island. With her art. That's the island legend, according to Harrow. It's all her doing.

A hundred years later—when their money was dwindling—they sent the island sons to find her. Again and again, we've brought her back, forced her to repeat her previous life. Using the jewelry as bait, Misty would recognize it. She'd love it and not know why.

They, the whole wax museum of Waytansea Island, they knew she'd be a great painter. Given the right kind of torture. The way Peter always said the best art comes from suffering. The way Dr. Touchet says we can connect to some universal inspiration.

Poor little Misty Marie Kleinman, the greatest artist of all time, their savior. Their slave. Misty, their karmic cash cow.

Harrow said how they use the diary of the previous artist to shape the life of the next. Her husband has to die at the same age, then one of her children. They could fake the death, the way they did with Tabbi, but with Peter—well, Peter forced their hand.

Just for the record, Misty's telling all this to Detective Stilton while he drives to the Waytansea Hotel.

Peter's blood full of the sleeping pills he never took. The death certificate that didn't exist for Harrow Wilmot. Misty says, "It's got to be inbreeding. These people are lunatics."

"The blessing is," Harrow told her, "you forget."

With every death, Misty forgets who she was—but the islanders pass the story along from one generation to the next. They remember so they can find her and bring her back. For the rest of eternity, every fourth generation, just as the money runs out . . . When the world threatens to invade, they'll bring her back and she'll save their future.

"The way you always did, you always will," Harrow said.

Misty Marie Wilmot, queen of the slaves.

The Industrial Revolution meets the guardian angel.

Poor her, the assembly line of miracles. For all eternity.

Shirtsleeves to shirtsleeves, just for the record.

Harrow said, "You always keep a diary. In every incarnation. That's how we can anticipate your moods and reactions. We know every move you'll make."

Harrow looped a strand of pearls around Grace's wrist and fastened the clasp, saying, "Oh, we need you to come back and start the process, but we don't necessarily want you to complete your karmic cycle."

Because that would be killing the goose that lays the golden egg. Yeah, her soul would go on to other adventures, but three generations later the island would be poor again. Poor and crowded with rich outsiders.

Art school doesn't teach you how to escape your soul being recycled.

Period revival. Her own homemade immortality.

"In fact," Harrow said, "the diary you're keeping right now, Tabbi's great-great-grandchildren will find it extremely useful in dealing with you the next time around."

Misty's own great-great-great-grandchildren.

Using her book. This book.

"Oh, I remember," Grace said. "When I was a very little girl. You were Constance Burton, and I used to love it when you'd take me kite flying."

Harrow said, "Under one name or another, you're the mother of us all."

Grace said, "You've *loved* us all."

To Harrow, Misty said, Please. Just tell me what's going to happen. Will the paintings explode? Will the hotel collapse into the ocean? What? How does she save everyone?

And Grace shook her pearl bracelet down around her hand and said, "You can't."

Most fortunes, Harrow says, are founded on the suffering and death of thousands of people or animals. Harvesting something. He gives Grace something shining gold and holds out one hand, his jacket sleeve pulled back.

And Grace holds the two ends of his cuff together and inserts a cuff link, saying, "We've just found a way to harvest rich people."

August 27 . . .
and Three-Quarters

THE AMBULANCES are already waiting outside the Waytansea Hotel. The television news crew hoists a broadcast dish from the top of its van. Two police cars are nosed up to the hotel front steps.

Summer people edge between the parked cars. Leather pants and little black dresses. Dark glasses and silk shirts. Gold jewelry. Above them, the corporate signs and logos.

Peter's graffiti: ". . . your blood is our gold . . ."

Between Misty and the crowd, a newscaster stands on camera. With the crowd milling behind him, the people climbing the hotel steps and entering the lobby, the newscaster says, "Are we on?" He puts two fingers of one hand to his ear. Not looking into the camera, he says, "I'm ready."

Detective Stilton sits behind the wheel of his car, Misty beside him. Both of them watch Grace and Harrow Wilmot climb the front steps, Grace lifting her long dress with the fingertips of one hand. Harrow holds her other hand.

Misty watches them. The cameras watch them.

And Detective Stilton says, "They won't try anything. Not with this kind of exposure."

The oldest generation of every family, the Burtons and Hylands and Petersens, the aristocracy of Waytansea Island, they fall in line with the summer crowds entering the hotel, their chins held high.

Peter's warning: ". . . we will kill every one of God's children to save our own."

The newscaster on camera, he lifts a microphone to his mouth and says, "Police and county officials have given a green light to tonight's reception on the island."

The crowd disappears into the dim green velvet landscape of the lobby, the forest clearing among polished, varnished tree trunks. The thick shafts of sunlight stabbing into the gloom, heavy as crystal chandeliers. The humped sofa shapes of boulders covered in moss. The campfire, so much like a fireplace.

Detective Stilton says, "You want to go in?"

Misty tells him no. It's not safe. She's not making the same mistake she's always made. Whatever that mistake would be.

According to Harrow Wilmot.

The newscaster says, "Everyone who's anyone is arriving here tonight."

And there, then there's a girl. A stranger. Someone else's child with short dark hair, climbing the steps to the hotel lobby. The flash of her peridot ring. Misty's tip money.

It's Tabbi. Of course it's Tabbi. Misty's gift to the future. Peter's way to keep his wife on the island. The bait to get her into a trap. A moment, a green flash, and Tabbi's gone inside the hotel.

August 27 . . . and Seven-Eighths

TODAY IN THE DARKNESS of the dim forest clearing, the green velvet landscape inside the lobby doors, the hotel's fire alarm goes off. One long ringing bell, it comes out the front doors so loud the newscaster has to shout, "Well, this sounds like trouble."

The summer people, the men, their hair all combed back, dark and wiry with some styling product. The women all blond. They shout to be heard over the alarm's din.

Misty Wilmot, the greatest artist throughout history, she's grabbing her way through the crowd, clawing and pulling herself toward the stage in the Wood and Gold Dining Room. Clutching at the elbows and hipbones of these skinny people. The whole wall behind the stage draped and ready for the unveiling. The mural, her work still hidden. Sealed. Her gift to the future. Her time bomb.

Her million smears of paint put together the right way. The urine of cows eating mango leaves. The ink sacs from cuttlefish. All that chemistry and biology.

Her kid somewhere in this mob of people. Tabbi.

The alarm ringing and ringing, Misty steps up on a chair. She steps up on a table, table six where Tabbi was laid out dead, where Misty found out about Angel Delaporte being stabbed to death. Standing above the crowd in her white dress, people looking up, summer men grinning up at her, Misty's not wearing any underwear.

Her born-again wedding dress tucked between her bony thighs, Misty shouts, "Fire!"

Heads turn. Eyes look up at her. In the dining room doorway, Detective Stilton appears and starts swimming through the crowd.

Misty shouts, "Get out! Save yourselves!" Misty shouts, "If you stay here, something terrible will happen!"

Peter's warnings. Misty sprays them out above the crowd.

"We will kill every one of God's children to save our own."

The curtain looming behind her, covering the whole wall, her own self-portrait, what Misty doesn't know about herself. What she doesn't want to know.

The summer people look up, their corrugator muscles contracted, their eyebrows pulled together. Their lips pulled thin and down by triangularis muscle.

The fire alarm stops ringing, and for as long as it takes to draw the next breath, all you can hear is the ocean outside, each wave hiss and burst.

Misty is shouting for everybody to shut up. Everybody, just listen. Shouting, she knows what she's talking about. She's the greatest artist of all time. The reincarnation of Thomas Gainsborough and Claude Monet and Mary Cassatt. She shouts how her soul has been Michelangelo and da Vinci and Rembrandt.

Then a woman shouts, “It’s her, the artist. It’s Misty Wilmot.”

And a man shouts, “Misty honey, enough with the drama.”

The woman shouts, “Pull down the curtain, and let’s get this over with.”

The man and woman shouting, they’re Harrow and Grace. Between them, they each hold Tabbi by one hand. Tabbi, her eyes are taped shut.

“Those people,” Misty shouts, pointing at Grace and Harrow. Her hair hanging in her face, Misty shouts, “Those evil people, they used their son to get me pregnant!”

Misty shouts, “They’re holding my kid!”

She shouts, “If you see what’s behind this curtain, it will be too late!”

And Detective Stilton gets to the chair. One step, and he’s up. Another step, and he’s beside her on table six. The huge curtain hanging behind them. The truth about everything just inches away.

“Yes,” another woman shouts. An old island Tupper, her sea turtle neck sagging into the lace collar of her dress, she shouts, “Show us, Misty!”

“Show us,” a man shouts, an old island Woods, leaning on his cane.

Stilton reaches one hand behind his back. He says, “You almost had me thinking you were the sane one.” And his hand comes out holding handcuffs. He’s clicking them on her, pulling Misty away, past Tabbi with her eyes taped shut, past all the summer people shaking their heads. Past the aristocrats of Waytansea Island. Back through the forest glade of the green velvet lobby.

“My kid,” Misty says. “She’s still in there. We have to get her out.”

And Detective Stilton gives her to a deputy in a brown uniform and says, “Your daughter who you said was dead?”

They faked her death. Everyone watching, they're just statues of themselves. Their own self-portraits.

Outside the hotel, at the foot of the porch steps, the deputy opens the back door of a patrol car. Detective Stilton says, "Misty Wilmot, you're under arrest for the attempted murder of your husband, Peter Wilmot, and the murder of Angel Delaporte."

Blood was all over her the morning after Angel was stabbed in her bed. Angel about to steal her husband away. Misty, the one who found Peter's body in the car.

Strong hands shove her into the backseat of the patrol car.

And from inside the hotel, the newscaster says, "Ladies and gentlemen, it's the moment of the unveiling."

"Take her. Print her. Book her," the detective says. He slaps the deputy on the back and says, "I'm going back inside to see what all this fuss has been about."

August 28

ACCORDING TO PLATO, we live chained inside a dark cave. We're chained so all we can see is the back wall of the cave. All we can see are the shadows that move there. They could be the shadows of something moving outside the cave. They could be the shadows of people chained next to us.

Maybe the only thing each of us can see is our own shadow.

Carl Jung called this his shadow work. He said we never see others. Instead we see only aspects of ourselves that fall over them. Shadows. Projections. Our associations.

The same way old painters would sit in a tiny dark room and trace the image of what stood outside a tiny window, in the bright sunlight.

The camera obscura.

Not the exact image, but everything reversed or upside down.

Distorted by the mirror or the lens it comes through. Our limited personal perception. Our tiny body of experience. Our half-assed education.

How the viewer controls the view. How the artist is dead. We see what we want. We see how we want. We only see ourselves. All the artist can do is give us something to look at.

Just for the record, your wife's under arrest. But she's done it. They've done it. Maura. Constance. And Misty. They've saved her kid, your daughter. She's saved herself. They've saved everyone.

The deputy in his brown uniform, he drove Misty back over the ferry to the mainland. Along the way, the deputy read her rights. He passed her off to a second deputy, who took her fingerprints and wedding ring. Misty still in her wedding dress, that deputy took her bag and high-heeled shoes.

All her junk jewelry, Maura's jewelry, their jewelry, it's all back in the Wilmot house in Tabbi's shoe box.

This second deputy gave her a blanket. The deputy was a woman her own age, her face a diary of wrinkles starting around her eyes and webbed between her nose and mouth. The deputy looked at the forms Misty was filling out, and she said, "Are you the artist?"

And Misty said, "Yeah, but just for the rest of this lifetime. Not after that."

The deputy walked her down an old concrete hallway to a metal door. She unlocked the door, saying, "It's after lights-out." She swung the metal door open and stepped aside, and it's right there Misty saw it.

What they don't teach you in art school. How you're still always trapped.

How your head is the cave, your eyes the cave mouth. How you live inside your head and only see what you want. How you only watch the shadows and make up your own meaning.

Just for the record, it was right there. In the tall square of light from the open cell door, written on the far wall of the little cell, it said:

If you're here, you've failed again. It's signed *Constance.*

The handwriting cupped and spread, loving and nurturing, all of it's her handwriting. In this place Misty's never been before, but where she ends up, again and again. It's then she hears the sirens, long and far way. And the deputy says, "I'll be back to check on you in a little." The deputy steps out and locks the door.

There's a window high up in one wall, too high for Misty to reach, but it must face the ocean and Waytansea Island.

In the flickering orange light from the window, the dancing light and shadow on the concrete wall opposite the window, in this light Misty knows everything Maura knew. Everything Constance knew. Misty knows how they've all been fooled. The same way she knew how to paint the mural. The way Plato says we already know everything, we just need to remember it. What Carl Jung calls the universal subconscious. Misty remembers.

The way the camera obscura focuses an image on a canvas, how the box camera works, the little cell window projects a mess of orange and yellow, flames and shadows in a shape on the far wall. All you can hear are the sirens, all you can see are the flames.

It's the Waytansea Hotel on fire. Grace and Harrow and Tabbi inside.

Can you feel this?

We were here. We are here. We will always be here.

And we've failed again.

September 3—
The First-Quarter Moon

OUT ON WAYTANSEA POINT, Misty parks the car. Tabbi sits beside her, each of Tabbi's arms wrapped around an urn. Her grandparents. Your parents. Grace and Harrow.

Sitting next to her daughter in the front seat of the old Buick, Misty rests a hand on Tabbi's knee and says, "Honey?"

And Tabbi turns to look at her mother.

Misty says, "I've decided to legally change our names." Misty says, "Tabbi, I *need* to tell people what really happened." Misty squeezes Tabbi's skinny knee, her white stockings sliding over her kneecap, and Misty says, "We can go live with your grandma in Tecumseh Lake."

Really, they could go live anywhere now. They're rich again. Grace and Harrow, and all the village old people, they left millions in life insurance. Millions and millions, tax free and safe in the bank. Drawing enough interest to keep them safe for another eighty years.

Detective Stilton's search dog, two days after the fire, the dog dug into the mountain of carbonized wood. The first three stories of the hotel gutted to the stone walls. The concrete turned to green-blue glass by the heat. What the dog smelled, cloves or coffee, led rescue workers to Stilton, dead in the basement below the lobby. The dog, shaking and peeing, his name is Rusty.

The images are worldwide. The bodies spread out on the street in front of the hotel. The charred corpses, black and crusted, cracked and showing the meat cooked inside, wet and red. In every shot, every camera angle, there's a corporate logo.

Every second of video shows the blackened skeletons laid out in the parking lot. A total of one hundred and thirty-two so far, and above them, over them, somewhere in the frame, you see some corporate name. Some slogan or smiling mascot. A cartoon tiger. A vague, upbeat motto.

"Bonner & Mills—When You're Ready to Stop Starting Over."

"Mewtworx—Where Progress Is Not Staying in One Place."

What you don't understand, you can make mean anything.

Some island car silk-screened with an advertisement is parked in every news shot. Some piece of paper trash, a cup or napkin is printed with a corporate name. You can read a billboard. Islanders are wearing their lapel buttons or T-shirts, doing television interviews with the twisted smoking bodies in the background. Now the financial services and cable television networks and drug companies are paying fat kill fees to buy back all their advertising. To erase their names from the island.

Add this money to the insurance, and Waytansea Island is richer than it's ever been.

Sitting in the Buick, Tabbi looks at her mother. She looks at the urns she holds in the crook of each arm. Her zygomatic major pulls her lips toward each ear. Tabbi's cheeks swell up to lift her bottom eyelids just a little. With her arms hugging the ashes of Grace and Harrow, she's her own little Mona Lisa. Smiling and ancient, Tabbi says, "If you tell, then I tell."

Misty's artwork. Her child.

Misty says, "What will you tell?"

Still smiling, Tabbi says, "I set fire to their clothes. Granmy and Granby Wilmot taught me how, and I set them on fire." She says, "They taped my eyes so I wouldn't see, so I'd get out."

In the bits of news video that survive, all you can see is the smoke rolling out of the lobby doors. This is moments after the mural was unveiled. The firemen rush in and don't come out. None of the police or guests come out. Every second of the time stamp on the video, the fire is bigger, the flames whipping orange rags out of the windows. A police officer crawls across the porch to peek in the window. He stoops there, looking inside. Then he stands. The smoke blowing him in the face, the flames blowtorching his clothes and hair, he steps over the windowsill. Not blinking. Not flinching. His face and hands on fire. The police officer smiles at what he sees inside and walks toward it without looking back.

The official story is the dining room fireplace caused it. The hotel's policy that the fire always had to burn, no matter how warm the weather, that's how the fire started. People died a step away from open windows. Their dead bodies found an arm's length away from exit doors. Dead, they were found creeping, crawling, crowding toward the wall in the dining room where the mural burned. Toward the center of the fire. Whatever the policeman saw through the porch window.

No one even tried to escape.

Tabbi says, "When my father asked me to run away with him, I told Granmy." She says, "I saved us. I saved the future of the whole island."

Looking out the car window to the ocean, not looking at her mother, Tabbi says, "So if you tell anyone," she says, "I'll go to jail." She says, "I'm very proud of what I did, Mother." She looks at the ocean, her eyes following the curve of the coastline, back to the village and the black hulk of the ruined hotel. Where people burned alive, transfixed by Stendhal syndrome. By Misty's mural.

Misty shakes her daughter's knee and says, "Tabbi, please."

And without looking up, Tabbi reaches over to open the car door and step out. "It's Tabitha, Mother," she says. "From now on, please call me by my given name."

When you die in a fire, your muscles shorten. Your arms pull in, pulling your hands into fists, your fists pulling up to your chin. Your knees bend. The heat does all that. It's called the "pugilist position" because you look like a dead boxer.

People killed in a fire, people in a long-term vegetative state, they all end up posed about the same. The same as a baby waiting to be born.

Misty and Tabitha, they walk past the bronze statue of Apollo. Past the meadow. Past the crumbing mausoleum, a moldy bank built into a hillside, its iron gate hanging open. The darkness inside. They walk to the end of the point, and Tabitha—not her daughter, no longer part of Misty, someone Misty doesn't even know—a stranger, Tabitha pours each urn off a cliff above the water. The long gray cloud of what's inside, the dust and ash, it fans out on the breeze. It sinks into the ocean.

Just for the record, the Ocean Alliance for Freedom hasn't issued another word and police have made no arrests.

Dr. Touchet has declared the only public beach on the island closed for health reasons. The ferry has cut service to just twice each week, and only to island residents. Waytansea Island is to all intents and purposes closed to the outsider.

Walking back to the car, they pass the mausoleum.

Tabbi . . . Tabitha stops and says, "Would you like to look inside now?"

The iron gate rusted and hanging open. The darkness inside.

And Misty, she says, "Yes."

Just for the record, the weather today is calm. Calm and resigned and defeated.

One, two, three steps into the dark, you can see them. Two skeletons. One lying on the floor, curled on its side. The other sits propped against the wall. Mold and moss grown up around their bones. The walls shine with trickles of water. The skeletons, her skeletons, the women Misty's been.

What Misty's learned is the pain and panic and horror only lasts a minute or two.

What Misty's learned is she's bored to death of dying.

Just for the record, your wife knows you were bluffing when you wrote about putting every toothbrush up your ass. You were just trying to scare people back into reality. You just wanted to wake them up from their own personal coma.

Misty's not writing this for you, Peter, not anymore.

There's nowhere on this island she can leave her story where only she'll find it. The future her in a hundred years. Her own little time capsule. Her own personal time bomb. The village of Waytansea, they'd dig up every square inch of their beautiful island. They'd tear down their hotel, looking for her secret. They have a century to dig and tear and hunt before she comes back. Until they bring her back. And then it will be too late.

We're betrayed by everything we do. Our art. Our children.

But we were here. We are still here. What poor dull Misty Marie Wilmot has to do is hide her story in plain sight. She'll hide it everywhere in the world.

What she's learned is what she always learns. Plato was right. We're all of us immortal. We couldn't die if we wanted to.

Every day of her life, every minute of her life, if she could just remember that.

September 10
1445 Bayside Drive
Tecumseh Lake, GA 30613

Chuck Palahniuk
c/o Doubleday
1745 Broadway
New York, NY 10019

Dear Mr. Palahniuk,

My guess is you probably get a lot of letters. I've never written to an author before, but I wanted to give you a chance to read the attached manuscript.

Most of it I wrote this summer. If you enjoy it, please pass it along to your editor, Lars Lindigkeit. Money is not really my goal. I only want to see it published and read by as many people as possible. Maybe in some way it can enlighten just one person.

My hope is this story will be read for generations, and it will stay in people's minds. To be read by the next generation, and the next. Maybe to be read by a little girl a century from now, a little girl who can close her eyes and see a place—see it so clear—a place of sparkling jewelry and rose gardens, that she thinks will save her.

Somewhere, someday, that girl will pick up a crayon and start to draw a house she's never seen. My hope is this story will change the way she lives her life. I hope this story will save her—that little girl—whatever her name will be the next time.

Sincerely,
Nora Adams

Manuscript enclosed

CHUCK PALAHNIUK

DIARY

Chuck Palahniuk's novels are the bestselling *Lullaby* and *Fight Club* (which was made into a film by director David Fincher), *Survivor*, *Invisible Monsters*, and *Choke*. He is also the author of *Fugitives and Refugees* and *Stranger Than Fiction*. He lives in the Pacific Northwest.